SUDDENLY SUPER

A TWISTED TALE NOVEL

JEN CALONITA

AUTUMN
PUBLISHING

AUTUMN
PUBLISHING

Published in 2023
First published in the UK by Autumn Publishing
An imprint of Igloo Books Ltd
Cottage Farm, NN6 0BJ, UK
Owned by Bonnier Books
Sveavägen 56, Stockholm, Sweden
www.igloobooks.com

0823 001
2 4 6 8 10 9 7 5 3 1
ISBN 978-1-80368-496-3

Cover illustrated by Giuseppe Di Maio

Printed and manufactured in the UK

SUDDENLY SUPER

A TWISTED TALE NOVEL

JEN CALONITA

To my own Super family, Mike, Tyler & Dylan

– J.C.

CHAPTER ONE
VIOLET

This was a bad plan.

A *very* bad plan.

"It's the perfect plan!" Kari McKeen argued, her lisp making her words stick together like toffee. "We go for an hour, then be back here before the movie gets out and our mums pick us up. They'll never even know."

Violet Parr had barely set foot in the Metroville Cinema and already she was regretting the decision. Two minutes after being dropped off in front of the cinema to see a slasher film Violet hadn't wanted to see in the first place, Kari was changing the plan. All because Lucy Daniels had walked by, seen Violet and invited them to Matt Reynolds's party.

A party.

Violet couldn't think of a worse nightmare.

Why hadn't she just stayed in, made a huge bowl of popcorn and watched cartoons on TV like she did every other Friday night?

Because her mum had been bugging her to make friends, that's why.

Look where that idea had got her.

Kari gripped Violet by the shoulders, getting that wild look in her eye she sometimes got when she'd had too much sugar. "Please? Violet, Lucy Daniels is inviting us to a party." She looked over her shoulder at the group of older girls standing a few feet away. "An actual party! And we get to arrive with a junior!" Kari's dark-blonde ponytail swayed as her head moved along with her hands. "We can't say no to that."

Violet sighed and looked over at Lucy, who was surrounded by friends. Kari was right about one thing – no one said no to Lucy. Not even Lucy's Uncle Lucius, who was Violet's honorary uncle but Lucy's actual one. Even though it was against the rules, Lucy was the one person she knew who was privy to the fact that once upon a time Uncle Lucius was the famed Frozone and Violet's parents were Mr Incredible and Elastigirl. Keeping the truth a secret was priority number one in the Parr house. But at Uncle Lu's, it appeared secrets weren't locked up as tight. Lucy had learnt the truth when she'd found her uncle's Supersuit behind a wall... in a wardrobe... concealed by another wardrobe. Violet wasn't surprised she had figured it out. Lucy's parents were archaeologists, so that family was good at cracking clues.

And doing impressions. Lucy did a spot-on imitation of her Uncle Lu and one of Violet's father that kept everyone in stitches at family dinners, which Lucy attended since she stayed with her uncle anytime her parents were away on a dig. Violet's mum was always going on and on about how sweet and 'accomplished' Lucy was, which just made Violet want to disappear even more. Literally. Which she had. In front of Lucy. On more than one occasion. At least Lucy already knew the family secret.

"So? What do you say?" Lucy asked, approaching Kari and Violet. With flawless brown skin and long, loose curls of black hair that tumbled to her mid-back, Lucy constantly looked like she was walking out of the pages of a fashion magazine. She was also class president, head cheerleader and the most popular girl at Metroville High. Lucy looked pointedly at Violet, folding her arms across her red-and-white varsity jumper. "Are you two coming?"

"Yes!" Kari crowed at the same time Violet mumbled, "I don't think it's a good idea."

"Come on, Vi." Lucy took her hand and swung it

through the air. "It will be fun."

Fun? Violet didn't even like to talk to people most days at school. Lucy knew this. How was she going to handle a party?

Kari looked at Violet pleadingly. The two of them were at the bottom of the Metroville High food chain. They didn't get invited to parties, and Violet was okay with that for many reasons.

Kari, apparently, was not.

"Yeah, fun! Everyone is going!" Kari cocked her head. "At least I think they are. I mean, I heard Matt Reynolds tell Jason Hoffman who was telling Jessica Sparrow in the hallway that they were listening to new records tonight and everyone should come because his parents were out to dinner with his dad's boss." She looked at Lucy. "Right?"

Lucy shrugged. "Something like that." She glanced at Violet. "So?"

Violet suspected this attention from Lucy was all her mum's fault. If she weren't constantly talking at family dinners about how she wished "Violet would come out of her shell", this wouldn't be happening.

Violet turned to Kari. "What if we don't make it back here before our mums come pick us up?"

"I'm good at math!" Kari pleaded too loudly for Violet's liking. "I looked up Matt's address in the phone book after school and he lives three blocks from here. It will only take us six minutes to walk over to the party and six minutes to walk back. The movie is two hours long, so we have one hour and forty-four minutes to be at the party."

Lucy smirked. "I like you. What's your name again? Carla?"

"Kari McKeen," she said happily.

"Violet, if you're really that worried about your mum, Kari McKeen's plan seems foolproof," Lucy agreed.

Both girls looked at Violet again for an answer.

The plan *did* seem logical, but… "If my mum finds out I left the movie theatre without permission, she'll be mad." There. She'd said it. Violet's palms were beginning to sweat. "What if my mum gets to the theatre early and sees us walking?"

Kari rolled her eyes. "Fine, we will leave after an hour and *thirty-six* minutes. That leaves us with plenty of time to go to Matt's party, get back here and be waiting out front. Come on," Kari moaned. "It will be fun going with Lucy's friends! Don't you want to have fun?"

Kari talked. A lot. Violet knew that annoyed some people at school, but Violet actually found a chatty friend a plus. Kari talking too much meant she didn't need to talk at all. At lunch, Violet usually just ate her sandwich, apple and pretzels and nodded here and there as Kari went on and on about something that happened in the science lab or on her last babysitting job (Kari was the most in-demand babysitter in Metroville because she was, as she liked to say, 'A sitter who stimulated babies' minds with flashcards and Mozart!'). To Violet, this was a perfect friendship.

Kari's need to talk meant Violet didn't have to reveal much about herself other than where she lived, how many siblings she had and who she had a crush on (and that reveal had been an accident). Her family was not normal, which was why she kept her distance from people. Stayed quiet. Faded into the background. She didn't want to slip up like her dad had. Him trying to relive his Super glory days, as Mum called them, and going rogue trying to rescue someone had blown his cover more than once, which had forced them to move. Again.

Kari was the first person Violet had spent this much time with. They'd been sitting together at lunch every day since school started last autumn. Listening to her friend talk was very soothing. Kari talked as they walked to maths class. She talked outside school in the morning. And sometimes when they partnered up in gym class to run the one-mile loop together, Kari talked during all four laps around the track, which Violet was amazed by. Who had the lung capacity to run and talk for a whole mile? The only person she could think of was her brother Dash, and he was a

Super with superspeed.

Not that anyone outside her family – other than Uncle Lucius, Aunt Honey and Lucy – knew that.

"If my mum found out I lied to her, I'd be grounded," Violet tried. Maybe getting grounded was something both Lucy and Kari would be afraid of too.

"Your mums will never know," Lucy said. "And Vi, I bet your mum wouldn't care if she found out you were with me." She looked at Kari again. "Our families are super close."

Inwardly, Violet groaned. Why did Lucy have to use the word *super*?

"Can I talk to Violet alone a second?" Lucy asked Kari.

"Sure!" Kari said, spitting by accident. "I'll go introduce myself to your friends." She ran off, yelling her full first and last name to the group of students a few feet away.

"Okay, tell me what's going on. If an upperclassman had invited me to a party at your age, I would have jumped at the chance," Lucy teased, and Violet just wanted to retreat into herself more. "You're going to be with me. People are going to be nice to you, if that's what you're worried about."

This conversation reeked of her mum. "That's not it," Violet lied. Even if it kind of was. A party where people were listening to records meant there would be dancing. She was *not* dancing. What was she going to do, stand in the corner and watch people dance? That was awkward. Violet took a deep breath, inhaling the scent of butter wafting from the cinema. Her mouth watered. Safe, wonderful popcorn.

"Then what is it?" Lucy's voice was quieter. "Are you afraid you're going to…" She waved her hands in the air like a magician. "Freak out and disappear? It's not going to happen."

Violet's heart fluttered. "But it *could* happen."

"It won't," Lucy said softly. "Relax."

"Easy for you to say," Violet whispered. It was hard to explain, and she realised she'd never actually tried to explain it before. "I can't control when I – *you know*. I could be anxious or excited. Nervous or happy. Which is why it's so scary. No one wants to be Super anymore. If I slip up… I…" She sighed. "I think about disappearing every day all day at school," Violet confessed, closing her eyes for a moment to block out the thought. "It could happen anytime."

"Going invisible sounds awesome," Lucy said wistfully, and Violet opened her eyes, peering out from behind her curtain of black hair to take in the older girl's far-off look. "If only my mum was on Uncle Lu's side of the family, maybe I'd be so lucky."

Violet wanted to tell her having powers was not lucky, but Lucy just kept talking.

"But this is about you, not me, and I promise you, if you come to the party, I will keep an eye on you. If you feel anything coming on, I'll get you out the door or cover for you."

Lucy was being nicer than she needed to be. "You promise?" Violet hesitated. "I guess we are only going for an hour. But my mum. I'm still worried she'll find out."

Lucy smiled slyly. "I have an idea about how to handle that. I may not be Super, but I do have a skill that could help us."

Violet paled. "No. You wouldn't. You couldn't… could you?"

Lucy winked and pulled Violet over to a payphone outside the cinema. "Watch me." Lucy slipped change in the phone and dialled Violet's house. "Mum?" Lucy mimicked Violet's voice exactly. She gave Violet a thumbs-up. "Lucy Daniels is at the movies too. I know. That is funny. Anyway, she wants us to see the movie that starts a half hour later with her. Can I?"

Violet's eyes nearly bulged out of her head.

"I know, that's so nice of her, right?" Lucy winked at Violet. "So can you pick me up later? Is that okay? I can? Thanks, Mum!" Lucy hung up and stared at Violet triumphantly. "Problem solved. I just bought you more time."

Lucy was the finest mimic Violet knew. If her mum bought Lucy's call, there was no getting out of this party now. Violet hung her head. "Okay," she mumbled into her hair.

"Kari, Violet is in!" Lucy called over to her.

Kari came running back. "Really? Yes!" Kari jumped up and down. Her trainers were pristine white. Violet could tell because Kari had rolled up the bottom of her jeans, which all the girls were doing lately. Violet had thought about doing it too, but she usually had nowhere to go. Tonight was a rarity. "This is going to be great! I didn't even tell you the best part." Kari grinned, the shiny metal of her braces reflecting off the bright cinema marquee lights above them. "Tony Rydinger is going to be there."

Violet's face reddened. "So what?" She quietly stared at her feet in embarrassment.

Lucy folded her arms. "Tony, huh? I know him. He's nice, Vi."

"It's not like he… I mean I've never spoken to… it's nothing," she stuttered. *Don't disappear,* she told herself. *Don't disappear!*

"Well, you can talk to him tonight!" Kari said. "Matt is going, obviously, since it's at Matt's house, which means Tony and Matt will both be there." Kari sighed and held her hands together reverently. "Can't you see it now? Matt and Tony falling madly in love with us? We'd have the cutest boyfriends in the whole school! We could double date!"

Lucy nudged Violet. "She's funny."

Funny, yes, but was Kari psychic? Because the 'Tony and Violet going out' fantasy was one she entertained a lot. What if tonight was the night Tony finally noticed her? Violet bit the inside of her cheek at the thought.

This wasn't just a party. This was a party with Tony Rydinger.

He was worth taking a risk for.

Violet squared her shoulders, stood up straighter and blew her hair out of her right eye to stare directly at Lucy and Kari. "Okay, you two win. Let's go to a party."

CHAPTER TWO
VIOLET

Six minutes later, after walking the three streets from the cinema to Matt's house while Kari talked Lucy's and her friends' ears off, Violet was having second thoughts.

From the street, she could see Matt's house was packed. The floor-to-ceiling windows in the living room revealed groups of teens in clusters, dancing, laughing and listening to music. Was Tony in there?

The sound of laughter permeated the early evening air and Violet froze. There were lots of conversations going on inside Matt's house. She would have to be part of some. Her breathing grew rapid. *Don't panic*, she told herself. *You can do this. Just stick with Lucy.*

"Ready?" Lucy asked as Violet dragged behind Lucy's friends.

"Ready!" Kari said, redoing her ponytail as she hurried up a long stone walkway dotted with flower beds.

"Umm…" Violet was not ready. Her brief bout of confidence had worn off a street and a half ago. "Maybe Kari and I should just go back to the movies." Kari ignored her and watched Lucy press the doorbell, the sound of gonging chimes momentarily drowning out the laughter inside. Someone came to the door, and Violet held her breath.

It was Matt. He was fair-skinned, had light blond hair, brown eyes and broad shoulders that worked to his advantage during football season when he was backup quarterback. "Luuuuu-ccccc," he said, pulling Lucy into a hug before greeting the rest of her friends. The group pushed their way inside, not looking back to see if Violet and Kari had made it in.

Violet watched Lucy disappear into the crowd and tried not to panic.

"Hi, Matt!" Kari gave him a big smile, revealing her braces. "It's Kari with a *K* not a *C*? I say hi to you in the hallway every day? Not that you say hi back, but it's fine. We're saying hi now."

Violet cringed.

Kari kept going. "You said you were listening to records

tonight and me and my friend Violet, Violet Parr, ran into Lucy Daniels – she's a friend of ours – and she told us to stop by."

"Hey, Kari from the hallway," Matt said, flashing her a grin that momentarily made Kari stop rambling. "Why don't you both come on in."

"Thanks!" Kari said, recovering and following Matt inside. "What new records did you get? I was going to go record shopping this weekend, but I didn't want to use all my babysitting money on new records if they weren't any good…"

Kari was moving fast, and Violet had to hurry to keep up. But where was Lucy? Violet had expected her to stick close by.

In the sunken living room, kids from school were sitting on cushions on the floor, eyes closed, listening to music playing at top volume. Others were leaning against sliding-glass doors that led out to a large garden. A third group was sitting at a table under a funky-looking lamp with spikes that reminded her of a porcupine. At the table was Tony.

Violet froze, her heart starting to beat faster than it did when she watched Tony run laps during gym class, his reddish-brown mop top flopping in the afternoon breeze. He had brown eyes that contrasted with his pale pink skin and crinkled when he laughed, which he was now doing, and he was wearing a navy blue turtleneck, which was a good look for him (anything he wore was a good look as far as she was concerned).

"Violet!" Across the living room, Kari was waving to her from the entrance to the kitchen. "Over here!" She was so loud; she could be heard over the record.

Violet hated to think what would happen if the record stopped and Kari was still calling her name. Tony might look up. Then everyone would stare at her some more. She needed to remain calm. *Don't disappear*, she made herself promise, scanning the room for Lucy again.

"Violet! Do you want a drink?" Kari popped open a cola and the cap went flying.

Violet felt her embarrassment deepen. How was she going to walk across this entire room without vanishing? Where was Lucy? *You can do this.* She took a deep breath and then hurried across the living room, being careful not to step on anyone lying on the green shag pile rug reading album liner notes.

She reached the kitchen and felt herself relax.

Kari handed her the open cola. "I followed Matt in here, but I'm not sure where he went. I realised you weren't behind me and I was like, 'Has anyone seen Lucy? She's our friend', but I'm not sure people believed me," Kari whispered.

"Then I saw you staring at *you-know-who* and called you in here so we could strategise."

Violet felt her confidence wane again. "I wasn't staring at anyone." She pushed a loose strand of hair behind her ear. "I was just listening to the record."

"Good beat, right?"

A boy passing through the room had stopped to talk. To her. Violet felt bile rising in her throat. Then she took another deep breath. "Yeah," Violet said, stretching her vocal cords. "Really good beat." *Good beat? That's all you could come up with?* She resisted the urge to smack her own forehead.

The boy nodded and walked over to his friends, but still. She had said actual words! She hadn't disappeared from sheer terror! Lucy wasn't even here to be her wingwoman.

Kari held up her cola. "Here's to our first party," she said with a giggle, and even though Violet wasn't sure she wanted anyone to know this was her first party, she couldn't help but want to toast to the fact she'd survived her first conversation without her head going AWOL.

"Party!" a pale girl with red hair cheered, clinking her own bottle with theirs, and then suddenly four more people walked over and wanted to cheer as well, some of them clinking their bottles so hard, Violet worried one would shatter, as that happened to her dad sometimes on account of his super strength.

But her dad wasn't here. She was. And right now she was Violet. Perfectly normal Violet.

She liked the sound of that.

"Did you bring any records tonight?"

Violet looked up. Now a girl with thick black eyeliner, olive skin and a high ponytail like Kari's was talking to her. She forced herself not to look surprised. "No, I forgot. Did you? Bring any records, I mean?"

Kari drifted away to talk to someone else, but that was okay because Violet had this girl to talk to. Violet was pretty sure her name was Denise. Denise was talking about some new record she loved that her brother stole from her. They got into a tugging war over it and the record cracked. Now her jerk brother was trying to make enough money from his paper route to buy her a new one.

Violet nodded, feeling in control of her emotions for once. "That's terrible. He *has* to buy you a new one," she agreed and took a swig of her drink. "Is he close to saving up enough money?"

Denise gave Violet a look. "I wish! He makes pennies at that paper route. I told him he should just talk to Tony Rydinger about getting a job at the Happy Platter."

Hearing Tony's name made Violet's heart thud. *Tony. Tony. Tony.*

"The Happy Platter?" Kari sidled up next to them and gave Violet a long look. "That's where Tony Rydinger works?"

"Yep," said Denise, grabbing a pretzel from a large bowl on the worktop. "His parents own the place. I think he clears the tables. He's got people jobs there before."

"We should go to the Happy Platter for breakfast tomorrow," Kari said decisively, and Violet felt her face begin to flame. "And then maybe you should get a job there." Kari nudged her. "Don't you think that would be a good idea?"

Denise frowned. "Are you looking for a job too, Violet?"

Denise knew her name and she hadn't even mentioned it to her. People *did* know her! That was exciting. What was not exciting was all this Tony and the Happy Platter talk. If she wasn't careful, she was going to get overwhelmed, and if she got overwhelmed, she might – NO. She couldn't let that happen. Violet stuffed several pretzels in her mouth to keep from having to talk.

"She'd *love* working there," Kari insisted, giving Violet a knowing look. "Wouldn't you, Violet? That place is so good."

The pretzels weren't working. Her hands were getting clammy. Was it getting hot in the kitchen?

"They have great chocolate chip pancakes," said Denise.

"They do." Kari batted her eyes. "I bet Violet *loves* them, don't you?"

Violet felt a bit woozy. Her heart was racing. *Don't panic*, she told herself. *Don't panic.* Where was Lucy? She needed to stay calm till she found her. Violet attempted to talk with her mouth full of pretzel pieces and practically choked. Kari slapped her on the back.

"Take a sip! And never put that much in your mouth," Kari scolded, talking to her like she was one of her baby-sitting charges.

"Are you okay?" Denise asked.

Violet nodded, but Kari wouldn't quit.

"So?" Kari asked again. "What job do you think you'll apply for at the Happy Platter?"

"*Kari,*" Violet said, feeling her face warm all over again. People could hear them! "Stop."

"You could be a waitress," Kari continued without skipping a beat. "You know what? Let's go ask Tony about openings right now!"

Violet's eyes widened. Her heart was fluttering so fast, she was worried it would leap out of her chest. Denise was staring at her strangely. Did she know Violet liked Tony? Violet's breathing became rapid. She started to struggle for air. Was the room shrinking? It felt like the room was shrinking.

Violet looked down at her right hand and blinked hard. Oh no. *Don't disappear,* she told herself. *Do not disappear! Lucy, where are you?* "That's okay," she managed to say. "I don't want a job."

"Yes, you do!" Kari trilled. "Come on!" She yanked on Violet's free hand, pulling her towards the table where Tony was sitting. Violet dug in her heels. Denise watched them curiously.

Violet's face flamed harder and she tried to focus. She felt her resolve waning. This wasn't good. She was anxious, excited, nervous and happy all at the same time. It was a vanishing act perfect storm. She had to get out of there. "What time is it? Don't we have to go?"

"We still have thirty-six minutes," Kari said cheerfully.

"You looking for Tony?" asked a boy grabbing a fistful of pretzels.

"Yes," Kari said at the same time Violet said, "No!"

"Tony!" the boy shouted over the music, making everyone turn around. "These girls are looking for you!"

At that precise moment, the music stopped.

Someone whistled.

Another person said, "Yeah, Tony!" while a third laughed. Everyone seemed to watch as Tony stood up.

Violet felt her chest constrict. Lucy was nowhere to be found. Kari was gripping her free hand and she was still holding her drink in the other. Tony started to walk their way, moving as if in slow motion. His eyes locked on Violet's. She inhaled sharply and her whole body seemed to sway. She pulled out of Kari's grasp and began to back out of the room, dropping the drink on a coffee table, not caring if there was a coaster. Her breathing was coming so fast that she was sure she was going to pass out.

Denise was looking at her. Kari was grinning madly. People seemed to be whispering.

"Who is that girl?" she heard someone ask.

The closer Tony got, the faster Violet moved, banging into the glass doors in the kitchen and fumbling for the door handle to get outside.

"Violet, wait!" Kari said, making things worse. "Don't you want to talk to Tony?"

Don't disappear! Don't disappear! But it was too late. Her left hand started to fade in front of her eyes. She could feel the tingles that meant her face would be going next. She was going to disappear in front of half of her school and she could do nothing to stop it.

They'd be exposed. They'd have to move again. The Supers Relocation Program would probably kick them out for excessive use. Mum and Dad would kill her.

Don't disappear! she said as her left hand did just that. Her right hand began to waffle.

And then she heard the crash.

"Sorry!"

Violet turned around.

Lucy was in the living room staring at a large white vase in pieces on the shag pile carpet. She briefly made eye contact with Violet. "I'm so clumsy! I can't believe I did that!"

Lucy had saved her after all.

Matt groaned. "That was my mum's favourite! She's going to kill me!"

People began to crowd around Lucy and the broken vase. Lucy motioned to the back door, which was wide open.

That's when Violet made her move. She slipped outside just as she felt her second hand disappear, then her head. In seconds, her whole body would be gone.

She ran around the back of the house, opened the gate and dashed into the front garden, prepared to run all the way back to the cinema. She felt her body glitching – appearing and disappearing in rapid succession as her heart beat out of control.

Tyres screeched, and a familiar car came into view at the curb.

"Violet Parr!" Helen Parr shouted through the open car window. "Get in this car right now!"

CHAPTER THREE
VIOLET

"Disappearing? In public? At a party you didn't have permission to go to? What were you thinking?"

Helen was gripping the steering wheel tightly at ten and two, her eyes on the road as they sped away from Matt's house. Next to her, Violet's body was finally visible again, but she almost wished it weren't.

"It was an accident! How did you find me, anyway?" Violet eyed her mother, taking in her attire: she was wearing a pink bathrobe and slippers and her short red hair was in curlers, her face free of makeup. "Did you follow me the whole time?"

"No," her mum said sarcastically. "I happened to be taking a drive through the neighbourhood when I saw a girl running with no head and no hands, and I put two and two together."

"Mum!" Violet moaned. "How could you?"

"I thought you were in trouble!" Her mum sounded exasperated. "Calling the house and saying you were seeing a later movie? I could hear the lie in your voice."

Lucy. Violet wasn't going to give her up, but she should have known the Violet imitation wouldn't have worked. No one put one over on Helen Parr. "I wasn't in trouble, Mum. Geez. I know what to do if I'm in trouble."

"Not in trouble? You were running without a head! It's a good thing I found you when I did. If I hadn't called Mrs Caruso across the street to stay with your brothers while I sped over here, someone could have seen you, and do you know what would have happened then?"

"Yes! Accidentally revealing my powers is all I ever think about! Unlike Dad, who is the reason we keep having to move!" Violet volleyed back.

"Now hold on – it's been a few years since our last move," her mum corrected her. "Your dad has been much better about keeping his powers under wraps."

Her mum tried to sound sure of herself, but Violet had her number on this one. She'd heard her parents argue about the use of powers before. "My point is, I was running so no one would see me without my head. How did you track me anyway?" she grumbled. "You were using one of your Super gadgets, weren't you?"

"Supers are illegal. Their gadgets, too, by association," her mum said stiffly. "I would never do something illegal to find my daughter who wasn't where she said she'd be the first night I give her some freedom."

Violet didn't buy it. "What did you use?" Her head swivelled to the back seat to look for evidence and she immediately spotted a small black gadget with a tiny screen. The gadget looked like a small TV screen with a map of Metroville on it. A small red flashing light moved across the screen, showing where they were driving. Violet suspected she was the target. She'd only seen a homing device like this once before in her dad's office. Her dad had actually blown up when he'd caught Violet tampering with its buttons. Apparently, the devices were illegal, just like Supers, but he and Mum still had theirs – one tracked Dad, one tracked Mum, but neither had used the item in years. "Aha!" Violet reached for it.

Her mum got to it first, extending her arm to four times its length and grabbing the gadget, which she placed in her lap. "Nothing to see here."

Violet sighed. This is what she got for having Elastigirl for a mother.

It was clearly a homing device, but it still didn't explain

how her mum had bugged her. Violet looked down at what she was wearing and spotted a small yellow peace button on her jacket. She didn't have a peace pin! Of course. "Mum! You used a homing device on me? They're illegal! You said to never touch one!"

"I said not to touch one unless there was an emergency. This was an emergency," her mum countered. "Do you have any idea how worried I was when I realised you weren't even at the theatre? I thought you'd been kidnapped!"

Violet folded her arms across her chest. "Mum, geez. You're so dramatic! I was fine. I was with Kari and Lucy." *Shoot. Shoot. Shoot.*

Her mum's eyes bulged. "Why were you with Lucy? So Lucy wasn't at the movies? Did you go with her to a high school party?"

She wished Lucy were here right now so she could say I told you so: her mum was not okay with Violet going to a party just because she was with Lucy. "We were only going for an hour and Lucy was with me the whole time." Okay, not true, but details weren't necessary.

"You went to a party for an hour?" Her mum braked hard at the light, sounding even more unhappy. "In one hour, you disappeared in front of people and could have blown everything." She shook her head.

Violet rolled her eyes at the window. Wasn't lying to your

parents about where you were a teen milestone? Thanks to being a Super, she missed out on even *that* rite of passage. "Well, you don't have to worry, I'm never going to a party again. I'm never going out again! I will stay home forever!"

Her mother's tone changed. "Violet…"

"No!" Violet boomed. "This is your fault anyway. 'Make friends', you said. 'Meet people' – how can I meet people and hang out when anytime I get nervous or excited, my emotions get the best of me and I disappear?" Her mum looked at her, frowning. "Do you know how stressful it is worrying about revealing my powers accidentally all day, every day? To be afraid I'll say the wrong thing in class and disappear out of embarrassment?" She thought of Tony. "Or pass someone in the hall and panic and lose my head?" She was on a roll now. "It's all I ever think about! I know I'm not supposed to use my powers! I don't even want them! You want us to *act* normal, Mum, but I want to *be* normal!"

"I didn't realise your abilities were causing you so much stress." Her mum's voice was lower now. "Why didn't you say something?"

"What was I supposed to say? Can I give them back? We both know that's not an option."

"I know that, but your father and I could have worked with you on how to control them. Your father would love that job," her mum said wryly, and they both knew why – her dad seemed to miss being a Super more than anything. Sometimes Violet caught him in his office, which held all his Super memorabilia, just staring at mementos from his past.

"I don't want to get better at my powers. I wish I didn't even have them. Our powers cause nothing but trouble."

"That's not true," her mum started to say.

"You know it is!" Violet argued. "Our powers are why we've moved so many times. They're why Dad was sued all those years ago and Supers had to disappear." She folded her arms across her chest. "I hate having powers." She stared at the dashboard, refusing to look at her mum. The silence between them made the car engine sound much louder, but Violet didn't care. She was mad.

Her mum finally spoke. "I know this isn't easy. And the fact that Supers are illegal makes it even harder, but your identity is your most precious gift. To fit in here in Metroville, we have to be like everybody else. Maybe if we work on controlling your powers, you'll feel more comfortable around your friends. But regardless of how powers do or don't make you feel, nothing gives you the right to lie about where you are."

Violet didn't answer, but she felt her stomach clench. Lying about your whereabouts was something a Super never did. Her parents had ingrained that into all three Parr kids from the moment they could walk and talk. Supers – illegal or not – would always be a target. Making sure someone knew where she was at all times was not only smart, it could mean the difference between life and death. It's why her parents always had comms links on them, even though they were retired.

"I'm sorry things have been so hard for you. I don't mean to make things more difficult, but you can't lie. I'm a mum, it's my job to worry. Even though I know we're safe in Metroville, and no one knows who we really are, sometimes I can't help but think…" She trailed off.

Curious, Violet finally turned to her. "Think what?"

"It's silly, really." Her mum made a hard right onto another street, making Violet tumble slightly. "You've heard your father mention Mastermind before, right?"

Violet resisted the urge to roll her eyes. "Only about a thousand times. Dad brings up stories about super villains at least once a week."

"Well, I fought Mastermind too. There was this one time, right after your father and I were married, before we had you, Mastermind and I were doing the dance we always did – Mastermind steals something, we get it back – and Mastermind said something I still think about to this day – 'You fear me now? Wait till you have children. You'll never sleep again'. I still think about that."

"But hasn't Mastermind been missing like fifteen years, as long as you've been retired?" Violet asked.

"Yes, but when you're a mum, you never stop worrying." She glanced at Violet again. "I want you to have friends and enjoy yourself, but you can't lie to me, Vi. And you cannot disappear from parties. Do you understand me?"

"I understand," Violet said, getting annoyed again. "But you can't use a homing device to track me. You have to trust me. I left the party when I lost my head, but I was going to go back for Kari before you forced me into the car. We were supposed to walk back to the movies together. She's probably looking for me."

Violet was guessing her mum was going to ground her and take away her phone privileges, which meant she wouldn't be able to call Kari and apologise. She'd have to wait till Monday to talk to Kari at lunch, and by then Kari was probably going to be so mad at her she wouldn't want to sit with her. The thought of eating alone in the canteen was terrifying. "What am I going to say when Kari starts asking questions about where I went?" Violet's heart began to flutter again at the thought. "What if she or someone else saw me lose my head? What if everyone at school is talking about me? Or won't talk to me? Because they saw me run out of a party?"

"Violet, stop whining!" Her mum stopped short at

the next stop sign and sighed deeply, her head hitting the steering wheel on purpose.

Violet could see her mum's face illuminated in the streetlight. Her expression was fraught. Something else was wrong besides this party business. "Mum?"

"I'm fine," her mum's muffled voice came from the leather steering wheel. "It's just been a long day that has now been made longer." She lifted her head and looked at Violet. "Between you and your dad, I—"

"Dad? What's wrong with Dad? Is Dad okay?"

Her mum paused, seemingly choosing her words carefully. "He's either in trouble or he's about to be." She looked at Violet. "I have to meet him at his conference tomorrow, which means I'm going to be gone all day. I was going to leave you in charge of Dash and Jack-Jack, but after the stunt you pulled tonight, I don't know if that's a good idea. I'll ask Mrs Caruso to watch the three of you."

"Mrs Caruso? Mum, no!" The thought of spending all Saturday with her elderly neighbour, watching TV game shows at full volume, sounded like the worst day ever. "She smells like black liquorice. No one likes black liquorice! I'm old enough to watch Dash and Jack-Jack. I'm responsible!"

Her mum snorted. "Responsible? Is that what you call sneaking off to a party?"

A car horn jolted them both and her mum started to

drive again, making the last turn onto their street. Violet could see their house up ahead, the lights on, the soft glow of the TV flashing. Mrs Caruso was probably watching sitcoms with Dash. If only Violet had stayed home with Dash, she wouldn't have had to worry about revealing her powers, or talking to other people. She wouldn't be in this mess. Didn't her mum realise that? "Mum, I—" Violet began again.

"Violet, that's enough for tonight." She sounded deflated. "I don't want to argue anymore. I'm asking Mrs Caruso."

"Mum, please." Violet's own voice matched her mother's quieter tone. Maybe if she was contrite, her mum would change her mind. "I'm sorry about the party, but you know I am capable of watching Dash and Jack-Jack. I've babysat them before. Kari babysits all the time. I'm fourteen. I can handle my brothers for one lousy day. I mean one *great* day," she corrected herself.

Her mum studied her for a moment, drumming her fingers on the steering wheel. "All right. You can watch them."

Yes! Violet thought. A whole Saturday on her own. No chores. No Mum vacuuming under her feet. Maybe she could even sleep in and convince Dash to take care of Jack-Jack in the morning if she told him he could eat that sugary cereal Mum kept on a high shelf in the kitchen. Then after lunch, she'd put Jack-Jack in the pram and walk over to Kari's to apologise. "I promise you won't regret this. I'm going to do a great job! That time Jack-Jack's nappy exploded at the grocery store in aisle three wasn't my fault. Dash forgot to put more nappies in the bag even though I had told him to, and…"

"Vi." Her mum put a cool hand on Violet's own. "I'm not worried about exploding nappies. Just promise me you'll keep your brothers safe."

"Safe? Mum, *please*." Violet resisted the urge to roll her eyes again. "I know to keep Dash away from the stove now. I won't let him try to make lasagna again."

"I don't mean the stove," her mum interrupted, her words slowing. "I mean, keep them safe in case anything happens. If you don't hear from me or your dad by bedtime, or at all tomorrow…"

In case anything happens? What was her mum getting at? Was this about that super villain again? "Mum, Mastermind is retired just like you! Stop worrying someone is going to grab us all the time."

"This is not about Mastermind," her mum said.

Violet may have been mad at her mum two minutes ago, but now she was concerned. "Is it Dad? Is he in danger?"

"No," her mum said, but she didn't make eye contact. "I just haven't been able to reach him, which is why I'm going to see him in the morning. I'm sure he's fine.

Now, there's plenty of leftovers. I've written out Jack-Jack's schedule already and left it in my office. I'll be back late tomorrow, but if you don't hear from me, put the boys to bed and—"

"Why wouldn't I hear from you?" Violet asked. What wasn't her mum telling her?

Her mother shook her head. "I'm sure I'm just being paranoid, but it's always better to be prepared."

"For what?" Now her mum was really starting to freak her out.

"Violet, please," her mum's voice sharpened. "Pay attention to what I'm saying. If anything is wrong, call Lucius. His number is on the board next to the kitchen phone. Tell him you haven't heard from me or Dad. He'll know what to do."

"What is going on?" Violet tried again.

Her mum kept going, not answering the question. "And if you can't reach Lucius, go to Dad's office and try me on the comms link, but—"

"Only in an emergency," Violet said for her. Her mum was a broken record about the comms link. All Super gadgets really.

"Atta girl. You remember what it looks like, right? Black flashlight with a red button on top?"

"Yes, I remember, but why wouldn't I be able to reach

you?" Violet pressed.

"Because I'm flying a jet. I might not be able to answer," her mum said, her irritation returning. "And if I don't answer the comms link…"

"Mum?" Violet was getting scared now.

"Everything is going to be fine." Her mum smiled. "I'm just giving you a worst-case scenario. That's what Mums do. Focus on your brothers tomorrow. That's your job."

"I will," Violet said, her stomach relaxing. It was just like her mum to be paranoid. Then she thought of something promising. "Hey, if I do a good job, does that mean I'm no longer grounded?"

Her mother gave her a look. "Oh no. After tonight's stunt, you're grounded indefinitely."

CHAPTER FOUR
VIOLET

"Vi! Violet! Vi! Wake up!"

Violet opened her eyes slowly. For a brief, shining moment she forgot what day it was and why Dash was standing over her. Then she remembered. She peered at his blue eyes and his pale face dotted with freckles. It was so close to her own she was sure they'd bump noses. Her brother smelt like marshmallows, which meant he'd found the sugary cereal. In the distance, she could hear Jack-Jack babbling and the sounds of the TV.

"Look what I found in Mum and Dad's room!" Dash hopped up on her bed, puffed out his tiny chest, and placed his hands on his hips, showing off a red unitard.

It had a giant black circle in the middle of the chest with

a gold lowercase letter i on it, which looked strange because usually the letter I on its own was capitalised. It had all the markings of a Supersuit.

"Fits like a glove," Dash said. "You've got one too. So does Jack-Jack."

"What were you doing in Mum and Dad's room?" Violet sat up fast and Dash lost his balance, tumbling off the bed.

"Mum was packing and I saw the suit on her bed. I asked her about it over and over again, but she got mad and told me to leave the room." He grinned. "But then the phone rang and Mum asked someone about borrowing a plane. I swiped these when she wasn't looking." He raised one eyebrow. "She had no clue."

Dash was wrong. Mum knew everything. But she didn't take the suits away from him, so she must have been in a real hurry. What was she doing packing Supersuits, anyway? And why would she have made ones for the rest of the family? This didn't make sense. Violet was too tired to process it. "Where is Mum now?" she said with a yawn.

"She left. She said you were babysitting all day and to listen to you." Dash climbed back on the bed and frowned. "It's not fair. Why do you get to be in charge?"

The argument with her mum from the night before came roaring back as the fog of sleep lifted. After Mum had said she was still grounded, Violet had stormed out of the car and gone right to her room. When her mum came by later to say good night, Violet had pretended to be asleep. She knew it was babyish, but she was still mad at Mum for spying on her. Technically her powers were Mum and Dad's fault, but now that she thought back on giving Mum the silent treatment, she felt kind of bad.

"Mum left?" Without saying goodbye?

"Yep!" Dash started to bounce on the bed again, his blond hair flying up and down. "She said to tell you she left you a note in Dad's office and I wasn't allowed in there. I don't care what time Mum wrote bedtime is. If she's not home early, I'm staying up later than I ever have before on a Saturday."

Violet hurried out of bed, adjusting her pyjama bottoms, which had ridden up to her knees overnight. "You have to listen to me. I'm sure Mum told you that."

Dash kept bouncing. "Maybe. But she didn't say what I had to wear today, so I'm wearing this. You've got one too." He held an identical red unitard in his right hand. "I put Jack-Jack in his. Wasn't easy." He bounced higher, the springs on Violet's twin-size bed groaning. "He doesn't like anything going over his head, but his nappy was so stinky I had to change him." Dash pointed a finger at her. "You're doing the next one."

Violet swiped the unitard from her brother and it disappeared the second it touched her hand. How did it do that?

Dash stopped bouncing and stared at her hand. "That. Is. So. Cool!"

Violet tapped the air where the unitard should be with her other hand and it reappeared. So the suit could disappear just like she could. It had clearly been made for her, but why? It didn't look like Dad's classic blue uniform or Mum's white one. Why did Mum have these? Mum, Violet thought, what are you hiding about this trip?

Dash tapped his own chest. "Aww, why won't mine disappear?"

From downstairs, Violet heard a high-pitched squeal and the sound of a dish getting thrown onto the floor. "What was on Jack's plate?"

Dash paled. "Spinach. I couldn't find anything else."

Violet groaned, grabbed her suit and headed downstairs to check on the baby.

She had to hand it to Dash. He'd moved the baby's highchair from the kitchen into the living room and plopped him in front of cartoons. Jack-Jack let out a high-pitched screech at the sight of her, banging his hands on his highchair tray. Violet sighed. Between his pale, bald little head with its short spike of blond hair and his big, blue eyes, it was hard to resist Jack-Jack, even when he was being a terror. An overturned bowl of spinach covered a patch of the living room rug. She really hoped spinach washed out.

"Take those suits off and put them back where you found them," she called to her brother. "And you're cleaning up this mess."

"Am not!" Dash grumbled.

Violet shook her head and walked past him into the kitchen, which was already a disaster. Several bowls, spoons and spilled cereal and milk covered the table. The tap was dripping, and Dash had left the milk out on the worktop. Violet sighed and put it in the fridge, leaving the rest of the dishes for a moment to check the wall phone. Was it working? If it was, why hadn't Kari called to yell at her yet? Violet picked it up and heard the dial tone. It was working. Maybe Kari was still sleeping. Or she was mad. She'd try her friend later after she figured out what to do with Dash and Jack-Jack.

Violet paused at the living room window. Outside, the sky was blue with a smattering of clouds. One of their neighbours was mowing his lawn, while two of Dash's friends were playing catch in the middle of the street. A tricycle bell chimed, and Violet watched kids ride by the house. It was clearly nice enough to get outside. Maybe she could take her brothers to the park and then stop by Kari's. Was she allowed to leave the house? Her mum hadn't said either way. Maybe there was more information in the note.

Violet headed down the hall to Dad's office and pushed the door open, sucking in her breath as she always did when she stepped inside the darkened room. Dad's office was usually off-limits. She knew her mum had only kept it unlocked today so that Violet could grab the note waiting for her on the desk or use the comms link in an emergency.

Mum's office wasn't so sealed. She kept her Super memorabilia locked in a chest in the loft. The only picture she kept on display was one of her and her old friend Snog, a fellow pilot from her flying days.

Flying. Her mum said that's what she was doing today, didn't she? Violet just realised she never asked where she was going. Where was Dad's latest conference, anyway?

"Violet?" Dash called from down the hall.

Violet quickly went to the door and shut it, locking it behind her. "You're not allowed in here. I'll be right out." Dash didn't respond. She looked at the desk, which was littered with papers and pencils. In the centre of it was a piece of paper with her name scribbled on the top.

Violet, keep Jack-Jack to a schedule and don't let Dash eat more than two bowls of that sugar cereal. Hang on to this note!

Below the note was an hour-by-hour checkoff schedule for Jack-Jack's naps, bottle feedings and sleep times. She'd signed it "Mum." Not "Love, Mum." Just Mum.

Mum was still mad at her.

"Is that the note?"

Violet spun around. Dash was standing behind her, in the office that she'd thought she'd locked him out of. She should have known he would speed by her and get into the room before she shut the door.

"You're not allowed in here!" Violet grabbed the note and stuck it in her pocket. "And why are you still wearing that red unitard?"

"It's a Supersuit and it's meant for me. I'm keeping it." Dash darted over to one of Dad's displays and picked up what looked like a miniature blue megaphone. "Hey, what's this thing do?"

"Dash," Violet's raised voice was a clear warning. "Put that back! We're not supposed to touch anything in here."

"I'm not going to break it," Dash said, pressing a button on the side before Violet could stop him.

"Dash, don't!" Violet jumped into the line of fire before thinking better of it. The megaphone fired and her body went numb. She tried to move, but it felt like she was swimming through mud. Every impulse told her to scream out, but no sound escaped her lips. Before she could panic, the sensation evaporated. Dash stood in front of her, eyes wide.

"What just happened?" Violet demanded, shaking out her limbs, which felt tingly.

"You froze!" Dash crowed, sounding excited. "A blue light came out of this thing and bam! You were e-mobile… er… a-mobile."

"Immobilised!" Violet snapped, reaching for the megaphone. "You could have killed me!"

"Nothing in here can kill us," Dash said, whipping back and forth across the room so fast, Violet's head couldn't swivel quickly enough to keep up. "Can it?"

"I don't know, and I don't want to find out." Violet reached for Dash again. She was afraid to attempt a force field for fear of breaking one of Dad's Super awards. He was always polishing those.

"Oooh!" Dash was on the opposite side of the room again. He held up a tiny yellow button with a happy face on it. "What's this do?"

The button looked a lot like the peace pin Violet had found on her jacket the day before. Why had it come from a box on display that had the word *WARNING* on it? "Don't touch that!" she said, and once again Dash did the opposite.

A red light beamed out of the button, projecting onto

one of Dad's beloved Super of the Year trophies. Two seconds later, the trophy shrunk to the size of a penny.

"It's a shrink ray!" Dash picked the trophy up. "Now it's smaller than your old dollhouse furniture!"

Violet groaned. "Dad is going to kill me! I think that was his favourite award!" Dash dropped the tiny trophy, smaller than her thumbnail, into Violet's palm, then took it back.

"Maybe if I press it again, it will get bigger?" Dash said, placing it back on the ground.

"Don't press it again!" Violet cried, but it was too late. The ray was shooting out at the trophy and poof! The trophy was back to normal size.

Dash smiled triumphantly. "Told ya."

Violet grabbed the trophy and put it back on the shelf, momentarily relieved before her anger kicked in. She did not need to be in more trouble than she was already. "Put everything back and get out of this office!"

"Can I take this mini pinball game?" Dash asked, appearing near the door and holding up the homing device her mum had used the night before. A red light was blinking over the ocean. That was weird – was this Mum's homing device or Dad's? Where was Dad's conference? On an island? That sounded more like a holiday than work.

"It's not a pinball game. Put it back where you found

it," she told him.

Dash groaned, dropped it on the desk and zipped out of the room. Down the hall, she heard Jack-Jack screech in delight at the sight of him.

Was it possible to be tired of babysitting already? Because she was.

"Jack-Jack, want to freeze for a second?" she heard Dash say and Violet stilled. He still had that freeze ray!

"Dash! I told you to put the other stuff back!" Violet ran into the living room where she found him about to freeze the baby.

"Make me," Dash said, doing laps around Jack-Jack's highchair, his speed kicking up wind. Jack-Jack started to laugh as Violet's black hair fluttered around her like she was in a storm. "Hey! Maybe I'll try this on Tony Rydinger so he talks to you!"

"How do you know that name?" Violet's eyes narrowed. "Have you been listening in to my calls with Kari? Dash? Dash!" Dash ran faster as Jack-Jack laughed harder, spitting bubbles.

What if the little pain in the neck teased her about Tony in public? And someone overheard? And news of her crush got back to Tony? Violet's heart tightened. "Give me that freeze ray!" she shouted, her anger mounting. Her whole body started to overheat. Before she knew what she was doing, she lunged towards him, trying to grab the back of his shirt.

"Missed!" Dash said, laughing.

Would Kari have to deal with this if she were baby-sitting normal kids? No. Violet had wanted an easy Saturday. Instead, Dash was creating a hurricane and threatening to shrink the baby. Being Super was so unfair. Violet felt her breathing grow shallow, her face and hands warm, and her body tingle as she reached out her hand in front of her.

An invisible barrier shot out, its hazy, purple edges barely visible as a force field as large as their dining room table appeared, powerful enough to knock Dash off his feet. Violet stood back in awe. Whoa. She'd never created a force field so large before.

"Hey!" Dash said, rubbing his side as he sat up and glared at her. "No force fields!"

Jack-Jack laughed harder, banging his forehead on the tray table and getting himself covered in spinach. He was going to need a bath.

"It's your own fault," Violet told him. "You know you're not supposed to use your powers when Mum and Dad aren't home."

"Neither are you," Dash pointed out.

Violet sighed. It was going to be a long day.

CHAPTER FIVE
VIOLET

When Violet awoke on the sofa, she had no idea what time it was. All was quiet except for the ticking of the clock on the living room wall. Her back hurt from twisting herself into a pretzel to fit on the sofa, and the TV was glowing in the darkened room. She had what looked like mashed potatoes crusted on her trousers and a pea in her hair. The rest of Saturday came back to her – nine million Jack-Jack naps and bottles and nappy changes, a quick trip to the park that ended when it rained, not leaving her time to pass by Kari's house and then a dinner of leftovers, which were now smeared on the furniture as well as Violet's trousers.

Mum would not be as amused.

Speaking of Mum, she hadn't called to check in on

them at all. Violet had waited up for her on the sofa and fallen asleep. Mum had said she might be home late, but through the closed blinds, Violet could see the faint glow of the brightening sky outside the window. Was it morning already?

Violet sat up. Dash was scrunched up on one of the other chairs, snoring under a blanket. And what was that lying on the floor next to him? Violet squinted to see. Was that the homing device? Had he stolen it back? "Dash," she growled to herself. He was not easy. She remembered they'd had a fight at bedtime when Dash wanted to wait up for Mum. Apparently, Dash had won that round, or sneaked back down to wait when Violet had fallen asleep. What time was it? Violet looked at the clock. It was 6:15 AM.

Where was Mum?

Violet stood up quietly, her heart starting to flutter. Mum would have called if she was not going to make it back the same day. She'd never left them alone overnight before.

What did Mum say to do if she wasn't back? Violet tried to remember. Call Lucius. But she couldn't call Lucius's house at six-fifteen in the morning. *Maybe she's home and went to bed without waking me.* Violet headed upstairs, her bare feet quiet on the carpeted steps. Mum and Dad's bed was empty. Trying not to worry, she hurried downstairs again, passed a snoring Dash, grabbed the homing device and went to Dad's office to see if she had missed anything. Maybe Mum wrote down where Dad's conference was so she could call there and ask for his room. She tried not to worry. It was not time to try the comms link yet.

How could she have been so mad at Mum that she failed to ask her something this important? Violet pushed the papers on the desk aside, sliding several off the table. A small white card with a phone number sat underneath the stack. The word *MIRAGE* was printed in big block print on a thick piece of card stock.

What was Mirage? Was that the name of Dad's conference?

Violet put the card down for a moment and kept looking. There had to be something she was missing. She opened two desk drawers, finding nothing but pens, loose-leaf paper and a yellowed pad with Mr Incredible pictures on it. In the photograph, her dad's hair was much fuller and his hairline lower – not that she'd ever tell him that. She closed the drawer with a thud and looked around the room again, spotting the unitard Dash had given her yesterday on the desk. She'd forgotten all about it.

Violet nudged it with her finger and the suit disappeared. She touched the space where the suit was again and it reappeared. Dash was right – this unitard was cool and it was clearly made for her, but why? Curious, she wondered for a moment what it would feel like on. She glanced towards the open door. She could still hear Dash snoring and the faint hum of the TV.

If she was ever going to get a moment of peace to try it on, it was now. Quickly she stepped out of her pyjama bottoms and slipped the suit on, wiggling into it. The unitard fitted like a glove – not too tight, not too loose. The fabric was breathable. The question was: would it disappear when she was in it? There was only one way to find out.

She closed her eyes, thinking of Tony and what happened at the party.

Within seconds, she felt herself begin to fade away.

"Violet?" Dash appeared in the doorway. "You in here?"

He couldn't see her. The suit was invisible! She couldn't help being impressed.

Dash looked in the room a moment longer, grabbed the homing device again, then walked away.

Violet reappeared, staring at the suit again in wonder. *Mum, why did you make this for me?* That's when she heard a beep.

Across the room a red light blinked on top of a small machine sitting on a folding table next to Dad's desk. Violet looked closer and saw buttons that said PLAY, REWIND, PAUSE, DELETE. The device looked a bit like the radio in the living room. Violet remembered Dad showing this to her once.

He said it was a voice recorder from his office, used to reach him if he didn't pick up the phone. He called it an answering machine. Violet pressed PLAY.

"Violet?" Mum's voice was loud and clear, the hum of what could be an engine or static rumbling in the background.

"Mum," Violet whispered. When had she left this? Was it when she and Dash were yelling at each other after Jack-Jack tossed a whole bowl of pasta at them at lunch and they'd had to wipe it off the walls?

"You're not answering the phone, so I'm sure you're busy with the boys, but I wanted to leave you a message. I'm sure you'll find this when you get my note about Jack-Jack's schedule. Hang on to that note! It could be helpful." Her mum paused. "I wanted to say I'm sorry about how we left things last night. I shouldn't have yelled at you about disappearing at the party. I know you didn't ask for this gift, but you have it and you're going to have to get used to it. I just want you to remember you have more power than you realise. You need to learn how to control it. Don't think. And don't worry. If the time comes, you'll know what to do. It's in your blood." *Click.*

If the time comes, you'll know what to do? What did that mean? Was Mum talking about her powers? Violet didn't want to learn how to use them! She just wanted to be normal. Why couldn't Mum accept that? The message was nice – at least Mum wasn't still mad at her – but it would have been great if she'd said something useful, like where Dad's conference was and why she wasn't back yet. Violet checked the Mr Incredible wall clock in the office. It was now close to seven. Was it still too early to call Lucius?

"You're in here!" Dash appeared in the doorway. The left side of his face had red sofa cushion marks on it. "Hey, you're wearing the suit."

Violet crossed her arms, but it did nothing to hide her appearance. "I was just trying it on. I'm taking it off and putting it back before Mum gets home."

Dash pulled at the collar of his blue striped pyjamas, revealing the red suit underneath. "I still have mine on too. Jack slept in his."

Violet growled. "Dash!"

"Where's Mum?" he asked, cutting her off. "Why isn't she back yet?"

Violet's palms began to sweat. "She'll be back soon."

"I thought she was supposed to be home last night. Didn't you say she was coming home last night? Violet? Didn't you?"

Violet took a deep breath. "She's on her way home."

"She is?"

Violet nodded. *I hope.* "I'm sure she is."

"But you don't know for sure." Dash started to look worried. "Did you call Dad? Where is Dad's conference anyway?"

Upstairs, they heard babbling. The baby was awake.

"Go get Jack-Jack," Violet said, hoping the distraction would buy her time. She threw her shirt on over the suit and pulled her pyjama bottoms back on. She'd have to take off the suit later.

Dash made a face. "Aww, why do I have to change his nappy? You're the one in charge."

"I am, which is why I'm telling you to go get him," Violet said.

"No!"

"Dash," Violet warned, her whole body warming up. If she had to make a force field to get him to do what she wanted, she would try to.

"No!"

Violet stepped towards him and the doorbell rang.

They looked at each other.

"Mum!" Dash went running down the hall to the front door.

"Dash, wait! Mum wouldn't use the doorbell!" Violet shouted as Dash peered through the peephole.

"It's not Mum," he whispered when Violet caught up to him. "It's a lady."

"A lady?" Violet frowned. "Is it Mrs Caruso?"

"Nope. She's tall and younger. She's wearing jeans. She doesn't look like a mum."

"Don't open the door," she instructed.

"Violet Parr? If you can hear me, open this door!"

Violet and Dash looked at one another.

"Your parents sent me. Please open the door! You're in danger!"

Danger? Dash's eyes widened at the word. Before Violet could even think things through, her brother was throwing open the door and a tall, slender woman with mousy brown hair was rushing through it, slamming it shut behind her.

CHAPTER SIX
VIOLET

"You are Violet Parr, correct?" the woman asked, her breathing coming fast, her chest rising and falling as she locked the door behind her.

Violet didn't understand what was happening. "Yes, but…"

"And you're Dash Parr?" she continued, eyeing her brother.

"That's me," Dash said.

The woman closed her eyes and leant against the door, clutching her chest. "I'm so glad I had the right house."

"Who are you?" Violet asked.

The woman didn't answer the question. She looked around nervously, her eyes taking in the home. "Has anyone been here this morning? Have you had a delivery? Or had anyone call the house?"

Violet and Dash looked at one another, confused. Her mum's big rule was never to talk to strangers, and now they were locked in their house with one who was asking a whole lot of questions that didn't make sense.

"We haven't even eaten breakfast," Dash said with a shrug.

"That's good." The woman stood on her tiptoes in white trainers to look out the door window. Her jeans were rolled at the bottom and she was wearing a baggy jumper. "I don't see anyone suspicious but that doesn't mean they aren't hiding out there. We should get away from the door." She walked into the living room and Violet felt uneasy. "Do you have a back exit we can use? Where is the baby?"

Dash looked at Violet and she could see the fear in his eyes. "Uh..."

Violet snapped to attention, feeling her emotions churn. *Protect your brothers*, she remembered Mum saying. "Hang on. Who are you? And what are you doing in our house?" Before the woman could answer, Violet held a hand up to stop her and looked at her brother. "Dash, go upstairs and change Jack-Jack," she instructed him.

He looked from his sister to the woman. "But..."

"Go!" Violet insisted. "And don't come downstairs till I tell you to." Dash raced up the stairs, and Violet narrowed her eyes at the woman standing in their living room. "Who are you?"

"I'm sorry to barge in like this," the woman said, running a hand through her shoulder-length brown hair. She had a fringe. Violet had always wanted a fringe but the thought of not being able to hide behind her hair had always stopped her. "I'm just trying to help, but I guess I'm not doing a great job. I didn't mean to scare you, it's just I'm scared myself." She rubbed her arms as if to keep warm. "We don't have much time."

I'm scared myself. The words made Violet uncomfortable. Still, she wouldn't show fear. "I'm going to ask you again: who are you?"

The woman looked at Violet. She had a heart-shaped face, amber eyes and smooth peach-toned skin. Violet couldn't gauge how old she was. Her clothes seemed young, but she was clearly an adult. "I'm a friend," she said and her chin quivered. "Of your parents."

"You know my parents?" The woman nodded. If they were supposed to go with a stranger, her mother would have called and told her. Violet was sure of that. But her mum hadn't called and she hadn't come home last night. Violet felt her whole body warming, her skin starting to prickle.

Something was wrong. "You still didn't answer the question. Who are you?"

The woman looked out the blinds in the living room. When she turned around, Violet could see the terror in her eyes. "I'll explain everything when we get out of here." Her eyes went to the staircase upstairs behind Violet. "Right now, you need to grab some things and get your brothers. We have to move. Fast."

Violet thought of the force field she hoped would be at the tip of her fingers if this woman took one step towards the stairs. Could she make one when she was this anxious? Violet held her ground. "I'm not going anywhere till you tell me who you are and what's going on."

The woman smiled. "You remind me of your mum."

Violet faltered. No one ever said that. Her mum was Elastigirl. She'd once saved a huge ocean liner full of people by using her elasticity to pull a damaged ship into port. *With her arms.* Violet couldn't even lift her head up when she was called on in English class.

"My name is Mirage," the woman said gently.

Mirage. That was the name on the card in Dad's office. For a split second, this news put her at ease – her dad knew this woman. It still didn't explain what Mirage was doing at their house. "And why are you here?"

"I'm a friend of Mr Incredible and Elastigirl. They sent

me to get you."

Violet inhaled sharply. This woman was using her parents' Super names.

"Yes, I know who they are, and I know who you are too," Mirage said, and Violet faltered. "If I were the enemy, would I know your parents' secret identities?"

She had a point.

"Rest assured, your secret is safe. Your parents sent me here to protect you and your brothers, which is why we have to go before the others get here."

"The others? What's going on? Where are my parents?" Violet asked. Mirage's eyes fell to the floor and Violet grew anxious. "Tell me what's going on, or I'm not going anywhere."

Mirage laced her fingers together. "You may want to sit down."

Violet's whole body began to tremble. "I don't want to sit." She folded her arms across her chest. "Where is my mum?" Her voice cracked slightly.

Mirage swallowed hard. She looked like she was thinking the question over. "What is the simplest way for me to explain this? Your parents were working for a top-secret branch of the government that I work for."

"You work for the government?" Violet said sceptically. "No offense, but you look kind of young. Like a babysitter."

At this, Mirage smiled. "Really? Thank you." She shook her head. "Anyway, your parents – did you know they were still in the Super business?"

Violet tensed. She knew the line she was supposed to spin if anyone ever brought up her parents' alter egos. "My parents are retired."

Mirage raised an eyebrow. "They were supposed to be, but I promise you they're not."

"Supers are illegal," Violet reminded her, hearing her ears start to ring. "My parents don't use their powers anymore." *Unless Dad needs to lift a sofa so Mum can vacuum.*

"That's not entirely true," Mirage said slowly. "Your parents were doing some deep undercover work with a branch of the government that is so top-secret, the world doesn't even know it exists."

Top-secret government work? Mirage couldn't be right, could she? Her Mum was constantly stressing they were retired, Supers were illegal and they had to fly below the radar. Her Dad wasn't thrilled about this, but he stuck to the rules – most of the time. "My mum and dad wouldn't want to get in trouble for doing Super work. They don't want to have to move again."

"No, they didn't want that," Mirage agreed, "but you have to trust me – they *were* doing top-secret Super work."

"For the Agency?" She'd heard her Dad mention the Agency before. She'd never met her dad's former boss, but she knew who he was. Every time her dad got in trouble for using his powers and they had to move, some guy named Rick Dicker helped clean up the mess.

Violet noticed Mirage falter. "You know about the Agency?"

Violet nodded.

"No, this is a different branch." Mirage looked out the blinds again. "Much more dangerous."

"Are my parents in danger?" Violet held on to the nearest chair for support.

Mirage didn't say anything at first. "I can see you're a smart girl, Violet. I'm not going to lie to you. Something went wrong on your parents' mission and they're in trouble. I was sent here to get you so you can help them, but we have to go now before it's too late."

So Mum and Dad weren't at a conference. They were off using their powers, which is what they always told Violet not to do. A spark of annoyance flickered inside her, but she kept it at bay thinking of the bigger picture: her parents were in trouble, and they needed their children's help. Could this be true? Violet's heart beat like a drum as she thought about something her mum had said the other night in the car. *If anything is wrong…* Was this what Mum had meant?

She'd told Violet to protect her brothers. She never mentioned Mirage. Still, her name was on a card in Dad's office. Violet was so confused. "Where are my parents now?"

"If you come back to headquarters with me, I will tell you everything." Mirage took Violet's hand. "Right now, the important thing is we get out of here before the others arrive. Now come on. We have to move quickly! Please." She glanced towards the door again. "I've already stayed too long and said too much." If Violet wasn't mistaken, Mirage looked frightened.

"Headquarters?" Violet pulled out of Mirage's grasp. She thought again of the note from Mum in her pocket. Mum had told her to first try Lucius and if that failed to use the comms link. She hadn't done either yet. She wasn't about to get in a car with someone she didn't know before she tried to reach her mum. "I'm sorry. I'm staying right here till I reach my parents."

Mirage gulped hard. "Violet, you can't do that. I was serious when I said you and your brothers were in danger." Her eyes darted back and forth. "Mastermind is coming for you."

"Mastermind?" Violet scoffed. "Mastermind hasn't been seen in fifteen years."

"You've heard of the super villain? Good!" Mirage seemed pleased. "Then you know how dangerous

Mastermind can be. Mastermind's on the way here as we speak. If you want to live, and you want to help your parents, you need to come with me right now. I'll tell you everything else once we're somewhere safe, but we're running out of time."

Mastermind was gone. If there was ever a moment to think Mirage was lying, this was it. Violet made an executive decision. She walked swiftly to the front door and opened it again. All was calm and normal as it would be on a Sunday morning. Just like yesterday, someone was outside mowing their lawn, and Dash's friends were playing in the street. She wasn't in any danger in her own house on her own street. *Everything is fine*, she told herself. *Mum and Dad are fine.* "I want you to leave."

Mirage stood there for a moment, then walked to the door slowly, as if she expected Violet to change her mind.

A siren sounded in the distance and Mirage tensed. "Violet, please..." she started to say and stopped herself. Instead, she reached inside a pocket in her jeans. "Fine. Call your parents. Check me out, but when you realise I'm right – *if* you're still alive – call me." She handed her a crisp white business card before walking out. It was the same card Violet had found on Dad's desk. "And if someone other than me rings this doorbell again?" She paused. "Run."

CHAPTER SEVEN
VIOLET

Violet slammed the door behind her, making sure it was locked.

"Who was that?" Dash asked from the top of the stairs. "What did she want?"

Violet peered through the blinds and watched Mirage walk to a small yellow sports car parked at the curb. Mirage reached into her bag, pulled out chic, cat's-eye black sunglasses, and put them on before getting in the car and driving away.

"Violet?" Dash badgered. "Who was that? Does she really know Mum and Dad? Where are they? Why did she want us to go with her?"

Violet massaged her temples, the way she saw her mum

do when Dash was blazing through a list of questions that he demanded answers for. The truth was, she didn't have any. All she knew was Mirage's card was in her dad's office, so he clearly knew her, but if her parents wanted them to go with the woman, they would have sent word. Wouldn't they?

Fine. Call your parents. Check me out, but when you realise I'm right – if you're still alive – call me. Violet shuddered, thinking of Mirage's words. *Mum and Dad are fine*, she told herself. *They probably just lost track of time.* She would try Lucius, and if that failed, she'd use the comms link. "Bring Jack-Jack downstairs and feed him breakfast," Violet told Dash. "I'll explain everything in a minute."

"Where are you going? Violet? Violet?" Dash called, but she ignored him and hurried down the hall to her dad's office again. She heard Dash audibly groan.

Violet went straight to the rotary phone. She knew Lucius's number by heart. Mum had made her memorise it when they'd moved to Metroville, since he and Honey were the only friends they had nearby. Her fingers were shaky as she dialled the numbers on the rotary wheel and watched the circle spring back. She knew it was early on a Sunday to be calling, but she had no choice. The phone rang two, three times, then four. Violet's fingers curled tighter around the phone receiver.

Even if Lucius was asleep, he would have heard the

phone by the sixth ring, wouldn't he? Or the seventh? Honey, his wife, would have picked up by the eighth… or the ninth. The phone continued to ring ten, then eleven times before Violet finally hung up. Where were they?

A dark thought occurred to her: could Mastermind have got to Lucius, too?

She needed to calm down. First, she would try the comms link. Violet scanned the room, looking for it. She spotted it next to a pencil holder full of Mr Incredible pencils. The comms link looked like a torch with a giant red button on top. One press of the red button and it would connect her with her parents, who carried an identical one on them at all times. Her dad had shown her how to use one before she even learnt how to write her own name. Violet stared at the comms link for a moment, suddenly paralysed with fear.

What if her parents didn't answer?

"Violet!" Dash yelled again. This time she heard Jack-Jack babbling. "What's going on?"

"Give me a minute!" Violet shouted back. "And don't come in here this time!"

Mum and Dad are fine, she told herself again. *Mum will answer*. Violet took the comms link and held it firmly in her hand for a moment before she clicked the switch to turn it on. She closed her eyes and pressed the red button.

"Mum? Can you hear me? It's Violet."

She let go of the button and waited for a response. All she heard was static.

She tried to calm her nerves. Her parents could be busy, or maybe they didn't hear her. Violet pressed the button again.

"Mum? Dad? Are you there? It's Violet. I need to talk to you right away."

Violet let go of the button and listened to static come over the line again. She waited longer this time. Static flooded her ears and her fingers grew sweaty around the device as she imagined the worst. Could Mastermind really be back and after her family? No. Her parents would have warned them.

They certainly weren't working for a secret branch of the government… were they?

Even if something were wrong, they would have got word to someone that they were in trouble, right?

Like Lucius? Who also wasn't answering.

Violet's stomach tightened.

If Lucius were in trouble too, would they have resorted to sending a *complete stranger* to warn their kids they were in danger?

Yes, a small voice in her head said. *If they had no other option.*

Her heart pounded faster. What if Mirage had been telling the truth and she'd just put her family in more danger?

"Mum?" Violet tried the comms link again. "This is an

emergency. Please answer. Mum? I need you to answer right away! Mum?"

All she heard was more static.

Don't panic, she told herself. *Mum and Dad are Supers. They can handle anything.* And they had. Her dad once fought off a great white shark.

"Violet?" Dash pushed open the door to the office, carrying Jack-Jack in his arms. The baby screamed in delight when he saw her, reaching his sticky hands out. In a trance, Violet took him, still wondering what her next move was. "Did you talk to Mum? Or Dad?"

Violet dug into her pocket for the note again and stared at it, willing it to tell her something new, but all that was written on it was Jack-Jack's schedule. Nothing about how to find her in an emergency. And this was an emergency.

"Violet? What's going on?"

Violet could feel her patience thinning. "Dash, I'm trying to reach Mum, okay? And Lucius. No one is answering." She knew her voice was strained.

"Then maybe you should call that lady," Dash suggested, moving around the office, again picking up various things he wasn't supposed to touch, like a box with a handwritten message on the side that said, *Thought you'd get a kick out of what I found in storage! – Lu.* Violet was too worried to stop Dash from going through it.

"Yeah," Violet said absentmindedly as Dash lifted the box's lid.

"Maybe she's at the door again," Dash suggested. "Someone's been banging for the last two minutes."

Violet froze. "Someone's at the door?" She stopped and listened. Someone was pounding.

Could it be Mastermind? Did super villains make house calls?

She reached in her pocket again, pulling out Mirage's number. Should she call it? Or was she just being paranoid? Maybe it was a delivery her mum was expecting and she was blowing this whole thing out of proportion.

The knocking grew louder. Violet put Jack-Jack on the floor and looked at Dash. "Stay here. And keep the door locked until I tell you to open it."

"Lock myself in Dad's office?" Dash couldn't help but grin. "Not a problem."

Violet went to the door. "Stay quiet."

"But…" she heard Dash say as she shut the door behind her and walked swiftly to the front of the house, peeking through the nearest window to see who was there.

It was two men wearing… tuxedos. They looked like they were headed to a wedding or delivering flowers. Not like super villain minions who would try to kidnap her and her brothers. Violet resisted the urge to laugh. She was driving herself mad! Mastermind was not after them. They knocked again and despite all the warnings Mirage had given, Violet felt confident opening the door.

"I think you have the wrong house," she said, feeling relieved.

Both men were wearing black sunglasses and standing at attention, their hands folded in front of them, their expressions serious. One was bald, the other had short black hair.

"Is this the Parr residence?" the man on the left asked.

So it wasn't the wrong house. Violet tensed. "Can I help you?" Slowly she reached for the door again, preparing to shut it on their fingers if she had to. Her black hair fell in front of one eye, shielding her from seeing them fully. She tried to control her breathing.

"We're looking for the Parr children," the second man said.

Warning signs went off in her head. *Mastermind's minions.* Her gut told her she and her brothers were in danger. Violet looked out at the street, frantically searching for Mirage's car, but it was gone. It was only then that she realised things were unusually quiet, when the street had been bustling a few minutes earlier. No one was playing ball out front. Her neighbour and his lawn mower had disappeared. Not a single car drove by. She bit the inside of her cheek. She needed to get her brothers out of the house. "I don't know the Parrs. You definitely have the wrong house. Sorry!"

Violet tried to shut the door.

The bald guy grabbed the frame and swung the door open again. "I don't think we do, Violet." He stepped forwards, grabbing her wrist. "You need to come with me."

She heard Mirage's voice in her head. *Run.* "Let go of me!" Violet shouted.

The man held firm and Violet did a move her dad had taught her. With her free hand, she reached for the wrist he was holding and twisted her body into him, forcing him to let go. Then she stomped as hard as she could on his foot. The man groaned in response.

"We need backup!" the other man said into the gadget on his wrist and reached for her.

Violet did the opposite, slamming the front door and running down the hall to the office, realising too late she hadn't locked the door behind her.

"Dash!" she shouted. "Open the door!" Turning around, she saw the two men right behind her.

"Stop yelling!" Dash said, opening the door. "Who was at the – uh-oh…" Dash said, seeing the men.

"It's the other Super kids! Grab them!" one of the guys shouted.

Violet slid into the room. "Close the door! Close the

door!" But it was too late. Something whizzed past her head and Violet looked down.

The intruders had tossed small metal balls into the room. They exploded, a heavy, dark smoke filling the room. Smoke bombs!

Violet spun around, coughing. She couldn't see her hand in front of her face. "Dash! Where are you? Where's Jack?"

"Violet!" she heard her brother call even though she couldn't see him. She heard Jack-Jack start to cry and Dash coughing too. "Where are you?"

She groped for the door, unsure if she should still try to close it or if she was locking them all inside. She felt someone grab her waist. She screamed.

"Got one!" one of the men shouted as Violet struggled to get out of his grip. "Spread out! There are two more Supers!"

"Let go! Dash! Grab Jack! Run!" she cried, scratching at the man's hands in desperation. She looked around wildly hearing people shouting and the commands of others entering the house. They were outnumbered.

"Use a force field!" Dash shouted from somewhere in the room as things began to crash.

A force field! Yes! Violet felt her fingers spark for a second, but she was so nervous they immediately fizzled out. She tried again, struggling harder, backing up and knocking whoever was holding her into a bookshelf. She heard her dad's trophies go tumbling. Violet couldn't focus. Her attention was too scattered – on Jack-Jack, on Dash, on the yelling – and she could barely move her hands. She couldn't summon her powers on command. The man began to drag her out of the room and her panic took hold. Mastermind had her parents and soon would have her and her brothers, and she couldn't even use her stupid powers to get out of this.

"Let my sister go!"

Violet looked up. The smoke had cleared enough that she could see Dash shoot something into the air.

A heavy stream of fire flew out of whatever he was using, igniting the ceiling. Dash screamed. Jack-Jack squealed like it was a show. Violet and the man holding her went slack at the sight.

"What is that?" Violet cried, getting loose and running to her brother as the fire quickly spread across the ceiling, expanding in seconds like a sprinkler fanning out on a lawn.

Dash's eyes widened as he glanced at the megaphone-shaped device in his hands. This one was red, not blue. "I thought it was the freeze ray!"

"Fire!" one of the men cried, running for the door as a bookcase became engulfed in flames. "Someone call Mastermind! We need to abort!"

Violet swept up Jack-Jack from the floor with one hand

and with her free arm reached for Dash. "The house is on fire. We have to go!"

"We can put it out, right?" Dash said as Violet searched for a path to exit. There were men in tuxedos everywhere she turned, some shouting for a fire extinguisher, others on their wrist gadgets calling Mastermind for help.

"There they are!" one of Mastermind's goons yelled, racing towards her again.

If they could make it down the hall to the garage, they might have a chance. And to do that, she'd need her powers. She had to try. She let go of Dash's hand, passing him the baby, and her hands flew out in front of her as she focused on the goons and her anger. Her whole body seemingly became electrified before a large force field shot from her hands and the men in the hallway went flying backwards. Violet's mouth opened in surprise, then she quickly made another force field around the three of them, like a protective bubble.

"How are you doing that?" Dash shouted as Jack-Jack giggled with delight.

"I don't know! And I don't know how long I can hold it either!" Every part of her body was pulsing as she felt the energy crackling through her. "We need to back out of the garage!" she said as the ceiling in the hallway caught fire too, smoke filling the room faster.

"Then move! You're too slow!" Dash complained.

He was right. She began backing up, but she wasn't quick enough. What if the force field fizzled? What if the fire made their back exit impossible?

Dash reached for something on the floor in their protective shield and held it up. It was his skateboard. "Jump on!" he said.

Violet stared at the board for a moment before realisation took hold. "Dash, I could kiss you!"

"Gross! Don't!" Dash dropped the skateboard on the ground, and Violet hopped on. Dash couldn't both push them and hold Jack. Violet had no choice but to drop the force field and grab the baby. Dash held on to the back of her shirt.

"The shield is down! Grab them!" the goons shouted.

Dash's feet churned and the skateboard started to move. The skateboard was going so fast the wheels were starting to smoke. Jack-Jack screamed with delight as the three kids rocketed down the hallway, slammed through the door into the garage and rushed down the driveway. In seconds, they were down the street, and Mastermind's men couldn't keep up.

When Violet looked back, she felt ill. Their house was engulfed in flames. The sounds of sirens whirred in the distance. Her stomach twisted and turned, but there was nothing she could do. Hopefully the firefighters would put the fire out in time. The important thing was that she and her brothers were safe.

"Can I stop now?" Dash shouted as they whipped around the corner of the street.

"No!" Violet said instinctively. They had to get somewhere far away. Somewhere safe. But where? Lucius wasn't answering the phone. Her parents might be captured. Their house was on fire. Violet bit the inside of her lip. She knew she only had one choice. "Get us to the back door of the supermarket, but slow down before the parking lot," she shouted. Dash slowed as they approached the shopping area, and Violet handed him the baby, who was squealing like he'd just spent an hour on their garden swing.

"We're alive to fight another day!" Dash cheered.

"How can you be excited?" Violet asked, sounding moody but not caring. "We almost died back there." *All because of our stupid powers.*

"Who were those guys?" Dash asked. He didn't even sound out of breath. "Violet?"

"Shhh!" Violet pulled the crisp white business card from her pocket, slotted a coin into the payphone, and dialled.

Someone answered on the first ring.

"Violet?"

"You were right," Violet whispered.

"Tell me where you are," Mirage said without hesitation. "I'll be right there."

CHAPTER EIGHT
MIRAGE

If someone had told her five years ago that she'd someday find herself in a tricked-out sports car speeding through a residential neighbourhood to pick up a frightened group of children on the run, she would have laughed them out of acting class.

But here she was and this was her current role: protective, considerate babysitter.

The call from the girl, Violet, had come in while she was on the phone with her acting teacher, Monique, complaining about today's 'scene'.

"It sounds like you were clearly dressed for the part," Monique had said. "And what do we know about dressing for the role we want to play?"

"Walking in our character's shoes makes us feel like we *are* that character," Mirage recited. She was parked a few streets away from the Parr's house at this point, and had pulled off the itchy brunette wig she'd decided on for the part (mousy brown hair seemed to scream 'babysitter'). Underneath, her real hair was a short, white-blonde bob. The baggy 'babysitter-ish' jumper she'd chosen that morning had also been removed. She now sat in a formfitting white silk shirt that was much more her everyday style than this jeans-and-trainers ensemble. She shuddered at the thought of having to change into the other outfit again. "I was sympathetic and spoke softly. I tried to channel the perfect babysitter," she lamented to Monique. "I was part mother hen, part older sister."

"And I'm sure you were wonderful," Monique said. "Just because the children didn't warm to you immediately doesn't mean you didn't do the job to perfection."

"Tell my boss that," Mirage said.

Syndrome – as her boss preferred to be called – wasn't happy when she had called to tell him the kids refused to go with her.

"What am I paying you for if you can't do your job?" he'd barked. "Just stay nearby. I'm calling in the reinforcements."

She'd flinched. "Are you sure that's a good idea? The girl knew about the Agency."

He scoffed. "Please, a kid can't contact them. We just need to get ahold of them and then my plan will come together."

Mirage hesitated. "And that plan is…"

"I'm working on it!" he barked.

She hated when he got like this. Manic. Worked up. Unreasonable.

He audibly exhaled. "Look, I'm stressed, okay?"

"I can tell," she said.

"I'm not going to hurt them. Just scare them a bit so we can get them to go with you. Then they'll call you. Believe me." He'd hung up before she could debate the idea.

Yep, Syndrome was losing it.

That's when she'd phoned Monique.

"I had no time to prepare for this role," Mirage said. "He literally gave me the job last night. There was no time to do character studies of the children's personalities or do research on babysitters in general." She'd never babysat a day in her life. Children weren't particularly fond of her. The feeling was mutual. But he'd insisted she take this part, which was different from all the other parts she'd played for this job. She wasn't even sure he had a fully fleshed-out plan. Who was she kidding? He didn't. What Syndrome wanted her to do was basically kidnapping, and then he'd figure out the rest later. She had no clue who this Mastermind was or what this nullifier he wanted to get his hands on could do. When she'd pointed out all the flaws in kidnapping Super children, Syndrome had doubled her salary on the spot. That made it hard to complain. (She'd been dying to have the money to go to a three-month intensive acting camp abroad with famed director Brad Bird. She knew three girls who'd been cast in regular sitcom roles after being part of Bird's camp.) Still, the nagging doubt remained.

"I'm sure you're just being too hard on yourself," Monique said. "When we have class this week, we'll role-play and you can show me the scene you performed. I'm sure I'll find your babysitter rendition top-notch. Where did you say this production was taking place again?"

"Errr…" Mirage paused.

Her current job was complicated, to put it mildly. She'd been working for Buddy Pine (aka Syndrome) for six months after seeing the advertisement on the board at her acting school.

> WANTED: Acting professional willing to play multiple roles for a short-term job that promises to be full of adventure. Pays well. Discretion is a must.

Short-term, long-term, it didn't matter. The "pays well"

line was what got her. If Mirage finally – *finally* – wanted to break into the business she'd dreamt about since she was a child, she needed help. Monique's acting school wasn't cheap, but it was one of the best in Metroville. At Mirage's first audition, the legendary acting teacher had said she thought Mirage had "great potential". Great potential was expensive.

"It's local theatre, with the promise of a national tour," Mirage lied.

What could she really say? She was working for a guy who could capture Supers, even though he wasn't one himself? Forget the fact that working with Supers in any way was illegal. Or that the job she'd taken – after signing an ironclad confidentiality agreement – helped her boss attract various retired Supers willing to help test a high-priced robot on a private island.

Monique wouldn't have believed her. Sometimes Mirage didn't believe it herself.

Having worked for Syndrome for several months now, she was starting to suspect he didn't actually work for a secret branch of the government like he claimed. He was an eccentric billionaire with an arsenal of brilliantly designed gadgets. The biggest one was an Omnidroid robot that got better and better with every Super it fought. When Mirage had inquired about the purpose of the Omnidroid,

Syndrome had asked her out to dinner. Was it a date or a business meeting? At first, she wasn't sure, but now that they'd gone out several times, and Syndrome had made his affections known, she had to admit to herself that she was casually dating her boss. This didn't feel smart, but neither did the job sometimes.

At least Syndrome had begun to open up to her. He told her the Omnidroid was the key to ridding the world of Supers once and for all. While they were illegal, Syndrome claimed they all wanted back in the action, and that's where he came in – hiring them to train his Omnidroid to beat every Super on the planet. Once the robot was ready, it, and so many other devices he'd created, could be sold to governments worldwide so they could protect their countries without having to look to Supers for help. "With my advancements, everyone can protect themselves and be Super," he'd explained. "And when everyone is Super, no one will be." The idea stuck with her. Why should some people have advantages that others didn't?

Before Syndrome, she'd never really had an opinion about Supers one way or the other. The town she'd grown up in had never had a visit from a Super when things went south. These Supers, before they were banned, were meant to be role models, but as Syndrome explained it, they thought they were "better than the rest of us". After he told her the story of how Mr Incredible had treated him back in the day, she had to agree – these Supers were no role models. Was his obsession with Supers a bit much? Yes. But was the pay so good she turned the other cheek? Absolutely.

She reminded herself of this reasoning every time she took on a new persona for her job. She'd managed to track down Supers in hiding by posing as everything from a waitress to an expat to an heiress. Her job seemed to be part spy (great for practising for a spy role!) and part actress, and Syndrome was thrilled with her results. "I could kiss you," he'd say when she tracked down another Super. Sometimes he did.

The job, the casual boyfriend, the excellent pay… it was all satisfying at first.

But lately?

She was starting to feel uncomfortable. Some of the Supers she found for Syndrome tested the Omnidroid and *died*. The first time it happened, she'd been upset, and Syndrome had reminded her of the confidentiality agreement first, and doubled her pay second. "Supers are always looking to prove themselves in ridiculous ways," he'd reminded her. "Fighting my droid was a risk they were willing to take."

She guessed completing the tasks Syndrome laid out for her was a risk she'd been willing to take too.

Syndrome, as odd as he could be, was magnetic. Mirage remembered the day she'd met him at her interview. She'd walked into the office and found a man with an athletic build, broad shoulders and even broader confidence. She'd been taken by his smile, which waffled between charming and mocking. He wore a fitted black jumper, dress trousers and an expensive pair of Italian leather shoes, which were lazily propped up on the desk in front of him. The gold watch on his wrist cost more than the rent on her flat for two years. He had flaming red hair that was gelled back, giving her a proper look at his porcelain white face and bright blue eyes that never left her face the entire time she was being interviewed. He was attentive, witty and, as she quickly learnt, intense. Maybe that's why she'd agreed to go on some dates with him.

This past week, when she'd finally tracked down a Super he'd been searching for, she could tell something had changed. Mr Incredible became his sole focus. He'd even made his own black-and-blue Supersuit, complete with a cape. He said every decent Super had a cape.

But unlike the other Supers, Bob Parr wasn't easily beaten. The Omnidroid had to keep getting tweaked to fight the man, and still it would lose. Just when Syndrome thought he had Mr Incredible beat, the guy beat the droid again. Even she was impressed. Syndrome, however, had gone off the deep end, not sleeping till he'd created a droid that could finally best the guy. And once he had him in his grasp, she thought he'd finish Mr Incredible off too. Instead, he'd held him captive like a pet.

And then his wife had shown up. Turned out she was Elastigirl. The droid captured her, too.

Syndrome's head practically blew off at that news. And that was before he learnt they had three kids at home. *Super* kids.

"Do you understand what this means?" he'd crowed to Mirage, hopped up in a way she'd never seen before. "I can finally get my hands on that nullifier Mastermind is letting waste away!"

"Nullifier?" she'd questioned, as some of the other workers rushed in, recording Mr Incredible and Elastigirl freaking out behind bars. Mirage didn't understand what was happening.

"I need those kids," he'd said, a strange look in his eye. "You have to go get them. Right away. Tell them their parents are in danger. Tell them…" He glanced back at Mr Incredible. "Tell them Mastermind is after their parents."

"Buddy!" Mr Incredible had railed. "I'm warning you… if you touch my kids…"

"Don't call me Buddy!" Syndrome screamed.

"We'll both tear you apart, limb from limb!" Elastigirl

had roared, sounding scarier than her husband. "Don't you go anywhere near our children! You hear me?"

Syndrome looked at his workers filming. "You get all that?" They nodded. "Good." He turned back to Mirage. "Go. Get. Those. Children."

"And do what with them?" Mirage cried. "You want me to babysit?"

"Yes! Consider it part of your job," he'd said.

Babysitting? "But…" she'd started to complain.

"Bring them to my place." His smile was eerie. "I've got the most brilliant of brilliant ideas. One that will give me everything I've ever wanted. Just leave the rest up to me."

Turned out his idea wasn't that brilliant, because getting the kids to agree to come with her had been impossible! She had no one to vent to other than Monique, whom she had to talk to in code.

"This sounds like an exciting job, dear," Monique said, bringing Mirage back to the present. "One that you're lucky to have."

"Lucky," Mirage repeated. She wasn't so sure of that. Syndrome was currently unhappy with her for being unable to convince Violet to come with her. Well, guess what? She wasn't that thrilled with Syndrome either. Why had she mixed business with pleasure? Why? This boss/relationship business was getting messier by the minute.

Then her other phone line had begun to ring. It was the child. Violet.

"Monique, I have to go," Mirage said, getting excited. "I… am being called to the set."

"See you at class, dear!" Monique said. "Good luck!"

Mirage cleared her throat. *You are a babysitter,* she told herself before picking up. "Violet?"

"You were right," Violet said, her voice sounding small.

Yes. "Tell me where you are," Mirage said sweetly. "I'll be right there."

Back went the wig. On went the jumper. She'd met the children at a supermarket in downtown Metroville. *You need this job,* she told herself as she drove. When she arrived at the supermarket, she found two excitable little boys (One was in nappies. Great.) and a scared teen. Violet's face was partially covered by her long mop of blue-black hair. She could tell already this child wasn't like her parents – her confidence hadn't come in yet. She was shy. She was nervous.

Mirage lowered her black cat's-eye sunglasses and looked at the children. "Get in! Quickly." *And don't let that baby drool on my leather seats.*

"Can you take us to my parents?" Violet asked.

"First we need to get you somewhere safe," she told the child, trying to sound confident.

Violet shook her head. "You said they were in trouble. We have to go help them."

She placed a cool hand on Violet's own and smiled in a reassuring way. "And we will. But first we need a plan. And reinforcements. You're being hunted," she whispered, not wanting the younger ones to hear. "We get you somewhere safe, then we will go after your parents. Understood?"

Violet looked unsure, but she nodded. "Buckle up!" she told her brothers as she slid in next to her in the front seat. "Thank you for coming to get us. I didn't know who else to call."

Mirage tried to look confident as she pulled away from the curb. "You did the right thing."

"Our house is on fire!" Dash yelled from the back seat.

"What?" Mirage tried not to look surprised, but she couldn't help it. Syndrome wouldn't have set their house on fire to get to them, would he?

"It was my fault," Dash said worriedly. "But it was an accident."

"I'm sure the fire department came and put it out," Violet said, giving Mirage a grown-up look that seemed to say *back me up here*.

"Yes, I'm sure the fire is out," Mirage agreed.

Dash had already moved on. "What do all those buttons do? Why do you have a phone in your car? What is that screen for? Does your car have a TV? Can we watch it? Violet, how do you know this lady? Is she a teacher? Is she, Violet? Is she?"

Mirage took a deep breath. That one was going to take some getting used to.

"She's..." Violet glanced at Mirage nervously, and Mirage completely understood the girl's expression. It was obvious the teen hadn't told her brother everything yet. How could she have when the attack on their home had occurred almost immediately after she'd left?

Mirage turned and smiled at the boy and the baby in the seat belt beside him. The boy looked just like his father. "I'm Mirage, and we're going to go on a little adventure. Is that all right with you?"

"Yes!" Dash said, returning to his happy state. "Can I press one of those buttons? Does this car go fast? Can you make it go fast now?"

This was going to be a long drive. Mirage adjusted her sunglasses and took off down the main road headed out of town, towards the water. What would a babysitter say in this moment? "Only grown-ups can drive a car, Dash. You know that." He groaned. "But I promise you, we're going to play some games once we get to our destination." She let the magic words drop. "The place we're headed is top-secret."

The boy's eyes widened. "Cool."

"Very cool," she agreed and gave Violet a small smile. The teen's hair was completely covering her face now and her arms were wrapped around her waist. For a second, Mirage felt bad for her. But then she thought again of who her father was and the threat this family posed to the world.

"We're going to your headquarters?" Violet asked.

Headquarters. Her boss's house. It was the same thing. "Yes. We'll plan our strategy there." Mirage turned to the back seat. "So, Dash, can I trust you to keep this place a secret?"

"Absolutely!" Dash declared.

"I thought I could. I could tell you were clever from the moment I saw you." She gripped the steering wheel tighter.

"That's me – clever!" Dash boasted. "And Jack-Jack could win a medal for pooping."

"Dash!" Violet scolded.

"What?" Dash made a face and folded his arms. "It's true. He's starting to smell and I don't think you brought nappies. Or a bottle."

Mirage wrinkled her nose. The boy was right. That baby needed a nappy change and she would not be the one doing it.

"Ba?" The baby said. "Ba?"

"Don't worry," Mirage assured them. "We'll get your brother everything he needs once we get there. For now, just sit back and relax. You've had a tough morning." She opened the windows wider to get some fresh air in the car and looked Violet's way again. The girl had her head down again and seemed to be staring at her trainers. "Why don't I tell you a bit about my friend whose house we're going to?"

"Friend?" Violet questioned. "I thought you were taking us to your boss?"

"He is," Mirage corrected herself, cursing her mistake. "He's my boss and my friend and he's going to help you. He's very excited to meet you all." That last part was true.

"He is?" Dash said eagerly.

"Yes! He's a big fan of your father's," she said. *Well, he was once upon a time.* "I already radioed ahead to say we were on our way. He's so glad you're safe."

"What did those men want?" Dash asked.

"Dash," Violet warned.

"It's all right," Mirage jumped in. "We should be honest with him. Then he won't be so frightened." Violet didn't say anything. "Those men work for someone who is hunting Supers and their families." Dash's eyes widened. "But you're safe now. Understood?"

"Kind of." Dash still looked confused.

Yeah, Mirage was, too. "For now, just enjoy the ride."

The town was in their rearview mirror and Mirage could see the water in the distance ahead of them. She hit the accelerator and the car took off, speeding down the wide-open road. Dash and the baby squealed in delight.

Fifteen minutes later they were on the outskirts of Metroville staring out at what looked like a forest at the water's edge.

"Where's your boss's house?" Dash asked as the car rolled up to a set of large metal gates.

She smiled. "Look up." She pressed a button and the car's roof retracted. The children turned their eyes to the sky.

"Whoa," Dash said. "He lives in a tree house?"

"You guessed it," Mirage said, although she personally wouldn't call the modern, circular home a tree house. Built on stilts and overlooking the city and the water, the house had 360-degree views of the surrounding area. It was a technological advancement in home design that Syndrome had created himself. Mirage punched a few buttons on the gate and a small blue blinking light popped out, which scanned her retina.

"Match! Mirage. You may proceed," said an electronic voice.

"Whoa," Dash said again.

Whoa indeed, Mirage thought as she pulled the car through the gates and directly into a garage camouflaged as a cave. She turned off the car and got out. The three children followed her, looking around in wonder at her boss's toys that also occupied the expansive cave: four other cars (including a ghastly Pizza Planet truck that was tricked out to be a decoy), two sports models, a small plane and several motorbikes.

"Are these all his?" Dash asked as he hurried along beside her.

"They are," she said, forcing a smile. Violet carried the baby, who was starting to whine and rub his eyes. Maybe the child would sleep when they got him upstairs. Mirage hoped Syndrome had ordered baby gear for this experiment of his. She had no idea how long he wanted to hold on to these three.

Deal with one problem at a time, she reminded herself, walking swiftly to the lift and waiting for them at the other end of the cave. She took another deep breath. There was no turning back now.

She pressed the button on the lift and a new laser eye popped out of a compartment on the door. The blue light pulsed and scanned the area.

"Match. Mirage," said the voice. "Identify others."

"Violet, Dash and Jack Parr," Mirage said, and the machine did a sweep of the children.

The lift door opened. "Please proceed upstairs."

"Cool!" Dash said for what felt like the millionth

time and raced into the lift. Violet and Jack-Jack followed.

Mirage hesitated. Syndrome hadn't said how long this new role was going to last, but already she wasn't sure she liked it. Children had raging hormones and unpredictable natures. She'd barely survived her own teens. How was she going to survive hanging out with these kids and staying in character the whole time? "It's only temporary", Syndrome had said.

Was it? That was one thing she'd learnt about her boss. His plans could change in an instance.

CHAPTER NINE
VIOLET

Am I doing the right thing? Violet wondered as the lift ascended at alarming speed.

She'd just called a perfect stranger to pick up her and her brothers, and now she was about meet the woman's mysterious boss.

After a lifetime of her parents drilling the 'don't talk to strangers' speech into her head, she'd just done the exact opposite.

What was she thinking?

That she was trying to save her family. What was it Mum had said Mastermind once warned her? "You fear me now? Wait till you have children. You'll never sleep again."

Mastermind was back. The villain had her parents and

was after her and her brothers. Lucius was missing. Violet had no choice but to trust Mirage.

The comms link was burning a hole in her pocket as the lift slowed to a stop. She hadn't had a moment since she'd called Mirage to try it again, but she was desperate to. She hoped Mirage was wrong: nobody was hunting Supers, and it was all a big mistake. If Mirage was right, which seemed far more likely, Violet hoped her parents had broken out by now.

Stupid powers.

Why did her parents start doing Super work again when it was illegal? It didn't make sense. Violet could feel her hands spark with electricity the more upset she got. Could Jack-Jack feel her fingers pulsing since she was holding him? She didn't want to hurt him. She tried to push the thoughts from her mind.

The lift doors opened and Violet squinted at the bright sunlight flooding the lift shaft.

"WHOA!" Dash raced into the massive living room.

The house looked like a glossy magazine spread about the lifestyles of the rich and famous, with a massive living room that featured floor-to-ceiling windows that overlooked the ocean and a lap pool that appeared to be on a wraparound deck. Every detail inside was modern, from the angular furniture to the sleek sculptures in each corner.

Trophies on a bookcase were the only personal touch. There were no photographs. It couldn't be more different from the Parrs' house – with its family albums, clutter and scattered toys – if it tried. Through an open doorway she spotted an equally large kitchen, and through another doorway, what looked like an office, where several people were sitting and tapping at computer stations.

Jack-Jack squealed in delight at the sight of a ball on a shag pile carpet rug and wiggled to get out of Violet's arms. Distracted, she put him down and let him crawl towards a large TV playing a cartoon and a stack of baby toys that appeared to be just waiting for him. Dash, meanwhile, had gone running towards a row of arcade games and a pinball machine lining one wall of the room. He reached the first machine and paused, looking back sheepishly.

"Is it okay if I play with these?" His cheeks burned.

Mirage's jaw went slack. "I… sure. I don't even know where they came from… these weren't here yesterday." She stopped herself, then smiled and said, "I bet these are for you to enjoy. Go on!"

Dash started the pinball game, and a cacophony of sounds filled the room, loud dings and beeping noises, making both Violet and Mirage wince. Dash cheered as his first high score rolled in.

"I thought you said we were going to headquarters?"

Violet asked, suddenly second-guessing her decision to come here. "This looks like someone's house."

Mirage nodded. "It is headquarters. I don't live here. My boss works out of his house."

"No one works from home," Violet pointed out.

Mirage smiled. "True, but his branch of the government is so top-secret, he has to. Most divisions don't know he exists. He has a remote location... offshore... but most of the time he works from here. In fact, he's in the office right now." Mirage walked to the door leading to the office and leant inside to talk to someone. She straightened and shut it before Violet could get a peek. "He's busy at the moment figuring out how to help your parents."

Violet moved to the doorway. "Then we should talk to him right now. You said my parents were in danger. We need to get supplies and go after them immediately."

"Yes," Mirage said, nodding like a bobblehead. She glanced back at the closed door. "And we will, but..."

"The government will help him, won't they?" Violet found herself talking fast. Her fingers sizzled and she felt light-headed. She was nervous. She was agitated. She was getting upset. It wasn't a good combination. She could disappear at any moment. "Even if other divisions don't know he exists?"

"I'm sure they will, but—" Mirage started to say, but

Violet cut her off again.

"So what we waiting for?" Violet felt her voice shoot up an octave as she started to hyperventilate. Her parents were in danger. Danger! "We can't sit here and play games when my parents need help. You said you wanted to help us!"

Mirage jumped back in surprise. "Violet...?"

"Yes?" Violet sounded irritated and she knew it.

Mirage waved her hands in Violet's general direction. "You seem to have lost your head!"

Violet looked down where her hands should be. They were gone. So were her feet and her hair. And apparently her head, too. So much for keeping their Super powers a secret. There was no need to talk to Dash about that privately now. "Don't freak out," Violet said.

"I'm not," Mirage said, even though she did sound a little freaked out. "I just didn't know you were... that they were... that your whole family was..."

"Super?" Violet finished. "Yeah, we are. At least everyone but Jack-Jack is."

Mirage stared at the space where her head should be. "Incredible," she whispered.

"Not really," Violet said with a sigh. "Not if you don't know how to control your powers. It's worse when I'm worried. Or scared. Or both. Not knowing what is happening with Mum and Dad is..."

"We're going to help them. You just have to be patient," Mirage said, her voice smooth and melodic. "You know how to be patient, don't you?" Violet didn't respond, and Mirage tapped her fingers on her small waist. "We have to focus. And to focus, we need to concentrate on our breathing. It's been a trying day, hasn't it? I need a two-second break before we move forward with our plans."

"A two-second break?" Violet said slowly. "What's that?"

"A breathing exercise I learnt from… my friend Monique. Try it with me."

Violet wasn't sure she was ready for this.

"I'm serious! This exercise works! You'll feel calmer. I know I will. Watch me first… er… if you can see me."

"I can see you," Violet said.

Mirage inhaled slowly, nodding five times as if she were counting, and then she exhaled for five, swooping her arms wide. Her shoulders relaxed. "Feels good! Try it. For me?"

Violet got the sense Mirage wasn't going to stop badgering her till she did as she was told. And there was the whole matter of being mostly invisible and not knowing how to reappear at the moment. "All right." Violet mimicked Mirage and inhaled for five and exhaled for five. She didn't feel better, but Mirage seemed to. She tried again. Her heart stopped racing. Her limbs tingled.

"You're back! See?" Mirage looked pleased. "It works."

"Okay, I'm calm. *Now* can you go get your boss so we can get going? We can call the Agency and tell them my parents have been kidnapped. When they hear Mastermind is back, trust me, they'll do something. Mastermind was one of the biggest villain threats Metroville ever saw."

"Did you say Mastermind?" Dash asked, appearing at Violet's side. "We just learnt about Mastermind in history class. That super villain once lifted the Metroville government offices and moved them to another country using a gadget. Mastermind lifted a building!" Dash said incredulously.

Violet seized up. "Did I say Mastermind? I didn't say Mastermind. Did I?" She looked at Mirage, who shook her head in agreement. "Go play pinball and keep an eye on Jack while I talk to Mirage, will you?"

Dash made a face. "Aww, I hate when you keep secrets."

Violet thought fast. "What's your pinball high score? Bet I can beat you. I'm coming over to try."

"No, you can't!" Dash zipped to the other side of the room as Violet hoped he would.

Violet lowered her voice to talk to Mirage again. "If it's okay with you, I don't want to tell Dash about my mum and dad being in trouble till we know more about what's going on."

"I understand," Mirage agreed. "I'll go talk to my

employer again. I should really let him know about your abilities." She whispered that last part as if Dash didn't know his sister lost her head sometimes. "I'll tell him how worried you are. I'm sure I can pull him away to come out and meet you all." A siren whirred on the game Dash was playing and he cheered again.

"I can come with you," Violet suggested.

"I think I should go alone. My boss is pretty private," Mirage explained. "It's best he and I have a word and then we can all talk. Have you even eaten yet today?" she asked brightly. "I am sure the kitchen is fully stocked." She glanced towards the kitchen, where Violet could see a table filled with every possible snack a kid could think of.

"They have pizza!" Dash crowed, running at lightning speed into the adjoining room and back again with a slice in his hands. He took a huge bite and grease dripped down his face onto his T-shirt. Jack-Jack reached for the food in Dash's hand and when he couldn't grab it, he immediately started to whine.

"Dash! You know Mum's rule – you can't eat anywhere but at a table," Violet told him.

"It's fine," Mirage said even though her voice was tight. "Eat up! And feed that baby," she added as Jack-Jack escalated to full-blown wailing. "Is he tired? Maybe he needs a nap." She looked at Jack. "Go to sleep, baby."

Violet and Dash looked at one another. "Uh… it doesn't work that way," Violet pointed out.

"I wish," Dash mumbled between pizza bites. Violet noticed he suddenly had three slices stacked on his plate, which meant he'd been back to the kitchen already for more food. If he overate, he'd have a stomachache.

Mirage smiled, revealing perfectly straight, very white teeth that gleamed brighter than the silver necklace she had on. "Well, whatever you need to do to get him to stop crying, do it. There's a spare bedroom off the kitchen. Maybe he can sleep on the bed."

Dash laughed. "Babies can't sleep on beds! They'll fall off."

Jack-Jack reached for the pizza again, mumbling "num-num". He cried harder.

"Then put him on the floor," Mirage said, sounding exasperated. "Try anything that will keep him quiet. My boss has work to do."

"Yes, work!" Violet picked up Jack-Jack, and he banged his head against her chest. Mirage exited one way and Violet went the other, grabbing a bag of nappies that had been left out for her before she continued to the spare room where she planned on changing Jack-Jack. He squirmed as she tried to pull off his snapped pyjama bottoms. She yanked them off. "Hey," she realised. "You're still in your Supersuit."

"So are you!"

Violet spun around. Of course, Dash was right behind her. This time he was holding a biscuit. Jack reached for it and Dash gave it to him.

For the first time in minutes, Jack stopped crying. Both Violet and Dash exhaled. Violet hoped Dash had more biscuits on him.

"I'm wearing mine because there was no time to take it off before those goons showed up at the house," Violet said. "But we have to put them back before Mum gets home."

Mum. Her heart lurched just thinking about the danger she and Dad were in.

"It was good we had them on at the house when all that crazy stuff started happening," Dash said, pulling at his collar to reveal his own suit. His face was pensive. "You think the house is okay?"

As much as she wanted to be mad at Dash, she knew today had been a lot already. "I'm sure the house is fine."

Dash smiled, relieved. "I'm going to go play more pinball!" He ran off again.

When Jack-Jack was changed and happy from having eaten his biscuit, Violet put him down and let him crawl on the floor, where he was fascinated by yet another white furry rug, which he patted like a dog before crawling out of the room.

Violet looked around. There was no sign of Mirage or anyone else who worked here. If there was ever a good time to try the comms link again, it was now. She slipped into the kitchen, pulled the comms link out of her pocket, and pressed the button. "Mum? Dad? It's Violet. Come in." There was only static. Violet sighed and shoved the device back in her pocket. Then she spied the phone on the wall.

Pressing her luck, she went over to it and quietly picked up the receiver, watching the doorway for signs of anyone. Quickly, she dialled Lucius's number. All it did was ring and ring. Where was he? Violet put the phone back on the wall and sighed again, trying not to get upset. She had no interest in doing Mirage's breathing exercise again today.

"… thought this through? How long is this going on for?"

Was that Mirage? Violet moved to the glass wall overlooking the outside deck and peeked through the curtains. She saw the back of Mirage's head as she talked to someone whose body was cloaked in the shadows. The other person spoke so low, Violet could only hear Mirage. She sounded upset. The other person sounded excitable and… were they jumping? Violet could see only the second person's shadow but they appeared to have big hair.

"That's not what I agreed to."

Violet tried to move closer, straining to hear the other person.

"I know this changes things, but you can't..." She was cut off. "I know, but... You think no one will notice? They're someone's children!"

Mirage was talking about them. Violet pressed against the glass, trying to hear what was being said. Was Mirage talking to her boss?

"You can't expect me to do that... No... That... But... I don't think you've thought this through. Wait!"

Violet felt her stomach tighten. Was this conversation about her or her parents or both? She put her ear to the glass to try to get a better angle and heard Jack-Jack squeal. Suddenly he was right in front of her. Mirage whipped her head around and Violet ducked, sure she'd been spotted. When she looked down, her whole body had disappeared – except for her clothes. Maybe she was in the clear.

She picked up Jack-Jack and paced the room. The baby didn't seem to be bothered by the fact Violet had no head again nor arms. Should she tell Mirage what she heard? Dash called for her and she headed to the kitchen.

"Violet, look! Look, Violet! LOOK!" He thrust a small, flat notepad-sized piece of metal in her face.

She stared at it for a moment. "What is that? A

mini TV?"

"It's a SpyGuy! *A SpyGuy*, Violet! And guess what?" Dash grinned. "Mirage said I could have it."

Violet frowned. "That looks expensive."

"It is."

Violet froze as Mirage came back into the room and stood watching them. Violet expected her to be annoyed if she'd seen her spying, but Mirage's expression was neutral.

"It's fine. My boss wanted Dash to have it. He's a bit tied up with everything going on." Mirage gave her a knowing look. "Unfortunately, he got some new information and got pulled away for a moment."

Violet tensed. "New information about my parents?"

Mirage looked uncomfortable. "I'm not at liberty to say, but I promise he will meet you soon. In the meantime, he wanted you to have the SpyGuys. You can have one too, if you want, Violet."

"Aaah!" Dash shouted, making Jack-Jack squeal with delight. "I can't believe I have my own SpyGuy! I always wanted one, but Mum said they were too expensive and not for kids." He paused. "But I'm not a kid. I won't break it. I swear." He clutched it to his chest, and Violet suspected if someone tried to take it from him, they'd have to pry it from his cold, dead hands.

"What's a SpyGuy?" Violet asked, confused.

Dash and Mirage exchanged a look.

"My employer invented it," Mirage told her. "It's a huge seller."

"Watch, Vi!" Dash hit a button and the small screen on the front flashed, blinking blue and black before a small toothbrush-sized compartment opened and spun around, a blue light scanning the room.

"Room secure," said the voice, reminding Violet of the device that gave them entrance to this house. "Hello, Violet Parr, Dash Parr, Jack Parr and Mirage."

Violet had to admit, the gadget was cool.

"It can send video messages," Dash told her. "Like on TV, and you can put it down in any room and the SpyGuy knows who is in the room, even if they're hiding. It's so cool." He hugged the device again. "Wait till I show Dad." He looked at Violet and his face crumpled worriedly. "Have you heard from Mum and Dad yet?"

"Not yet, but Mirage is going to help us reach them. Right?" Violet glanced at the woman tentatively.

Mirage folded her arms across her chest. "Right. Violet, can I talk to you privately for a moment?" Her voice was strained as she left the kitchen. Violet trailed her to the living room carrying Jack-Jack.

She saw me, Violet thought. "Sure." She put Jack down again in front of a toy while Dash played with the SpyGuy.

Mirage opened a sliding-glass door and Violet followed her outside, trying not to feel rattled. "I know you're anxious to go after your parents, but I talked to my employer, and based on his intel, he thinks the safest thing to do is to keep a low profile for now. You can all stay here indefinitely."

Violet didn't understand. "Stay here? So who is going to go after my parents? Is he?"

Mirage played with a strand of her brown hair. For a moment, Violet thought she saw some blonde peeking out from underneath. "We are. I mean, my employer is. We're taking care of it."

Violet didn't like the sound of that. "I want to speak to your boss."

"He really can't talk right now," Mirage said, side-eyeing a glass wall that Violet suspected was her boss's office. "He's very busy getting together plans to go after your parents."

"I want to hear what he's doing," Violet insisted, and Mirage started to protest. "I know my parents better than anyone. I can help."

"You're a child," Mirage said, her frustration showing. "Just let us handle this."

"And how are you handling it?" Violet pressed. She hated when adults thought they knew everything! Violet knew her parents' war stories, their moves, their enemies.

She was an asset. Mirage's boss should want to talk to her. "I want to see your boss. I came here as you asked. Now I want to see him."

"I told you, he's busy." Mirage inched sideways to block Violet's view of *something*.

The movement made Violet want to see what was behind her. "Too busy to see the kids he wanted to protect?" Violet asked loudly. "Fine! If you won't take me to him, then we're leaving." She marched towards the lift.

Mirage tried to get in front of her. "You can't! You're safe here! Mastermind is looking everywhere for you and your brothers. Do you want to get yourself captured?"

"I won't get captured," Violet insisted. "I'll find my parents on my own and rescue them. We're going." Violet went to pick up the baby again as he banged on a drum set.

"Wait! Please!" Mirage said desperately. "You can't leave. You need to listen to us."

"Listen?" Violet felt her emotions begin to heighten again. "I don't even know you. In fact, I'm starting to think it was a mistake coming here."

Mirage stepped in front of her. "Violet, please. Your parents wanted us to protect you."

"We don't need you to do that," Violet said, looking for Dash, who was suddenly nowhere to be found. "Lucius will help us."

"Who?" Mirage asked.

Violet spun around. "Frozone? If you're friends with my mum and dad and know Supers, you'd know who he was." She blew her hair out of one eye. Where was Dash?

"I do," Mirage tried to cut in, sounding flustered. "I know it's hard to understand, but we're trying to help you."

"How?" Violet demanded. "By holding us hostage?"

"That's not what we're doing," Mirage said coolly.

"Then why are we just sitting here? We have to go after my parents! We have to get them back from Mastermind! You said he is after us! He already has them!"

Her shouting startled Jack-Jack, who started to cry.

Violet sighed. She hated this sensation – feeling calm one moment, then angry the next, so mad she couldn't catch her breath, knowing this combination was sure to unleash powers she didn't know how to work right. "If your boss is too busy to help me, then I'll find someone else who will! I'll... I'll... I'll call the Agency myself!" she said, thinking fast. Not that she had any clue how to contact the Agency.

Mirage's eyes widened. "You can't! There could be spies! Moles! You could put your parents in even more danger!"

Violet crossed her arms, her expression darkening like her mood. "And who is going to stop me?"

"I am," said someone appearing behind her.

Violet turned around. A man with bright red hair that stood up like it had connected with a light socket watched her with an eerily wide smile. He held out his hand. "Hi, Violet. I'm Syndrome. Sorry to keep you waiting. I've been dying to meet you."

CHAPTER TEN
VIOLET

Violet limply shook Syndrome's hand.

This was Mirage's boss?

He was so… young. Mirage was too, of course, but compared to Syndrome she looked like a grown-up. A grown-up babysitter.

Syndrome reminded her of Dash. A boy playing dress-up. She'd never seen a grown man in a Super uniform before. Sure, her parents had tons of pictures of themselves in their uniforms, but that was in the old days, when Supers weren't 'retired', which was Mum-speak for 'illegal'.

Syndrome was clearly not retired. And he couldn't care less that Supers were illegal. He was proudly wearing a black-and-white uniform with a large white letter *S* on the chest and white gloves and boots. His eyes – which were bright blue – were partially concealed by a black mask, like the ones her parents used to wear. The smattering of freckles across the bridge of his nose made him appear even younger.

"Syndrome just showed me all his inventions!" Dash said, appearing behind Syndrome, who ruffled his head. "He makes such cool stuff! You have to see everything!"

"You two were together?" Violet side-eyed Mirage. Is that why Syndrome couldn't talk to her? He was with Dash?

The baby stopped crying and crawled over to Syndrome, clearly intrigued, and yanked on the back of his black cape, which was lined with blue silk.

"Ah, this must be Jack!" Syndrome tickled the baby under his arm and he squealed.

"Jack-Jack's not a Super, either, like you," Dash explained and looked up at Syndrome again.

"You told him about your powers?" Violet accused. Sure, she'd basically done the same thing by disappearing in front of Mirage, but Dash was younger. Mum had drilled it into their heads not to reveal themselves. She figured he would listen to that rule.

Dash shrugged. "He already knew."

"We're not supposed to talk about our powers," Violet said, her heart pounding, her reflexes kicking in.

Syndrome put a hand on her shoulder. "Relax. Your

secret is safe with me, Violet." He ran a hand through his hair. "Honestly, I'm ecstatic to hear Mr Incredible and Elastigirl have Super kids! What a secret to keep from the world! I want to hear everything you three can do!"

"Oh, Jack-Jack can't do anything," Dash interrupted. He's just a baby. You look like a Super at least."

Syndrome put his hands on his hips and laughed. He leant down to Dash's level. "I do, don't I? And what did I tell you? I'm even better than a Super. I create gadgets that make *everyone* feel Super." Syndrome showed off the glove on his arm. It had multiple blinking lights and buttons on it. He clicked one and his boots rose off the ground, white-blue fire shooting out from the soles. Dash's and Jack-Jack's mouths fell open. He clicked another button and a laser shot out from his gloved pointer finger on his left hand. Mirage ducked. The laser homed in on a tree in the garden beyond the open sliding-glass doors. It lifted the tree into the air, its roots now visible.

"That is AWESOME!" Dash crowed as they all raced outside to the deck to see the airborne tree. Dash banged into a sculpture of a man flying as he ran out the door, and the relic started to wobble.

Mirage caught it. "Careful!" she scolded. Jack-Jack jumped, frightened by her tone, and reached for Violet.

She doubled back and picked him up, then returned to

the deck in time to see as a group of workers running across the lawn like an army of ants. They seemed to be trying to figure out what to do with a tree that was now standing upside down, its roots in the air.

"Sorry!" Syndrome chuckled. "I'm getting carried away! I can show you more tricks later, Dash. Wait till you see how these gloves I designed can control the SpyGuy." He landed and patted Dash on the shoulder. "I can get you a set of gloves too if you want to try them out. And I want to see you run the track I have here at the house."

"Cool!" Dash said.

Violet pulled her brother backwards by his T-shirt. "I don't think that's a great idea," she said, thinking of the whole 'protect your brothers' promise she'd made Mum. "Kid. Gloves with lasers. We don't want to burn your house down the first hour we're here."

Dash bit his lower lip and glanced at Syndrome. "I set our house on fire this morning."

Syndrome looked surprised. "You did?"

"These guys broke into our house and they were chasing Violet, and I said, 'Not my sister!' and I used one of the gadgets in my dad's office and boom! Fire!" Dash looked down at his trainers, which were untied. "My mum and dad are going to be so mad."

"Nah! You were being brave!" Syndrome said. "I'd be

proud if I were them. You were protecting your sister. Like Mirage and I are protecting you right now while those bad guys are out there looking for you."

Dash looked at Violet worriedly. "Do you think they'll find us here?"

"Not to worry, Dash. I fly below the radar. No one will find you here." He patted Dash on the head again. Dash seemed appeased. "Why don't you take the baby inside and have some more pizza while I talk to your sister for a minute."

"More pizza?" Dash said, excited. "You mean I haven't had too much yet?"

"No way!" Syndrome said before Violet could get a word in. "Have more biscuits, too. You can have whatever you want here!"

"Num-num?" Jack heard the word *biscuit* and homed in on it. "NUM-NUM?" He started reaching his hands wildly for the air as if he expected a biscuit to materialise. The whining was back in full force.

Mirage rubbed her temples. "Someone please get that baby a biscuit."

"Come on, Jack!" Dash said, taking the baby from Violet.

Syndrome waited till Dash had slid the door shut to turn his attention back to Violet. "So, I hear you're thinking of leaving?"

Violet looked down at the ground, feeling unnerved, and pulled her arms around her chest. "If you're not going to rescue my parents, then I have to go."

"She wanted to talk to you about what you were doing to help her parents and I explained you were busy," Mirage explained.

"Never too busy to answer questions," Syndrome said. "You've had quite the day! We all have! More Supers in the world." He shook his head. "This was a twist I didn't see coming! Why don't we sit down? I have some news too."

"About my parents?" Violet asked eagerly.

"Everything okay?" Mirage sounded concerned.

"Come sit." Syndrome motioned to one of the chairs on the deck. It had a turquoise cushion that looked the exact colour of her dad's Supersuit. Syndrome sat down on the opposite one.

Sit? Whenever adults said to sit down it was because they wanted to have a talk. And in Violet's experience, 'the talk' was never a pleasant one. "That's okay. I'll stand."

"You should sit," he said again, patting the chair a second time.

"I don't want to," Violet insisted. "Just tell me. Did you find a way to rescue my parents? I can describe the men who were at our house. They were wearing tuxedos, and I think if we go back to the house and find anyone lurking around, or search my dad's office…"

"Violet…" Syndrome's tone was sharper. "I need you to sit."

She sat down, her heart beating wildly. "I'm sitting."

"Listen, kid, there's no easy way to tell you this, but your parents are gone."

Violet was certain she misheard him. Gone? "Gone as in they got away?"

Syndrome's stare was penetrating, his expression neutral. "Your parents didn't make it."

Violet reached out to hold on to the nearest chair to keep from falling over. The world started to spin and she heard ringing in her ears. "Didn't make it where?" she whispered.

Syndrome swallowed hard and placed his head in his hands for a moment before continuing. "I know this is hard to hear, but they're dead."

"Dead?" Mirage covered her mouth with her hand, a silver spoon ring on her second finger glinting in the sunlight. "What happened?"

Syndrome ran a hand through his hair. "There was nothing we could do. By the time my men got there, Mastermind had already killed them."

Violet felt cold. Her hands began to shake, then her arms. She sank to the floor. *Mum and Dad are dead?* Her parents couldn't be dead! She felt her whole body electrify, the heat encasing her body almost overpowering her. For a second, a small force field formed in front of her, knocking over the table next to the chair Syndrome was in. He didn't flinch.

"You're wrong. My mum said she was meeting my dad at his conference! She was only supposed to be gone for the day! She wasn't supposed to be fighting villains," Violet said, her cries intermingling with her shouting. Mirage put a hand on her back. When Violet looked up, she noticed Mirage was crying too.

"I know this is a lot to take in, but it's true," Syndrome said, sounding remorseful. "Your dad was working with me, in a branch of the government that doesn't even have a name it's so top-secret. He was helping us test a robot I developed called the Omnidroid."

"My dad already has a job at an insurance company," Violet said, almost on autopilot. "How could he be working for the government? Supers are illegal." Violet's chest hurt. Bad. She felt like her body was burning up.

Syndrome stared at her. "That was his cover. No one could know Supers were still working behind the scenes. Your dad didn't even tell your mum – at first. This bot, when completed, was meant to be able to stop any threat that came to Metroville, and eventually the world. It's why I called on your father – the best Super I've ever known – to test it." He leant back in the chair and looked at her. "I don't know if you knew this, but your father and I go back years. I was his biggest fan."

Violet had never heard her dad mention someone named Syndrome before, but she wasn't going to say that. She gripped the top of the chair, wishing she had the power to crush metal, like her father did, as she listened to Syndrome continue.

"I've been working on this Omnidroid for years, testing its abilities and making it bigger, badder. I went through quite a few Supers to get it ready to fight Mr Incredible. I had to make some major modifications. Sure, it was difficult, but having it ready to fight someone like your father meant it was tough enough to face any villain." His expression darkened. "I just didn't count on Mastermind learning what we were doing."

"I thought Mastermind was retired," Violet said numbly. Her head was spinning. She was having a hard time following the conversation.

"That's what we all thought, but I guess word that I was developing something so powerful that it could even stop Mastermind was too much for the super villain to handle. Mastermind has always been envious of my ideas and inventions," Syndrome said bitterly.

"What did Mastermind do to my parents?" Violet needed to know.

"You don't want to hear this," Syndrome insisted. "This is a lot to process. If you want to take a walk around the grounds, or use your powers or something... Mirage said you can disappear? I don't know if that's exactly a stress-reliever, but..."

"I don't want to walk around!" Violet shouted. "I want to know what happened to my mum and dad."

"Violet, don't torture yourself with details," Mirage said. "You're in shock. We all are. I can't believe your parents are..." She trailed off.

Violet's tone sharpened. "I need to know what happened. Please." She practically pleaded. "What did Mastermind do to them?" she whispered.

Syndrome's expression softened. "All right." He looked at Mirage. "She has the right to know. She's a big girl. She can handle the truth." He turned to her. "Can't you, Violet?"

Violet took a deep breath. "Yes."

"It was a routine training exercise," Syndrome explained. "Everything was going great – your dad was running around the island fighting the latest version of the Omnidroid when Mastermind shows up out of nowhere!" His voice grew animated. "Now I know Mastermind was before your time, but you have to understand, Mastermind used to be major.

Whoa, did those two have some tussles! Their battles were legendary, I tell you!"

"I know who Mastermind is," Violet snapped. Why was he stalling?

"Syndrome," Mirage said quietly. "About her parents…"

"Right! Well, Mastermind knocked me out before I could be much help with anything. When I awoke, Mastermind's people were hauling away my Omnidroid and had already locked your dad in a Super-proof holding chamber where his powers wouldn't work. I overheard Mastermind monologuing to your dad about how he'd no longer be a threat, and that's when I realised the villain had finally done it. Mastermind had created a nullifier to strip Supers of their powers." He leant forwards. "And the first test was going to be on your dad that very night."

Steal her dad's powers? Violet's heart beat so fast she was sure it would bolt right out of her chest. "That's impossible." Her mum had said their powers were permanent. Weren't they? "You can't take someone's powers."

"But what if you could? Think about it," Syndrome said. "If nobody was Super, then anyone could be."

Violet was quiet. A power-stripping device? She'd dreamt of something like that being possible for as long as she could remember. She wanted to be normal so badly, unlike the rest of her family. Her dad lived for his powers. Mastermind trying to take them would have enraged her father. Maybe it made him reckless. "But how did Mastermind know where you were? And that my dad was testing this droid with you somewhere top-secret?" She didn't understand.

"I don't know the specifics!" Syndrome said, getting agitated. "All I know is Mastermind found us and I saw this nullifier with my own eyes. Mastermind couldn't wait to use this thing on your dad. Want to know why? Because if it worked, the invention would level the playing field between Supers and the rest of the world." Syndrome leant forwards and spoke, his voice barely a whisper. "And it did work. Within seconds, the nullifier reduced your dad to a weakling."

"Where were you when this was happening?" Violet's blood started to boil. "Why didn't you try to help him?"

"I tried!" He waved his arms emphatically. "Mastermind knocked me out and I fell behind a computer monitor and was hidden from view." He stood up. "When I came to, Elastigirl had shown up and Mastermind nabbed her too. With the little strength I still had, I recorded this from my glove."

Syndrome pressed a button on the table in front of him. A screen popped up and video footage appeared. It was of her father.

"Dad!" Violet cried, touching the image as it began to

play. He was wearing his old black-and-turquoise Supersuit. His hair was a mess, hanging in his eyes. She didn't remember it being that long. When was the last time he'd had it cut?

He was being held behind electrified bars. It was hard to hear what he was shouting, but he looked angry. The screen jumped and suddenly Violet's mum appeared in the same cage. "Mum!" She was wearing a replica of the suits Dash had found. What was her mum doing in a new Supersuit?

"Your dad was the only one meant to be on the island, but I guess when he didn't show up at home, your mum followed him." Syndrome closed his eyes and stopped speaking.

Her mother looked like she was shouting at the top of her lungs too, but Violet couldn't hear anything. "I can't hear what they're saying!"

"Oh. Sorry." Syndrome touched another button and the audio started to play.

Her dad was shouting. "I'm warning you… if you touch my kids…"

"We'll both tear you apart from limb to limb!" her mum shouted. "Don't you go anywhere near our children! You hear me?"

Violet remembered the threat Mastermind had made to

her mum. *You'll never sleep again.*

"You can't take our powers!" Her dad was flipping out now. "These are our powers! They're our life!"

"They're everything we stand for!" her mum jumped in. "If you try to use that thing on us, and it works, we will never stop coming for you. Ever!"

"We will hunt you down and destroy you with our bare hands!" her dad added.

But her father was cut off as the screen filled with bright-white light and then went black.

Violet's whole body felt like it might erupt into flames. She saw her hands appear and disappear in rapid succession, then her head. Mirage gasped. Violet felt herself glitching but couldn't stop it, nor did she care to. *Mum. Dad.* "Was that an explosion?" She felt like she couldn't breathe. "What happened to them? Was that Mastermind's weapon?"

"Yes," Syndrome said sadly. "The nullifier took both your parents' powers and ended my video footage. Your parents were knocked unconscious from the blast."

"Isn't a nullifier a spray?" Violet asked, thinking of what she'd seen Kari use for her asthma. "Why was there an explosion?"

"You're thinking of a nebuliser, I think?" said Mirage.

"Try to keep up, both of you. It's a nullifier, not a nebuliser. And I have no clue how it works, just that it worked." He sounded agitated. "Look, I saw it happen! Your parents were so obsessed with being Super! So irate about losing their powers! They couldn't even fathom a world without them. They were going on and on and on about how they'd fight Mastermind to their dying breath to destroy that nullifier and make it hard for Mastermind to carry out the plan on other Supers. And I think Mastermind knew – Mr Incredible and Elastigirl wouldn't stop coming. They were going to do everything they could to avoid the nullifier being used on other Supers. Mastermind doesn't like being threatened. I guess Mastermind was worried these two ordinary people were going to make life hell. There was no choice but to…" Syndrome trailed off.

"No choice but to what?" Violet was thinking too fast to get the words out. Her heart was pounding. She felt her head appear and disappear again. She couldn't breathe. "What are you saying?"

"Villains don't like loose ends," Syndrome said grimly. "If your parents had shut up, maybe Mastermind would have been satisfied with just taking their powers. But Mastermind knew your parents were going to get in the way. They had to be eliminated." He looked at her. "I'm sorry, Violet. Your parents are gone."

"No. NO!" Violet tried to cover her face with her hands and felt tingling. Her face and hands were both invisible.

Why did her parents have to be so attached to their powers? These ridiculous, uncontrollable powers she didn't even want! Her emotions threatened to overwhelm her. She felt her fingers spark and fizzle out. She couldn't make a force field on command if she tried. What would she do with it if she could? Who would she aim it at? There was nobody to fight here. She felt herself disappear completely.

"Whoa," Syndrome said, jumping up as he stared at the headless girl with no limbs, only her clothes remaining. "Did you see that? She disappeared! That's just… incredible!"

Why did people keep using that word? A sob escaped Violet's lips.

"Violet?" Mirage's voice was clear. "Remember the breathing exercises I taught you. Try to relax. I know this is a lot to process, but you have to try."

"I don't think I can," Violet said, a sob escaping her lips. Her parents were gone. It seemed impossible. They were Supers. Her dad was Mr Incredible! Her mum was Elastigirl! They couldn't be dead! "Why did they have to be so stubborn?" Violet screamed. "If they'd just shut up about their powers, they would still be here with us. What's wrong with being normal?" She was shaking so hard her clothes were visibly trembling. "Why couldn't that be enough for them?" *They were killed because they were obsessed with their powers. Powers I don't even want!*

She started to cry.

"I don't know," Syndrome said sadly. "I'm normal and look at what I can do." She cried harder. "Violet, stop crying now and listen to me," he snapped. "Now isn't the time to fall apart. You have to be strong. You have two brothers in the other room who need you!"

Dash and Jack-Jack. It was her job to protect them. Her job to look out for them when Mum was... when Mum was... Her last conversation with her mum had been a fight. She swallowed hard, feeling worse than ever.

The sound of Jack laughing in the other room filled the air and Violet winced.

She felt her face reappear and she looked at Syndrome. "That's why Mastermind's goons came to our house. They wanted to capture me and my brothers."

"I know," Syndrome admitted. "I sent Mirage to get you to keep you safe because of who your parents are. But now that I know you're Super too? This changes everything."

Violet suddenly felt cold. "What do you mean?"

"Does anyone else know about your powers?" he questioned. "Other than your parents? Anyone seen you use them?"

Violet felt her face flush. "Maybe," she said, sounding small.

"Who?" Syndrome demanded.

"My dad's friend, Lucius, who is Frozone, and the Agency."

Syndrome paced the deck. "The Agency knows about your ability to become invisible and Dash's speed? Is there more you can do?"

Violet hesitated. "I can make force fields."

Syndrome seemed to mull this over. "Force fields. Speed. Invisibility," he repeated to himself. "Anyone else know? Anyone at all?"

Violet paled. "Maybe Mastermind since Dash and I used our powers to get away from the house." She felt like she might pass out. She'd just doomed her siblings. How could she have been so careless? "Is Mastermind going to kill us, too?"

"Not on my watch," Syndrome said, but even he sounded unsure.

"How are you going to keep us safe?" Violet freaked.

"Violet's right. You're not a Super!" Mirage reminded him. "You said Mastermind is eradicating Supers! If someone finds them here…" Mirage sounded as panicked as Violet felt.

"I know! I know! I'm thinking." Syndrome paced some more and Violet and Mirage watched him. "There has to be a way to keep you three safe." Finally, he stopped pacing and punched the air. "Okay, I think I have an idea that will work."

"Great, what is it?" Mirage pressed.

"I think Mastermind will leave Violet and her brothers alone if the villain doesn't think they're a threat," Syndrome said slowly. "And if you don't have powers, you're not a threat."

"But they have powers... OH." Mirage's eyes widened. "You want them to stop being Supers?"

"Exactly!" Syndrome said, nodding.

He and Mirage looked so pleased, as if they'd just created world peace. Violet stared at them blankly, getting annoyed. "You can't just stop being a Super," she said bitterly, and inside, she was enraged. "I think what you mean is you want to let Mastermind capture us," Violet said slowly, "and take our powers and hope we aren't killed. Is that it? That's a bad plan!"

"That's not my plan!" Syndrome said, snapping at her. "I've got a better plan than *that*."

"And what is that?" Mirage demanded.

Violet and Mirage stared him down.

"My plan is... my plan is... okay, my plan is risky, but it if we pull it off, you're home free," Syndrome said to Violet as he started to pace. "Don't worry about the details yet."

"It's my job to worry about my family," Violet reminded

him. "Tell me what you're thinking and I'll tell you whether I'm willing to risk my brothers and my lives to make it happen."

Syndrome laughed. "Wow, you sound like your dad! Okay, I'm spitballing here, but I'll tell you what I think we need to do. Ready? I think we have to steal the nullifier, use it on you and your brothers, and strip your powers. Think about it! If you willingly gave up your powers, and didn't make waves about the nullifier being used on other Supers, you wouldn't be a threat to Mastermind anymore. Right?"

For someone spitballing, Violet had to admit, his plan was a good one. She thought about the idea for a moment. Having powers had been the bane of Violet's existence ever since she first discovered that she could literally lose her head in a panic. Now those powers had cost her Mum and Dad. She hated being Super! Would it be so wrong to willingly give up her brother's and her powers to avoid her parents' fate? The move was so risky. So much could go wrong, but if they pulled this off, maybe her family would be safe. *Mum and Dad*, she thought again, wanting to cry. *How could you do this to us?* She just wanted to curl up in a ball and grieve, but there was no time for that. This feeling of despair could pull her under, make her lie flat on the floor and never get up again.

Or...

She could get up and fight for what she had left – her brothers. Her mum had asked her to protect them, and that was her job now. She had to fight for her family. Violet's head was spinning, but she managed to reappear. "I think this could work. Let's do it! Take our powers. I don't even want them," she declared.

"Violet, hold on," Mirage said. "You haven't even talked to your brother about this."

"Mirage is right," Syndrome said, staring at her. "Sleep on this. Talk to Dash."

"No," Violet said forcefully. "This is my decision. My mum left me in charge of my brothers and I think she'd want me to do this if it could help save us. Let's get rid of our powers. I won't miss them."

He nodded. "If you're sure."

"I'm sure." Violet felt an uneasy calmness come over her at the thought of being normal. "But how are we going to get that nullifier and strip our powers before Mastermind comes after us?"

"We need to break into Mastermind's compound and steal the nullifier before Mastermind comes for you," Syndrome said. "And to do that, I think I'm going to need help – Mastermind knows every gadget I've ever created. This is one time I could use a Super to get the job done. Someone who can be invisible, fly below the radar."

Violet's eyes widened and she looked at Mirage, who seemed stricken. "You need me," she realised.

"Yes," Syndrome admitted. "I need you to use your powers so you can give up your powers! Insanity! Look, I know I'm asking a lot. This is an insane plan! Certifiable! You can tell me no if you want." His stare intensified. "But if we do this... if we get the nullifier, use it on you and your brother and let Mastermind know you're no longer a threat and you won't make waves, I really do think you'll be safe."

Safe. Violet thought of her brothers. They were all she had left in the world. She was so angry at her parents right now. So heartbroken. So upset, but she wouldn't forget her mum's last wish. Using that nullifier could save them. "Let's do it, then. Steal that nullifier. Where do we start?"

Syndrome ran a hand through his red hair. "Start? A plan like this takes some time."

Violet groaned.

"It does!" Syndrome said. "And besides, after all you've been through today with your parents..."

She couldn't think about what happened with Mum and Dad right now. It was too painful. She had to push her pain aside and deal with it later. Right now she needed to focus. She would get that nullifier or die trying.

A shot of anger coursed through her and Violet felt her whole body come alive. Suddenly the rest of her reappeared, her expression deadly as she stared at Syndrome and Mirage. "We start work now! Let's get the nullifier and use it ourselves. Then I never have to hear the word *Super* or talk about powers ever again."

CHAPTER ELEVEN
VIOLET

"Now hold on!" Mirage interrupted, looking at Syndrome aghast. "You can't have Violet help you steal a weapon from a major villain! She's a child!"

"A *Super* child," Violet corrected her. "Well, at least till we get the nullifier." She was so delirious, she laughed at her own sick joke. Syndrome joined in.

Mirage ran a hand through her hair. "But this is so dangerous! You barely survived when Mastermind attacked your house."

Protect your brothers. The memory of her mum's voice made Violet's heart feel like it would break into a million pieces all over again. She pushed the thought aside.

"What are we going to do? Stay locked away our whole lives? We have school!"

Okay, so maybe Violet wouldn't exactly miss school. Dash certainly wouldn't. Who really needed algebra anyway? Still, she would miss seeing Tony Rydinger. "And what about Jack-Jack? He's just a baby. We can't live here forever and spend our lives looking over our shoulders for Mastermind to attack. Syndrome is right. If we willingly give up our powers, and Mastermind knows we're normal kids who won't get in the way, we should be safe. Right?"

Syndrome grimaced. "I hate to say it, but yes." He looked at Mirage. "There's just no other way to protect these kids."

Mirage threw her hands up. "So what? You're going to steal the nullifier, use it on yourselves and then say, 'Here, Mastermind. You can have it back now'?"

"*Mirage*," Syndrome growled. "That's enough."

Violet paused. "Oh wait. That's a good point. Won't Mastermind come after us anyway for stealing the weapon?"

"Let's tackle one problem at a time." Syndrome scratched his head and stood up, clearly thinking about this. His cape flapped in the light breeze. "Get the nullifier, use it, then we deal with getting it back to Mastermind." She nodded. "But Mirage is right to be worried…" He stared at her forlornly. "If anything happened to you three on this mission, I would never forgive myself."

"Something *will* happen if we don't get rid of these powers," Violet said hastily. "I want to be rid of them! I don't even know how to control them."

Syndrome cocked his head. "You don't?"

Violet shrugged. "I guess my parents didn't practise with us because being a Super is illegal. My dad was more excited about seeing what we could do than my mum. She said protecting our identities was more important." She sighed. "Which was hard to do when I couldn't figure out how to control when I disappeared and reappeared. You try being in middle school and disappearing when you get embarrassed. And don't get me started on the force fields."

"Force fields could come in handy with Mastermind." Syndrome tapped his chin. "And Dash said he can run at the speed of light?"

"I'm not sure about light, but yeah, he can run fast," Violet agreed. "Mum wouldn't let him go out for the track team."

"Interesting," Syndrome mumbled. "And you're sure the baby has no powers?" Violet shook her head. "Force fields, invisibility and speed against Mastermind. I don't know. It's still risky."

Was Syndrome back-pedalling? No! She couldn't let him change his mind now. "We don't have a choice," Violet said firmly. "You said it yourself, we'll use our powers one more time so that we never have to use them again."

Her parents were dead.

She, Dash and Jack-Jack were orphans.

Mr Incredible and Elastigirl, arguably the greatest Supers to ever exist, were gone.

The Super who had held up falling bridges and the Super who guided planes to safety when they were in despair had both been taken out by a super villain because of their abilities. Violet didn't want herself or her brothers to ever have to go through that. "Please?" she wasn't beneath begging. "You're the only one who can help us. We have to get that nullifier."

"You said yourself you don't know how to use your powers," Syndrome pointed out, sounding frustrated again. "I can't believe your parents never prepared you for this moment. You're not a real Super! How do you expect to steal the nullifier from Mastermind if you can't make a force field on command or go invisible when necessary? Maybe I'm overreaching here. I don't know if you can do this."

"I can! I swear!" Violet insisted.

"You could train her, Syn," Mirage suggested. "Maybe give her some lessons on how to fight? You've worked with Supers for years and developed weapons to stop villains. What if you used the Omnidroid? It's the perfect training weapon."

"Yes!" Violet liked that idea. *Thank you, Mirage*. "Train

me! Show me what to do and how to get to Mastermind."

Syndrome mulled it over, pacing back and forth. "I could do that. I'm a great mentor. But we don't have much time!" He lamented. "If Mastermind senses we're coming, or someone tipped off the Agency that Mr Incredible and Elastigirl have gone missing…"

"Or Frozone," Violet added. "I've tried reaching him several times and I can't."

"Frozone?" Syndrome looked at Mirage.

She held up a SpyGuy and showed Syndrome a picture of Uncle Lu in his Supersuit. "He's the one I told you about. He can freeze things and make ice out of water."

"I have never dealt with Frozone. We didn't call him in to test the Omnidroid," Syndrome told her. "But you say he's nowhere to be found?" Violet shook her head. "Problem: if the Agency finds out multiple Supers are missing, they could start digging around. Then it's just a matter of time before Mastermind panics and tries to move the nullifier to a new location."

"Let's go right now, then!" Violet suggested. "Train me and then we'll break into Mastermind's today!"

Syndrome held up his hands. "Slow down, kid. We still need a few days to work out details." She started to protest. "Training doesn't happen overnight! We need a few days at the minimum. You're safe here for now. I want you to be ready.

This is going to be a dangerous mission." He glanced beyond the patio at the world beyond. "Are you sure you're ready for this, Ms I Don't Know How to Use My Powers? Mirage is right: I can't protect you once you're at Mastermind's."

Violet stood up straighter. Her whole body burned as she thought about confronting a super villain. "I'm sure."

Syndrome nodded. "All right. I'm going to prepare my training facility. Do some recon work on Mastermind's place and map out the best infiltration points. I have an older version of the Omnidroid for you to square off against. In the meantime, talk to Dash. We're going to need him in on this mission too if we want to succeed."

"But he's so young," Mirage started to say. Syndrome shot her a look, and she stopped talking.

Violet frowned. Mirage was right, though. It was one thing to put herself in harm's way, but she had to keep Dash and Jack-Jack safe. "On second thought – no Dash. I don't want him getting hurt. My powers are enough."

Syndrome's gaze narrowed, his eyes piercing beneath their black mask. "All right. Then get ready. The real work begins tomorrow."

"Tomorrow," Violet repeated, feeling adrenaline course through her, "we stop Mastermind."

Without another word, Syndrome turned and walked away. Violet glanced at Mirage, who watched him leave.

"Okay, I guess Syndrome is going to go… work, and we will head back inside so you can take care of the baby and let Dash know you're staying. And if you're staying…" Mirage drummed her fingers on her hips again, "I guess we should get some rooms made up."

She wasn't going home again. It made sense. Mum and Dad weren't there. For a moment, Violet felt an overwhelming sense of panic, but she talked herself down. *Mastermind knows where we live. The house caught fire. Lucius is missing. You are safe here*, she reminded herself. *Dash and Jack are safe. Just breathe.* Maybe Mirage's breathing exercise could help her again today after all.

"I'll need a cot," Violet told her. "And baby food."

"A cot? Baby food?" Mirage asked, sounding stressed.

"Yes," Violet said. "I can't leave, so you'll have to get some. And clothes. We need a change of clothes, or laundry? Can you wash everything? I don't even have pyjamas for Jack-Jack, and he pees through everything."

Mirage looked ill. If Kari were the one taking this all down, she would have told Violet, "No problemo! Be back in a jiff!" But Mirage was clearly perplexed. Violet had to guess getting kid stuff wasn't normally part of her job requirement with Syndrome, who had his own business.

"Is that okay?" Violet asked. She pulled the note out from Mum again and looked it over. Food, nappies, clothing. That should cover it for now. *One day at a time*, she told herself. *First, we get rid of these powers.*

Mirage's expression brightened. "Yes, of course. Whatever you need." She walked inside ahead of Violet. "I'll just get my purse and go… shopping. For baby clothes. And food. And find a cot." Her smile was tight. "You're all right here while I'm gone? Don't disturb Syndrome. I'll pop in and see him before I go."

"We won't bother him," Violet assured her. "I'm just going to talk to Dash."

Mirage looked around, somewhat unsurely, and Jack-Jack peered up at her, babbling. He raised his arms as if he wanted to be picked up and Mirage recoiled, frightened.

"I'll be back soon," she said.

"Okay." Violet watched Mirage head to the lift and disappear. Dash was still at the arcade game. He could play that thing for hours.

"Where is she going?" Dash asked, not looking up from the blinking lights and sounds of the machine.

"To get baby stuff for Jack-Jack," Violet said, her heart feeling heavy again at the sight of her brother. She knew she'd have to tell him about Mum and Dad eventually, but for now, they had to stay focused. Tomorrow… after she got the nullifier and stripped their powers and were finally normal like most of the world… she'd tell him what happened and they'd figure out what they were going to do next. "It looks like Mum and Dad are going to be gone longer than expected," she said lightly. "And since there was a fire at the house—"

Dash turned and looked at her worriedly. "Did the house burn down?"

"No." She hoped not. She should really find a way to check. Could she call Kari? That was safe to do. Mastermind didn't know Kari, right? "But since Mum and Dad aren't home… we're going to stay here for a bit. All right?"

Dash looked pensive. "Okay. Is this about the bad guys?"

A lump formed in her throat. She stroked Dash's hair. "You don't have to worry about the bad guys," she said, trying to sound confident, when really what she felt was mad. Mad that they were even in this situation because Mum and Dad couldn't accept losing their powers. She tried to push the thought away. "No one is going to hurt you."

"How do you know, Vi?" he asked, sounding smaller than normal. "How?"

Violet felt her whole body warm with a dark rage she'd never felt before. *Mastermind, you are going to pay for what you've done. You can have our powers, but you can't destroy my family.* When she spoke, her voice was strong and clear. "Don't worry, Dash. I'm going to make sure no one tries to hurt us ever again."

CHAPTER TWELVE
VIOLET

Violet woke up to the sound of people arguing.

It's not like she'd never heard adults fight before. Her parents had arguments all the time over silly things like who was going to help Dash with maths homework, or what time Dad was going to be home for dinner. They always got into arguments on 'bowling night', which was code for Dad-and-Lucius-listening-to-the-police-scanner-and-doing -illegal-Super-stuff night. That's what got her mum so mad. It made Violet angry too. If only her mum had realised then that powers were the root of all problems, maybe she'd be here right now.

With all the varied thoughts in her head, it took Violet a second to remember she wasn't home in bed listening to her parents right now. For one brief, beautiful moment she forgot the truth. Then it all came flooding back to her. Mum and Dad. Syndrome. The nullifier. Her brothers. The pain threatened to crush her, but she fought it back with one word: normal.

Once she stole Mastermind's nullifier and stripped her and her brothers' powers, they'd be free.

No more worrying about disappearing.

No more force fields accidentally shooting out and breaking one of Mum's picture frames.

She and Dash would finally be like Jack-Jack: ordinary, non-Supers.

"How long? It's a simple question."

The argument was growing louder. Violet sat up in bed to listen to the conversation. The rooms Mirage had made up for the kids had everything they could possibly want or need. Violet's bedding was purple (her favourite colour), the pillows were plentiful (which she always liked) and there was a stack of teen magazines just waiting for her to consume. Mirage had picked up several outfits for Violet when she'd gone shopping, and shockingly, they all looked like they would fit and like things she would wear, which was impressive. Whenever Mum shopped for her, they warred over a pair of jeans her mum thought were great and Violet hated. Violet looked across the room at the cot Mirage had laboured over putting together for an hour last night. Jack-Jack was fast asleep, a green stuffed bear tucked under his arm. He was Violet's responsibility now. She swallowed hard and grimaced, pushing the pain down deeper.

"... I can't keep this up. It's dangerous. They're children!"

That was definitely Mirage talking. What couldn't she 'keep up'? The quieter mumbling had to be Syndrome's.

"Don't call me sweetheart. I'm not a babysitter! And you owe me a paycheque!"

Violet heard a door slam. The voices stopped. She glanced at Jack-Jack, expecting him to wake up at the noise. The clock read 8:00 AM. He was usually up way earlier than this. She should take advantage of the quiet. Her heart craved something normal, and for a moment, she had the overwhelming urge to talk to Kari, even if her friend might still be mad at her about Friday night. Talking on the phone to her best friend was the most normal thing she could think of.

Quietly Violet slipped out of bed, slid her feet into the plush purple slippers Mirage had bought her and crossed to the phone in her room. She picked up the receiver and heard the dial tone. Looking back at the door fast to make sure no one was walking in (who knew if Syndrome would be okay with her calling a friend?), she dialled Kari's number.

"Hello?" came a sleepy voice.

Violet cringed. It was still early for a Sunday. "Hi, Mrs McKeen?" Violet whispered, trying to sound positive. "It's Violet Parr. I'm sorry to call so early. Is Kari awake yet?"

"Hi, Violet. Kari slept at her cousin's last night. They were babysitting my nieces." Her mum chuckled. "You know my Kari – never misses a chance to babysit."

Violet tried not to sound disappointed. "Could you tell her I called? And that I'm not home, but I'll try to call her again later?" She hesitated, winding the phone cord around her fingers nervously. "Speaking of home..." She cleared her throat. "Any chance you drove by mine yesterday?" She clutched the receiver tight.

"No. Sorry. Can't say I have. I'll tell her you called, Violet. Bye."

"Bye."

The fact Mrs McKeen didn't know about a fire at the Parrs' had to be a good sign for the house. Maybe their home had only minimal damage. Violet heard Jack moving around in the cot and hung up the phone, unwinding the cord she had wrapped around her fingers. When she turned around to go get Jack-Jack, she found the baby sitting on the rug in front of her.

"Hey!" She eyed him suspiciously. "How did you get out of your cot?" She picked him up. "Did you climb out?"

Was that even possible? She'd never seen him climb out of his cot before.

"Num-num," Jack-Jack said, squishing her cheeks. "Num-num?"

"No biscuits. We don't have biscuits for breakfast, although if there was ever a time to have biscuits for breakfast, it would be now."

By the time she'd given Jack a bottle, changed him, dressed him, then changed his nappy again, Dash had already got up and was sitting at the massive kitchen table underneath a funky gold light fixture, eating cereal. The rest of the house was quiet. There was still no sign of Syndrome or Mirage. Violet had to assume Mirage didn't live there, but she had definitely heard her voice earlier that morning.

Spying the box of Sugar Crunch Cereal on the worktop, she shook it in the air. "Dash, Mum doesn't let you have this."

"Hey!" Dash protested. He swiped it back before she knew the box was even out of her hand. "I was eating that!"

"It's junk!" Violet countered as she plopped Jack-Jack in a new highchair to keep him busy. She dropped a few pieces of cereal on his tray and made sure the latch was tight around his waist so he couldn't climb out.

Dash jutted out his chin. "Syndrome says I can eat anything I want here, anytime I want it."

"He did, did he?" Violet wasn't sure that was the

best idea, but they had bigger problems to worry about at the moment.

"Yep! He says I need energy for today, and I want this cereal."

Energy? For what? Violet rolled her eyes at Dash. "Fine."

Dash poured himself another bowl, and Jack-Jack reached his hands out to have more food. Dash shook a few more pieces of cereal on his tray as Violet reached for a bagel and cream cheese to smear on it. She also made a point of taking an orange from the large bowl on the table that held every type of fruit imaginable. "Have some fruit, too." She threw him an apple and he caught it triumphantly.

Jack-Jack laughed, and Violet and Dash looked over at the highchair.

The baby was gone.

"Where'd he go?" Violet could hear him, but she couldn't see him.

Dash kept eating. "You probably didn't strap him in right."

Violet felt something brush against her leg and looked down. Jack-Jack was at her feet, petting her furry slippers. "Jack-Jack!" She picked him up and stared at him. He blinked back with big, confused eyes. "You can't climb out of your highchair." She marched him back over and strapped him in again, tugging on the buckle twice to make sure he was secure.

"Num-num?" Jack asked. "Num-num?"

She gave him some more cereal instead.

Babies were a lot of work.

"You're all up early, I see!" Syndrome walked into the room wearing his Supersuit again. It made Violet wonder if he ever wore anything else.

Mirage appeared right behind him, wearing another baggy jumper and a pair of jeans with trainers, her brown hair looking a bit frizzy. She radiated crankiness. Maybe she wasn't a morning person.

"Everyone ready for training?" Syndrome asked.

"Wait, *everyone*?" Violet repeated. She thought she was the only one training this morning.

"YES!" Dash jumped up from the table and stood with his hands on his hips. "I practised running in my room, too. Watch." He took off like a shot, rounding the table so fast he left indents in the carpet.

"Nice!" Syndrome high-fived Dash when he came to a stop. "Guess what? I set up a racecourse for you outside that you're going to run after breakfast. I have a few of my team down there setting up an obstacle course, too."

Dash's eyes widened. "Cool! An obstacle course? Sounds like track." He frowned. "Mum won't let me run track even though I'd be so good at it."

"You'd be killer!" Syndrome agreed. "I'd totally let you run track, and hey, today you're going to run all day. I am even setting up a few of the robots I'm testing so that you can practise avoiding enemy fire and lasers."

"YES! Lasers! I am faster than any laser! I mean, I think I am."

"I don't think that's a good idea," Violet said as Jack-Jack looked from Violet to Syndrome. "Why does Dash need to train? I thought I was the only one… you know." It occurred to her that Dash was going to ask questions when she took off for a few hours.

"You know *what*?" Dash pressed, picking up on the vibe immediately. "What does Violet get to do that I don't?"

"Grown-up stuff," Violet told him.

Dash rolled his eyes. "You're not a grown-up!"

"I'm more grown-up than you!" Violet reminded him, getting annoyed.

"I'm more grown-up than you," Dash mimicked.

"Stop copying me!" Violet shouted.

"Stop copying me!" Dash repeated.

Violet was two seconds away from calling for Mum when she remembered she couldn't. She grew quiet.

"I need coffee," Mirage said, making her way across the room to the coffeepot.

"Clean up your breakfast," Violet told her brother, then

looked at Syndrome. "I don't think Dash is old enough to train for anything. And he really can't use lasers." Dash loudly dropped his bowl in the sink.

Syndrome nodded. "Gotcha. This is to keep him busy, while you're busy! Something to do and stretch his legs. See how fast he can go." Dash appeared at his side looking like an eager puppy. "And the lasers? They're just simulations. Nothing that could hurt him."

"See?" Dash said, giving her a hard look.

Violet wasn't going to win this one. "All right, fine. But be careful."

Syndrome and Dash high-fived again.

"Violet, if you're done eating breakfast, I'll get Dash set up on the track and then we'll get to work ourselves," Syndrome told her as he grabbed an apple from the bowl and took a bite. "We can all head down together."

Jack-Jack slammed the highchair tray, sending cereal flying in the air. He laughed hysterically and then did it again. Violet tried to pick up the pieces that had fallen on the floor. "What about Jack-Jack? I can't bring him to training. If Dash is practising too, what do we do with him?"

They all looked at Mirage.

"Fine," Mirage said flatly. "But when Dash is done, he takes over baby duty. I have a job, you know." She ran a hand through her hair. Violet noticed she was wearing makeup today. "And errands to run. Apparently, I didn't buy enough baby food to last the weekend."

"Another problem solved!" Syndrome said. He smiled at the group. "Today is going to be" – he leant in close to Dash – "*super*."

"I'm so excited!" Dash exclaimed. Violet couldn't tell if it was all the sugar cereal or actual excitement, but she was happy to see him happy. He didn't know the truth. He should be happy.

"Good! Because once you're trained up by me, no one will be able to hurt you or your family ever again. You'll see. I make an excellent mentor," Syndrome boasted as he led the way out of the kitchen.

Violet wanted to remind Syndrome that Dash was losing his powers. What did he need training for? But she wasn't about to tell Dash what was going on yet. Instead, she followed Syndrome and Dash to the lift. When the doors opened, a woman in black goggles and a grey uniformed bodysuit that covered even her head was waiting inside. Violet noticed the flak jacket she had over her uniform. She held a weapon at the ready in both her hands.

"Morning, Eugenie!" Syndrome said pleasantly.

"Morning," she said blandly, staring straight ahead.

"Don't mind Eugenie," Syndrome said as the doors closed behind them. "She's one of my employees. You'll meet a lot of them today."

With a *swoosh!* they plummeted. Violet's ears popped.

The lift stopped and the doors opened again. This time three more people in grey suits with black goggles were waiting for them. Syndrome walked right past them to a waiting open-air buggy that pulled up almost on cue.

"Come on!" Syndrome said, hopping on next to the driver as the sunlight peeked through the trees surrounding the house. "We've got a lot to do!"

Dash immediately went running for the vehicle. Violet walked slower, feeling the sunlight on her face. The air was warm, the sky was clear. It was a beautiful day.

And her parents weren't there to see it.

Violet's heart lurched. She suddenly had the urge to scream and cry at the same time. Neither would be a good reaction. Instead, her hand moved to the pocket in her black leggings. Tucked inside was her mum's schedule for Jack-Jack and the comms link. As ridiculous as it was to hold on to these things, Violet clutched them like an anchor.

"Violet, come on," Dash called to her, bouncing up and down in his seat as Syndrome talked quietly to him. "I want to get to the racetrack! A real racetrack!"

Violet climbed aboard and the vehicle took off, moving swiftly along what looked like a giant elevated train track, whooshing past trees at a rate that made the world around them blur. After a few minutes, the vehicle stopped at a clearing.

"WHOA!" Dash shouted, jumping from the buggy.

Violet stayed in her seat, momentarily stunned.

Syndrome wasn't kidding about the racetrack. He had a high school–sized running field and a dozen workers in grey-and-black goggles were lined up around it, just waiting for them.

"This is all for me?" Dash asked.

"Just for you! You said you wanted to run track, didn't you? Here you can run all day and no one is going to stop you or tell you how fast you can go!" Syndrome said.

"I can't wait! See you later, Vi!" Dash took off so fast, he was a blur. She could hear him still yelling happily even though he was half a mile away already.

"Be careful!" Violet shouted and turned to Syndrome, who was stepping out of the vehicle. "You built all this?"

"I have lots of space here to test out my toys." Syndrome leant on the buggy, crossing his legs and making his white boots squeak. "And when I say *toys*, I mean *weapons*. You need a place to see how they work, you know? I've got one place I use offshore for specific experiments, and then my private facilities here are good for everything else." He turned to a worker. "Run the target practice simulation with him after he's warmed up. Then bring out the Omnidroid v.8x and see how he does with the zero-point lasers. I'll be back to check on him." He hopped back in the buggy. "I'm taking Violet over to the dome."

"Yes sir," said the guard closest to the buggy.

Violet stared off at her brother. "Are you sure he's okay here alone?"

"He's going to have fun," Syndrome insisted and tapped the side of the buggy. The guard driving began to speed away from the track. "I wish I could say the same for you."

Violet did a double take. "What does that mean?"

Syndrome turned to look at her as his red hair whipped around his face. "Look, Violet. Can I be honest with you?"

"I think so," Violet said, feeling slightly queasy. She wasn't sure if it was from the ride or how serious Syndrome suddenly was.

"Dash is a kid. We want him to have fun with his powers while he still has them, but you, you're practically an adult."

"I'm fourteen," she felt the need to say; whether it was to prove she was older or younger, she wasn't sure.

"I don't know if you've talked to him about your parents yet," he said. Violet started to explain her reasoning, but he cut her off. "That's your business. He's a kid, but you know the stakes. If we don't get ahold of Mastermind's nullifier and the super villain finds you first…"

We could die like Mum and Dad. Violet shuddered at

the thought, trying to block it out. Her hair was covering her eyes now and for a moment she was glad. She could hide from the world, but not from the truth. "I know," she whispered, her heart starting to thump madly.

"So this training – which you requested, let me remind you – is not going to be easy like Dash's is. He clearly knows how to run, even if he doesn't get to stretch his legs much under all your parents' rules. But you? If you're really going to break into Mastermind's and get that nullifier, you need to learn how to use your powers. We don't have a lot of time to practise."

"I can do this," Violet promised, even though she could feel her nerves threatening to make her lose her breakfast.

He leant in closer. "For your sake, I hope you're right."

Syndrome faced forwards again, and Violet tried not to panic as she watched the buggy arrive at a glass atrium. It looked like a glass bubble or a massive terrarium filled with trees and plants. The vehicle sped right up to it and a door opened, allowing them inside, where the air was much warmer and stickier. Bird chirps and animal sounds filled the air. The buggy stopped, and both the driver and Syndrome stepped out.

"Okay, you stay right here while I get some training exercises ready. Don't go anywhere! Ha!"

"I won't," Violet told him. The man constantly sounded like he was giving pep talks. His voice alternated between deadly serious and aggressively cheerful, like a vacuum cleaner salesman going door-to-door. The kind her mum always turned away as quickly as she could. Violet looked down at the leggings she was wearing and the new T-shirt she had on. The shirt was sort of itchy, as if it had never been washed. It made her long for her mum and the smell of fresh laundry that Mum was always begging Violet to help her fold. (Violet was great at coming up with excuses explaining why there was no time for her to actually fold the laundry.) Her mum used this detergent that smelt like—

BOOM!

The top of the buggy was hit by something hard that dented the roof. Violet screamed.

BOOM! BOOM! BOOM!

Whatever it was came down on the roof again, and again, leaving a dent so large that Violet was sure the entire car was going to be pancaked. She scrambled to get out, her breath coming fast as she practically fell out of the side of the buggy onto the hard dirt.

"Syndrome?" Violet called.

There was no answer. What was going on?

BOOM!

Violet looked up. Before she could even scream, she saw a long black metal claw coming straight for her.

CHAPTER THIRTEEN
SYNDROME

If he wanted to, he could squash the kid like a bug.

As Syndrome stood in the control centre watching Violet get attacked, for a brief second he thought about allowing the Omnidroid v.8x to do just that.

Killing Mr Incredible's kid? He could retell that story for years!

But no. He had to keep his head here. What he was trying to accomplish was so epic, so unexpected, so spectacular, he couldn't fall victim to the quick and easy kill. He had actual Super kids at his disposal that he could mould as he pleased. Oh, to think of the possibilities!

Sure, the non-Super baby was a disappointment, but the older boy, Dash, was like a sponge, soaking up every word he said. That speed of his could come in handy.

But Violet? She was the clear prize. The minute Mirage sent back intel on the girl, Syndrome knew if he played his cards right, he could turn that shy, moody wallflower into a grief-stricken rage machine. Who better to teach her to channel rage and bitterness into brilliance than he?

Over the years, he'd learnt that if you push the right buttons, anyone could become hell-bent on destroying the people who wronged them. That's why he was so successful today. He may have loathed Mr Incredible, but really, he should have thanked the guy. He hadn't become a billionaire obsessed with making Supers obsolete by being a fanboy in the Mr Incredible Fan Club. He no longer had any interest in being a sidekick.

Mr Incredible giving him the cold shoulder as a kid had been exactly what he needed to become someone with tech advancements that every country wanted to get their hands on. His weapons were a threat, and as he'd teach Violet, being a threat gave a person power. Violet was a threat too. Even if she didn't realise it yet. And if he finally got his hands on that nullifier... oh, the possibilities!

It was only nine in the morning and already he could tell this was going to be the best day ever.

"Syndrome!" Violet's screams echoed through the domed enclosure.

He wasn't sure if she realised yet that he could hear her loud and clear. (She'd missed that he'd planted a small mic on her T-shirt when they'd got into the buggy.)

"Syndrome! Help me!"

From high above, on multiple monitors and through the windows, he watched Violet hang by her feet, the blood rushing to her head as the Omnidroid held her in its clutches. He let her hang there for a moment. He'd built this place to be a mirror image of the landscape on his private island, which allowed him to test versions of the Omnidroid in both locations. It was also the perfect place to take a Super to her knees.

Finally, Syndrome pressed the speaker button and spoke calmly. "Help yourself."

Violet stopped flipping out for a moment, and he saw the wheels inside her brain turning. *Yes, Violet. This is a game and I make the rules. You want to live? Fight.*

A spark burst from her fingertips, and he held his breath as the kid shot a force field from her hands. It fizzled out within seconds. She could do better than that!

"It's not working!" Violet cried. "I can't always make one on command!"

Syndrome bit his lip, tasting blood. Excuses. He hated them. From his workers, from Mirage, as alluring as she could be, from Supers begging for their lives. This kid had all kinds of powers – unfair advantages that he'd never had. And she hadn't even bothered to learn how to use them. "Time to figure it out!" He touched another button on the panel in front of him. The Omnidroid began to swing Violet around wildly while she screamed in terror. Finally, he released the grip on the arm so that it dropped her – a safe distance – to the ground. Violet jumped up and ran into the trees, hitting one of the walls of the dome hard.

"I can't find an exit!" she shouted as the Omnidroid turned and came after her. She threw her hands out in front of her and tried another force field. A pitiful one shot out and popped, the hazy purple glow of the kid's energy dissipating quickly.

That wouldn't do. Syndrome pressed a few buttons, and a laser in the Omnidroid's eyes targeted Violet, landing on her chest. She looked down in horror.

"Exit?" It was hard to keep the glee out of his voice. "We're not leaving this place till you learn how to defend yourself. Break walls! Destroy robots! Take over the world! See that laser focused on you? It means you're this robot's target now. If you want to live, you better learn to make a force field or hide really well using your invisibility, because where you go, this little number follows, and if it gets ahold of you again…" The droid's claws pinched the air menacingly.

He saw Violet's expression turn from fear to anger. "I

told you! I don't know how to control my powers!"

The droid swung a metal arm dangerously close to her head.

"Guess it's time to learn."

Violet started to run again, ducking through the trees, trying to hide behind a rock.

"There's no hiding, Violet. Want to hide from the Omnidroid? Disappear."

He could see her chest rising and falling. "I am trying!"

The droid swung for her head again, missing a second time. He wasn't really going to kill her, but she had to believe that might be possible.

"Haven't you done it before?" he asked. "You did it yesterday."

"Yes!" She ducked behind a rock as the Omnidroid scanned the area, looking for her. "But it happened by accident!"

"Because…?" Couldn't the kid see what he was getting at? "What was happening at the time? Were you scared, happy? Nervous? Anxious? How did you disappear?"

The droid shot a laser at a nearby tree that came down at her feet. Violet cried out and started running again.

"All of the above," Violet said. "Please, help me!"

"I am helping you!" he snapped, despite his best attempts to stay calm. "You think if Mastermind finds you, and thinks you're anything like your parents, clinging to their powers, you'll live? Nope. You need to stay hidden. You need to be invisible. Tap into that feeling – think of something that scares you. And if this droid isn't really doing it for you, then think of something else that does frighten you."

He saw Violet run into a clearing, scale a large rock and stand in direct view of the Omnidroid. Its roving mechanical eye turned towards her, shining the laser on her chest again. On all his monitors, the sirens went off. "Target on lock," he heard the computer say.

"Come on, kid, do it!" he yelled.

Her chest was moving so fast, he was sure the kid was going to pass out, but then she closed her eyes, took a deep breath and *POOF!* She was gone! All that remained were her clothes. Hmm… They'd have to figure out how to deal with that.

"Target lost," the computer announced.

"You did it!" He looked down at his monitors for a second and lost sight of her. Where did she go? His cameras zoomed in on the dirt on the ground, and he saw her footprints heading towards the tree line. Then he spotted a headless girl with no limbs. "Found you," he said to himself. He turned the Omnidroid her way again. "Now the key is to hold it. When you get to Mastermind's, you're going to need to stay hidden for as long as possible so you aren't picked up on any of the security cameras. Understand?" Violet didn't answer. "Violet?"

"Understood," she said and flickered into view again.

The Omnidroid fired a laser blast a few feet from her.

He watched as the kid took another deep breath, closed her eyes, and all but her clothes disappeared a second time. "That's it!" he said excitedly. "Now, question: can you fire a force field while you're invisible?"

He stared at her floating clothes again. Nothing happened.

"I don't think so."

Syndrome rolled his eyes. That was a bummer.

"Then reappear. Let's try some force fields next." He hit a few buttons on the control board again and the Omnidroid came her way, moving faster this time. The droid clutched her in its claw before she could even react.

"It's squeezing me!" Violet shouted.

"Then use a force field. Shoot your target and make it let you go!"

She was swinging back and forth, her head whipping around as she tried in vain to pull herself free. He watched her fingers spark, once, twice, then flicker. Another claw came for her head and she screamed. This droid could easily break her in two.

"Make a force field, Violet! You're running out of time,"

he warned, enjoying himself.

Violet's breathing was coming so fast now she couldn't even form sentences. She reached up and pounded on the claw. "But if I hit the droid now, I'll fall! I'm too far up!"

"Figure it out, Violet! Make a force field!"

Her fingers flickered again and a small force field formed, purple light glowing in the dimly lit forest. It worked for a split second and Syndrome held his breath, hoping it would grow bigger. Instead, it disintegrated.

"I can't hold it," she said, sounding small. "I'm being squeezed too tight. You have to let me go! I can't do this."

"You can do this!" he said, pounding his fist on the computer screen so hard he was sure it would crack. "You have to do this!"

"I can't." Was she going to start sobbing now? "I don't know how to hold it."

Weakness was the one thing he couldn't tolerate. A Super who could grandstand, who could pretend they were better than everyone else? They demanded a level of respect. Someone who grovelled to be saved? He had no use for them.

This kid could do it. He could feel it. But maybe fear wasn't the motivator here. She'd tapped into something to become invisible. He didn't know what it was, though. Was it her pain? If that was the case, maybe he needed to exploit that here as well.

He pressed the speaker again. "Then you're going to die, Violet. Is that what you want? To leave your brothers all alone in this world?"

"No!" she shouted, her limbs disappearing again.

He could see her leggings and her shirt wiggling wildly as she still struggled to get free. She looked like a bug caught in a zapper. She reappeared and a small force field shot out. It was a start.

"You have to do this on your own! Do you think I had anyone out there to help me? No. When I was a kid, the Super I wanted to work with told me: 'Fly home, Buddy. I work alone'. He could have ruined me. But I didn't let him. I got strong. I came up with tech that renders Supers useless. I'm a billionaire! I learnt how to take care of myself." He threw his head back and laughed. "Look at that – you got me monologuing! We're supposed to be working on how to keep you and your brothers alive! You need to fight! Your parents are gone! You're all they have left!"

"I know that!" Violet screamed. "Mastermind took everything from me!"

So, Mastermind… that was the key. He could play into that.

"Yes, Mastermind did. That villain killed your parents! Took their powers and still killed them. You think if

Mastermind learns you have powers and finds you, you'll be safe? After how your parents reacted? I'd bet my money you're doomed. Your only hope is to steal that invention and use it on yourself while you have the chance."

She tried to spark another force field, and it grew bigger this time. She held it a few seconds longer before it popped again. She screamed out in anguish and the force field that came next was bigger. Grief. He had to tap into her grief.

"Save your brothers, Violet. You need to get that nullifier from Mastermind first and use it to save what's left of your family! Are you going to let Mastermind destroy your brothers?"

Violet let out a guttural scream and a force field shot out in front of her, sending the Omnidroid staggering backwards. The claw unclenched and Violet dropped to the ground. Syndrome could see her face – angry, red, laser-focused on the droid in front of her. She shot her hands out in front of her and moved forwards, blasting the robot again and again as she held steady, screaming at the top of her lungs in a way he suspected she'd never screamed before.

As a result, the force fields grew larger and moved quicker until the Omnidroid backed up as far as it could go, banging into a rocky incline that made it unstable (a flaw of the v.8x that he would need to fix). The droid fell over. Violet shot a final blast at the machine and the robot's control panel was engulfed in flames. It would take some serious work to rewire that. Workers came running from every direction to put the Omnidroid out.

"Nice job!" Syndrome cheered.

Violet was breathing hard. She looked up at the control room – he didn't realise she could even see him up here – and stared at him darkly. "Let's go again."

Impressive.

This Omnidroid was done for, so he'd have to get another one out of the hangar, but who cared how many she destroyed? Her dad had done the same thing. She was clearly Mr Incredible's daughter. Thanks to him, the kid understood what she had to do now.

"How do you feel?" he asked.

"Powerful," she admitted, looking at her hands in wonder. "I've never used my powers like that before."

No, you haven't. "That was incredible! Your powers are only going to get stronger the more you use them and the more you focus. Channel your anger. Your pain. Whatever helps you with invisibility, use it. Rage can be your friend, Violet."

"Rage?" she repeated, trying another force field and blasting a rock to smithereens.

"Yes. Did you feel how strong that force field was when we were talking about Mastermind? That's the key here:

when you tap into your anger about Mastermind taking your parents, you can make those force fields as large and as fast as possible."

"I can do that!" Violet's face contorted, looking darker now. She braced her legs and shot her hands out in front of her, shooting a force field so fast that it smashed through one of the glass panels of the dome. Broken glass rained into the arena and workers dived for cover.

But Syndrome just stood there and smiled. *Tap into that rage, kid!* He pressed another button.

"Send in a new Omnidroid," he told a worker. "We're running the simulation again. We can patch the dome later."

Look at what he'd accomplished with one training session. Imagine what he could do over the next few days. See what a good mentor he could be? He knew he had been right about the kids! And here Mirage had said taking them and putting them in harm's way with Mastermind was a bad idea. Sometimes he just didn't get what she was thinking. They'd worked together for two years and been a thing for the last few months. He liked her well enough, but he hated her questioning his ideas. Didn't she know by now he always had a plan? And his plan this time was a good one. In a few days' time, he'd have everything he'd ever wanted right at his fingertips. *Watch out, Mastermind. Violet's coming for you.*

Imagine what he could do with some more time with

these kids? It made him wonder.

Syndrome smiled wider. If only he could see the look on Mr Incredible's face when he realised his Super children were now super villains.

There was no stopping him now.

CHAPTER FOURTEEN
VIOLET

They practised for three days. Violet and Syndrome ran simulation after simulation with Omnidroid after Omnidroid. Her speed increased. Her force fields came more naturally. She started to learn how to disappear with the ease of taking a breath. By her fifth Omnidroid, Violet felt like a natural Super. This bot she actually evaded and outmanoeuvred within twenty minutes, destroying it with a force field so large it blew out another wall of the dome. That's when they finally called it quits on the training.

While his workers seemed harried by the destruction, Syndrome was thrilled. "I knew you could do it!" he said, rising into the air, propelled by his jet-fuelled boots and towering over her. "The minute I saw you, I said to myself, this girl has untapped power just begging to be unlocked! And boom! With my training, we unlocked it! You are unstoppable! We are ready!"

"You think so?" Violet questioned, but really she was just trying to be modest. For the first time ever, she *did* feel unstoppable. She was powerful. In control. Full of anger and rage. It was a strange feeling... but she kind of liked it. Was that wrong?

For what might be the first time ever, she wasn't afraid of reacting and losing her head. Syndrome had tapped into something inside her that made using her powers feel as easy as flipping a light switch. Who knew becoming invisible could be as easy as blinking? Or that forming a force field could be as simple as throwing out her hands in front of her? Having Syndrome in her ear all morning – taunting her, pushing her, reminding her of all she'd lost – helped her channel her emotions in a way she never had before.

The only catch? It seemed like if she wanted her powers to work, she had to stay angry about losing her mum and dad, something she still didn't want to dwell on at the moment. But if she wanted to steal the nullifier from Mastermind, she had to use Super skills she still didn't want but was starting to understand.

And now that she was starting to understand them, was it possible there was a small – very small – part of her that maybe, kind of, sort of… liked her powers?

Violet couldn't help thinking of the possibilities.

How useful would it be to listen in on conversations if she could go invisible any time she wanted?

Or to protect her brothers from any and all future threats? What if there was another Mastermind out there in the world who wanted revenge against her parents and their offspring? If she gave up her powers, how would she protect Dash and Jack-Jack?

She looked down at her hands. In seconds, she disappeared, then returned just as easily. *I want to be normal!* she had always told her mum. But did she?

"Let's get back to the house and get ready for this mission!" Syndrome told the driver whisking them back to his house for a briefing before she headed to Mastermind's fortress.

She was about to go on her first Super mission. It was all happening so fast. *Focus on saving Dash and Jack-Jack. Protect your brothers. That's what Mum would want.* It wasn't until she exited the buggy and took the lift up to the main level of the house that she realised she'd had her hand in her pocket the whole ride, clutching her mum's comms link.

Dash and Mirage were waiting for them as the lift doors opened, Mirage held a squiggly Jack-Jack by his armpits. He screamed with delight at the sight of Violet. Mirage, however, looked mutinous as the baby swung back and forth in her arms, acting as if he were on the swings at the park. "This baby is a menace!"

A menace? Violet frowned. "What did Jack-Jack do?"

"Look, I've tried to be a good babysitter the last few days while Dash did laps around the track and you learnt how to beat up robots, but Jack is impossible," Mirage complained. "He can't sit still or be quiet. He needs constant attention!" The woman sounded exhausted, while Jack-Jack giggled with delight.

The baby's face was covered in what looked like chocolate, with more caked on the onesie he was wearing. Crumbs had embedded themselves on the outfit where his knees should be. He obviously was not bothered by any of it.

"I tried explaining he's a baby," Dash said as he munched on crisps from the large bag he was holding. (Mum would never allow him to eat right from the bag.) "But I don't think Mirage has babysat before."

"Not true," Syndrome said, giving Mirage a look Violet didn't understand. "You babysit all the time, don't you, Mirage?"

It was as if Syndrome had flipped a switch. Mirage suddenly pulled Jack to her chest and pasted an eerie smile on her face as the baby tried to get away. "Of course. Sorry. I think I'm just tired from the last few days. I'm normally very maternal." She patted Jack's head awkwardly. "In fact, I was thinking we should probably come up with a chore chart for you all while you're here – taking turns watching Jack. And bedtime schedules. Doesn't that sound fun?"

Dash threw his head back and groaned. "Chores... no!" He flashed her a grin. "And I don't have a bedtime when I'm on holiday."

"This isn't a holiday!" Violet said at the same time as Mirage.

"Every day is a holiday when you're here, right Dash?" Syndrome asked and high-fived him.

Jack-Jack let out another ear-piercing scream of delight and Mirage winced.

Violet took him from her and Jack-Jack babbled, looking wide awake and ready to move even though it was definitely past his nap window. "Did you try to give him a nap?"

"Yes." Mirage looked affronted. "He wouldn't sleep. You didn't tell me he could climb out of his cot."

"He only started doing that a few days ago," Violet admitted, feeling guilty she'd forgotten to mention this before. Mum never would have forgotten something like that. She would have written it down, like she'd done with his schedule for Violet. It was still in her pocket.

"And he got out of his highchair today too," Dash said. Jack-Jack clapped for himself as if he could understand what they were all saying.

"I found him in the kitchen," Mirage told them. "He had a biscuit in each fist! I put him back in his cot four times."

"How did he get the biscuit jar?" Violet wondered. She distinctly remembered seeing it on a kitchen worktop when she left today. Jack-Jack couldn't climb up there.

Dash shrugged. "When you really want a biscuit, you get a biscuit." He popped another handful of crisps into his mouth. It took all Violet's energy not to rip the bag out of his hands.

"He clearly cannot be left alone for one second," Mirage told Syndrome. "And I have other work to do, as you know. Plus, you might remember I need to leave work early to go see my friend Monique."

"We've got a lot going on here," Syndrome said absentmindedly as he pulled out a SpyGuy and punched in a code. Immediately a blueprint of a house pulled up. "Violet's assignment is this afternoon and I can't have distractions."

"That is happening today?" Mirage sounded surprised as she looked from Syndrome to Violet. "She's completed enough training? It's only Tuesday! I thought becoming a Super takes time?"

"It does, but we don't have forever," Syndrome said

curtly. "With my tutelage, Violet's ready. You should see her go!" He sounded manic again. "We can't risk Mastermind finding Violet and the boys before… you know." He glanced Dash's way. "I'm sorry but you'll need to reschedule your class and watch Dash and Jack while Violet's on her mission today."

"A mission?" Dash's eyes widened. "I want to go!" He pulled on Violet's arm. "Can I come too? Violet?"

"No," Violet snapped. *Focus. Think of Mastermind.* "You're not old enough to go on a mission."

"Class? What class?" Mirage spoke over the escalating noise in the room, her voice jumping an octave. "I said I'm seeing my friend Monique. I can't reschedule. We meet the same time each week."

"*Mirage*," Syndrome said, smiling even though he sounded strained. "We've talked about this. I need you to work overtime. Just this once?"

"It's not just this once… it's been all week," Mirage said, her annoyance growing. "You know Monique is important to me."

"You're not old enough for a mission either!" Dash continued to argue with Violet.

"I'm older than you!" Violet reminded him as Jack-Jack watched the two of them, amused.

The noise in the room escalated to the point Jack-Jack

started to whimper. Three workers came running in, shouting. Then Jack started to full-blown wail.

"Sir?" The first worker was carrying a handheld monitor that looked like a larger version of the SpyGuy. "We have an issue that needs your immediate attention."

"Issue?" said the second worker. "I'd call it a major problem. It was a problem when I saw it pop up on the monitor an hour ago, Gerard. Now it's a potential disaster!"

"Can it wait?" Syndrome snapped. "We're in the middle of something important here."

"No, it can't wait. Not if you..." He glanced at the kids then back at Syndrome, tapping his earpiece. For a moment Violet thought she heard yelling. "There's been a breach on the island."

Mirage and Syndrome looked at each other, then Syndrome pulled the worker aside, Syndrome whispering heatedly with the worker and gesturing wildly. "Then fix it! Fast!" The workers ran out of the room and Syndrome turned back to the others sheepishly, running a hand through his red hair. Violet couldn't help thinking he looked unnerved. "New plan. I need to go. Now. Mirage, I need you here to monitor Violet's mission and watch the kids. It's not a request."

"Excuse me?" Mirage scoffed.

"Wait. You're not coming with me?" Violet felt her

stomach lurch. "I'm going alone?"

Syndrome put a hand on her shoulder. "It's better this way. This is one time not being a Super works against me. Infiltrating Mastermind's compound hinges on getting past security undetected, and without invisibility I can't do that. If Mastermind catches wind I'm there, it will only put you in more danger." He looked slightly worried. "We have had run-ins before."

"Run-ins?" Violet asked as Jack-Jack tried pressing a sticky finger in one of her eyeballs. When had Syndrome crossed paths with a super villain before?

"Syn?" Mirage tried, but he continued to ignore her.

"It's a long story, one we don't have time for." Syndrome punched up a few things on the screen he was holding. "This week is the first time Mastermind's been spotted since Supers became illegal. Now, I don't know why Mastermind is back in Metroville, but Mastermind would never go anywhere without that nullifier. We need you to get that device now or we'll lose the chance. Mirage can monitor the car while she watches the kids."

Mirage threw her hands up. "Anything else you expect me to do while you're gone?"

"Um, no, I think that's it." Syndrome seemed distracted as he squeezed Mirage's arm. "Thanks, sweetheart. Violet?

We're going to have to speed this mission talk up. Follow me."

"Hang on," Mirage said, grabbing his arm now. "Can I talk to you before you go deal with your *problem*?"

The way she emphasised the word *problem*, Violet got the impression it was one Mirage was familiar with.

"No time," Syndrome said. An exasperated Mirage turned and strode into the kitchen, mumbling to herself. He looked at Violet. "Let's go." He walked fast, his cape getting tangled in his legs.

"Coming," Violet said, giving Dash a look that said, *Don't even try to follow.*

Dash wasn't any happier. He turned away from Violet, but she could still hear him clearly. "I'm telling Mum and Dad about this."

Violet paused, startled. She felt the blood rush to her ears, the pain of loss threatening to overwhelm her. *This time tomorrow you'll be safe and I'll tell you everything*, she vowed to herself. She pushed the pain down again. "Dash, you can be mad at me all you want." She shifted Jack from one arm to the other. "Mum put me in charge while she's… gone."

Dash cut her off and jutted his chin out defiantly. "In charge? Syndrome's the boss here."

"Well, I'm still the boss of *you*," Violet said, her voice growing stronger. She could feel her fingers spark as her anger grew. "And I'm trying to protect you." *Like Mum wanted.*

"You two finished?" Syndrome snapped. "Violet, we need to move." He started to walk towards his control room again and Violet followed. She almost banged into him when he spun around suddenly and looked at Dash. "And Dash? I haven't forgotten about you," he said, his voice softening. "I tell you what – next mission we'll go on together. How does that sound?"

Next mission? Violet thought. There wasn't going to be a next mission. If all went well, by tonight, neither of them would have powers anymore.

"Fine," Dash said, but he still sounded mad and moody. "Can I go play pinball now?"

"Go," Violet and Syndrome said at the same time.

Jack started to whine, begging to get down and follow Dash, and Violet obliged. Dash could watch him while Mirage was busy and she talked to Syndrome about her mission.

Mission.

Was she really doing this?

Breaking into a super villain's compound and stealing their greatest weapon?

Her stomach started to do flip-flops.

Don't think, she heard her mum's voice in her head. *And don't worry. If the time comes, you'll know what to do. It's in your blood.*

Being Super was in her blood. She could see that now. She was doing this. She would protect her brothers from Mastermind if it was the last thing she did.

Violet hurried behind Syndrome into a dark room, illuminated by various screens and monitors that lined the walls. Lights flashed on the control boards, and one of the screens was flashing with the word *Breach!* Beneath the word she could see the outline of what looked like a volcano. *Where is that?* she wondered as she heard the faint sounds of people yelling and an explosion. Syndrome turned down the volume on one of the screens and pointed to a monitor that had a blueprint of a house on it.

"Here is where you're headed." He tapped another button and an arial view of a large estate appeared on the screen. He clicked something to make the image on the screen appear 3D, allowing Violet to see inside the complex. "Getting inside is tricky, but not impossible. You'll have to get around security at the main gate, but then there's a tunnel underneath the house used for deliveries that are arriving at all times as Mastermind sets up here in Metroville again. You'll be in a car that looks like a delivery van."

"Delivery van," Violet repeated, committing the details to memory.

"This thing is legit," Syndrome exclaimed. "It's driverless of course, but it will appear as if you have a driver."

"A driverless car with a fake driver?" Violet repeated, confused.

Syndrome grinned. "A hologram program created by me personally. Wait till you see it! Might be my best work. If only I could figure out a way to program the hologram to walk and move instead of it needing to stay stationary to function." He waved his hands around. "Workload for another day. Anyway, you'll sweep right past security with that thing and be on the grounds."

"If you say so." Violet was still nervous, but at least he'd thought this through. "What will the car say it's delivering?"

His blue eyes glittered mischievously. "Double-fudge brownie pizza."

"Brownie pizza?" Violet couldn't help feeling sceptical. "That's what is going to gain me entrance to Mastermind's compound?"

"Yes," Syndrome insisted. "Every villain has their weakness. Mastermind's is brownies." He got a far-off look in his eyes. "Trust me. We all have vices that could destroy us."

"Sir? We really have to go," said a worker who looked more anxious than Violet felt during a presentation.

"Two seconds." Syndrome pointed to a spot on the map. "Now, there may be some guards once you arrive at the underground service entrance there, so the key is to be invisible when you arrive." He slapped his forehead. "Wait a minute! I forgot about your clothes! They don't disappear when you do. How are we getting around that?" He hit the monitor in front of him and everyone jumped. "Now what?"

"Actually, I think I have something that might help with that." Violet hesitated before explaining. "I found this suit at home that seems to work with my powers. Actually, Dash found the suit and I have mine with me."

Syndrome stared at her curiously. "A Supersuit?"

"My mum made them for all of us, I think. It looks like a Supersuit, but mine actually becomes invisible when I touch it, so I think if I'm wearing it, I'll be completely invisible too. Dash and Jack have theirs, too, although theirs don't make them invisible, obviously."

"Obviously!" He clapped his hands. "Hot dog, that's brilliant! Score one for Elastigirl! Great! Wear that." He laughed to himself, shaking his head. "Problem solved!"

Violet smiled, relieved. One problem solved, at least.

"Okay, moving on." He hit another button and a 3D view of the house's floors came into view. "The guards will be kept busy unloading the vehicle while you head into the service lift, which will take you up to the kitchen. Cross the kitchen and keep going. From there, you'll need to get down a long, narrow hall unseen." The image of the hallway seemed to go on forever. "The door you want is at the very end of the hall. It may be locked so take this." He handed Violet a small red device that had a suction cup on one end. "It can open any locked door."

Picking locks. Okay, not something she'd ever done before. "Then what?"

"Get through the door. Make your way downstairs again to the lower level, which is nestled right into the cliff. My intel tells me the nullifier is being held in a safe down there," Syndrome said.

"Lower level," Violet repeated. That was pretty vague. "In a safe. Where did you get this intel?"

"Sir?" A worker looked up from a monitor. "The jet is here. You really need to get on it. They need backup immediately."

"Trust me. If you follow my directions, you're going to get in and out unseen." Syndrome clapped Violet on the back and started to walk away. "I'll check in as soon as I can, and remember, Mirage is here, monitoring the vehicle. Just get going. We want you there by nightfall when Mastermind gets snacky. You'll need to get the nullifier, get back to the car, and then it knows what to do to get you off the premises and back here. It's all been plugged in already. The plan is foolproof."

"But won't Mastermind come after me to get it back?" Violet wondered, thinking again of something Mirage had worried about too.

Syndrome scoffed. "Mastermind will have no clue where to find you." He headed to the door. "I guess that's it! Good luck today."

"You're leaving? So soon?" Violet knew her voice sounded small, but she could feel her heart pounding, the panic taking hold. Her parents were gone. She was about to face a villain, alone. This was worse than a teacher springing a surprise test. They weren't going to run a simulation or test the lock picker? Wasn't he going to give her more details about the security system or tell her about other Mastermind inventions she should watch out for? Violet had so many questions she wasn't going to have answers to. "I'm not ready."

"You have to be. We're out of time." He turned and clasped her by the shoulders. "Just remember what I taught you today. Stay focused. When you get to Mastermind's, remember why you're there: to get a gadget that could keep Mastermind from killing you like the villain did your parents. Don't mess this up."

Great pep talk, Violet thought, but it still worked. She felt her rage building again.

"Get that nullifier and get back here fast." An alarm blinked on one of his gloves. "You need to get going. The car is waiting for you downstairs. Wait till you see it! Way better than that Incredibile your dad used to drive! This has features you couldn't even think of. Oh! I almost forgot." Syndrome grabbed something from the nearest table and handed it to Violet. It was a digital watch. "Here. This is a way for us to stay in touch. The second you get to Mastermind's, start the timer. It will alert me you've made it inside. When you've got the nullifier, send me another alert." He pressed a button on the watch and the screen lit up with several different features. "I'll communicate with the vehicle to make sure it's ready to whisk you out of there."

"Sir?" the worker tried again to get Syndrome's attention.

"There's a bunch of cool things the watch can do, but I don't have time to show you now. The one thing I should point out is the emergency feature." He tapped what looked like a dial on the side of the watch. If you're captured, or in trouble, hit this so we know."

"You'll come for me?" Violet said hopefully.

"Someone will," Syndrome said, looking distracted as he typed something into the nearest computer.

Violet bit the inside of her cheek. This was real. It was

happening. "Okay."

"Sir?" A worker swallowed hard as he interrupted them again. "We really have to get you to the island."

"Yes. Okay. Good luck, kid. I'll check in with Mirage as soon as I can." He grinned as he nodded to another worker, who led Violet out of the room. "You've got this."

You've got this. She hoped Syndrome was right about that, and all the intel on Mastermind. The worker gave her a fifteen-minute warning before she needed to leave, so Violet rushed to check on Jack-Jack before going to her room to put on her Supersuit. She found Jack-Jack on the floor, playing with a ball, while Mirage sat dejectedly on the sofa in front of him. As soon as she saw Violet, she perked up.

"How did it go? Are you ready for your mission?" she said cheerily. It was a complete one-eighty from how she'd been just a few minutes earlier.

"Uhh... yeah. Where's Dash?" She glanced towards the arcade games, which sat unused.

"Oh, he wanted to take a nap. Maybe Jack-Jack will do the same so I can monitor you while you're gone." Mirage showed Violet a handheld screen that had a purple light pulsing on a map. "I can track your car on here, and you can talk to me through the monitor in the car so you won't feel so alone."

"That makes me feel a little better," Violet admitted.

"But I'm sorry you're stuck babysitting. I know that's not your job." Violet wasn't sure what Mirage's job was, actually.

"It's fine," Mirage said right before Jack-Jack threw the ball at her face. Mirage handed it back to him with a tight smile. "That's my job this week it seems."

"But now you have to miss your class." Violet felt bad about that.

"Class? No, you must have misheard me, I don't have a class," Mirage said quickly. "My job is to be here with you. That's what Syn needs so that's what I'll do, even if I'm wasting my talent at this place and…" She exhaled loudly. "Sorry. This was supposed to be a temp job and now, here I am a year later, and…"

"Your talent?" Violet questioned.

Mirage waved her hand dismissively. "Why am I bothering you with all this? I'm fine." She exhaled, doing her breathing exercise. "I am Mirage and I am fine. You need to go get ready. The car is already waiting."

Violet started to head to her room when Jack-Jack screamed again. Mirage rubbed her temples. This woman clearly needed a holiday. Mirage had got them out of the Parr home when Mastermind's goons had attacked. Now it was Violet's turn to help her. "You know, if it's too much watching Dash and Jack-Jack today, with Syndrome not here, you could hire a babysitter."

"Babysitter? You mean someone other than me?" Mirage repeated, and Violet nodded. She seemed to mull the idea over. "Where would I find a babysitter?"

"My friend Kari is the best babysitter in Metroville. I'd feel safe knowing Jack-Jack was with her if you were in a pinch." Violet grabbed a pad from the coffee table and scribbled Kari's number on it. "If you need her, just say you're my aunt or something and I'm away with my family."

The baby started to screech and squirm again. "Num-num. Num-num," he whined, and Mirage skirted to the other side of the sofa.

"She's good," Violet promised. "She babysits every kid in town. She's worth the five dollars an hour."

"Five dollars an hour, you say?" Mirage looked at the piece of paper with interest. "And she's reliable?"

"Absolutely," Violet said. Most of the time. Mirage didn't need to know that Kari had dragged her to a party they didn't have permission to go to.

Mirage smiled as Jack-Jack squealed at the top of his lungs. "Well, I'm sure I won't need her, but thank you. My role today is to make sure you stay safe on your mission, even though Syn would clearly be better at this job. But when you're trying to do too many things at once…" She sighed. "Sorry. Again. Not your problem." She smiled too brightly. "You focus on your mission and go get that nullifier."

CHAPTER FIFTEEN
VIOLET

Violet had seen pictures of her dad's Incredibile. This car in Syndrome's car park was nothing like it.

Dad's car, which he often talked about lovingly and longingly while Mum looked on, shaking her head, was a sports car. The car Syndrome had assigned to Violet was a bright yellow estate with a white-and-red PIZZA PLANET logo painted on one side. From several steps away, Violet could see a tall stack of boxes in the back seat marked BROWNIE PIZZA. Violet hoped nobody from school spotted her cruising around delivering dessert pizza.

She opened the passenger side door and reluctantly climbed into the front seat wondering when the hologram would appear as a driver. There were several modifications to the dashboard, which she had to admit were cool. In front of her were two large monitors – one showed where she was going and another one mapped where she'd been.

"Hello, Violet Parr," said the car as she sat down. "Would you like your seat warmed?"

"Oh! Um, no thank you," Violet said, patting the dashboard, which lit up at her touch.

"The interior temperature of the car is twenty degrees," said the car. "Would you like a snack for your trip?" A panel above the glove compartment shot out showcasing a row of sweets like it was a concession stand at the cinema.

"I'm good, but thanks." She was too nervous to eat.

"All right," said the car. "Please let me know if and when you might need laser beam attack function or a missile launcher. Could I interest you in our aeronautics or parachute features?"

Violet bit the inside of her cheek. Why would a car need a parachute? And why did this car have a missile launcher? It occurred to Violet that with one accidental press of a button she could mess up the mission before it started. "Just a regular drive would be great, thank you," she said, and the car took off. The hologram, however, didn't appear. Violet hoped the windows were tinted so no one noticed a driverless car and a girl on a joyride.

As the car made its way along city streets, Violet kept her

eyes on the road in front of her. This section of Metroville was one she wasn't familiar with. The homes were larger, the streets more spread apart, and she hadn't seen an actual person in miles. The pulsing dot on the map suggested that Mastermind's compound was located at the top of one of the mountains they were driving towards, overlooking the whole city. If Violet weren't so terrified of what she was about to do, she'd be excited to see the view from up there.

She took a deep breath, inhaling the smell of chocolate from the brownies in the back seat. The car was quiet as it zoomed along the narrow road with impressive precision. She thought about calling Mirage just to hear someone other than the voice in her head, but why stress the woman out more? She'd looked terrified about being left alone with Jack-Jack again.

"Just focus," Violet told herself, tapping her fingers on her legs and looking down at her Supersuit (which was surprisingly comfortable and seemed to breathe like Egyptian cotton). In a hidden pocket, she'd packed her mum's comms link and her note that was already starting to look worn. "You can do this." She looked at the watch Syndrome had given her. One of the buttons said SET TO STUN. Did that mean she could point the watch and stun someone? Might not be the best idea to test that in a moving car. She continued her pep talk. "A mission is no big deal.

Who cares if you're trying to break into Mastermind's super secure compound and steal the villain's greatest weapon?"

"You're breaking into Mastermind's house?"

Violet whipped her head around and gasped. "Dash?"

On the floor of the back seat, Dash peeked out from under a Pizza Planet delivery jacket and looked at her sheepishly, his cheeks colouring. "Surprise!"

"What are you doing here?" Violet demanded, feeling a spark of anger when she realised he was in his Supersuit as well. "You're supposed to be back at the house with Mirage! She's going to freak out!"

"No, she won't. She doesn't even know I'm gone." Dash shrugged. "She thinks I'm napping." He held his stomach, blocking the *I* on the suit's chest, and laughed. "As if I nap!"

Violet glared at him. "You've messed up everything. I'm calling Mirage to come get you."

"Don't!" Dash begged. "I can help you."

"No!"

"Why not?" Dash groaned. "You need me."

I do, but I don't want to lose you, too, she wanted to say, but she couldn't. Her heart was pumping hard again as she stared at all the buttons on the dash. Which one did she use to call Mirage? Why did these buttons all say things like FIRE SHRINK RAY instead of something simple like MAKE A CALL? "Sorry, Dash. This is a solo mission and – aha!

There's the speak button." She pressed it.

The car spoke first.

"Hello, Violet Parr. Dash Parr," it said. "Your vehicle is headed to 1024 Overlook Drive, Metroville."

"That is awesome," Dash whispered.

"Uh, car? Can you turn around and take us back to Syndrome's?" Violet asked politely. "We've got a stowaway on board."

"I'm not a stowaway! I'm your sidekick!" Dash argued, the two of them talking over each other like they always did when they argued.

"I don't need a sidekick," Violet told the car. "I need him safe, at home, back at Syndrome's."

"Negative," the car said. "Route is confirmed and on lock: 1024 Overlook Drive, Metroville."

Violet groaned and pressed herself back against the seat as the car started to climb up a mountain. The sky was darkening, the red in the sky giving way to deep blues. City lights began to light up the skyline. Enjoying the car ride and the view was supposed to be the easy part of the mission. "Great. Mission over before it even started."

"No, it's not. I brought all kinds of gadgets." Dash pulled a bag out of the back. "If you're trying to stop the bad guys, you can't do this alone. You might need my speed or some kind of gadget to do… whatever it is you're doing."

She forgot he didn't actually know the mission.

"Look at all the stuff I brought to help us – two SpyGuys and a bunch of gadgets from Dad's office." He opened the bag and held up the megaphone she recognised from the other day at the house. "I have the freeze ray and the shrink-and-grow button, too." He showed her the happy face button again that almost destroyed Dad's trophy.

"You stole Dad's stuff?" Violet narrowed her eyes at him. "When? How? I didn't see you steal anything before we ran out of the house."

"You say *stole*, I say *borrowed*," Dash told her triumphantly. "I also grabbed this." Dash held up the tiny homing device she'd let Dash play with in Dad's office the other day.

It reminded her of the SpyGuy, but smaller, and she knew it was expensive. (Dad was always saying, "Be careful! I can't get another one of these!") She was going to say the same exact thing to Dash until she realised there was a small blinking light over a tiny island in the ocean. Violet grabbed it from him.

"Wait, who is this homing device tracking?" Violet asked.

Dash shrugged. "I'm not sure. I did see Mum with it before she left though. Maybe Dad? Is his conference on an island? Sounds like a holiday."

"But it can't be Dad's location, can it?" Violet said, thinking out loud. "How can it be working if…?" She stopped herself.

"If he already left?" Dash suggested. "I know! Shouldn't Mum and Dad be on their way home by now? When are they getting back?"

"Soon." Violet stared at the screen, trying to work out what was happening. Why would the light still be blinking if Dad was dead? Wouldn't it have been destroyed if her parents had been killed in an explosion? Or did they drop it in their scuffle with Mastermind?

"Violet?" Dash interrupted her thoughts. "Is this mission about the bad guys that came to the house?"

She saw his small face scrunch up tight underneath the black mask he was wearing, and her heart melted a bit. They'd been through so much the last few days. She could only imagine what he was feeling being kept in the dark. She was doing it for his own good, wasn't she? Hiding the truth was her protecting him, wasn't it? She couldn't let Dash face Mastermind. She couldn't lose him, too. "Yes," she said slowly. "I'm going after the bad guys."

He thought for a moment. "And the bad guys work with Mastermind?"

He was figuring everything out. How could she lie now?

"Yes, but Dash—"

The car came alive with the sound of a phone ringing, interrupting her answer. Violet looked around for a receiver, but saw none. She still couldn't find a phone button either.

"Don't you think you should answer that?" Dash asked.

"Yes, but I can't find a phone!" Violet said, looking at each button on the dash carefully again.

"Violet?" Mirage's voice filled the car. "Are you there?"

"Mirage?" Violet shouted to the ceiling, relieved. "I'm here and so is Dash." She shot him another grumpy look.

"He is? Thank goodness. I've been looking everywhere for him!" In the background, Violet could hear Jack-Jack whining again. It made her stomach hurt. "I went to check on him and when he wasn't in his room, I thought… well, I'm just glad he's safe."

Dash's cheeks turned brighter, and he shrunk down in the seat, trying to hide behind the Pizza Planet jackets.

"Can you turn this car around so I can drop him off?" Violet asked as Dash shook his head vehemently no.

The car had turned onto a winding road now that chugged higher along a narrow dirt path. The car knocked Violet around like one of Dash's marbles.

"Destination approaching, one mile," the car said as they passed a large sign that said NO TRESPASSING. "Private road."

"One mile?" Mirage could obviously hear the announcement. "It's too late to turn back now. You'll have been spotted on Mastermind's security system already. Turning around now could send Mastermind's goons after you."

Goons? There was no one out here but their car. The road ahead was pitch black. If there was a house on this mountain, there were no signs indicating it either. Violet gave Dash a mutinous glance. "But I need to be invisible to get inside. What am I going to do with Dash?"

"I don't know, but you better think fast."

"Nobody's faster than me!" Dash said proudly. "I can get past any villain! That's what Syndrome told me."

Violet did a double take. "What?"

"Yep! Syndrome said I was old enough to act Super, even if Mum and Dad never let me *be* Super. Today's that day." Dash sat up and placed his hands on his hips, taking on a Super stance and a dreamy look in his eye that was very familiar.

He looks like Dad, Violet thought. *He acts like Dad too.* Her stomach tightened. Unlike her, Dash loved having powers, even if he didn't get to use them. How was he going to react when she told him he'd have to give up being Super?

The car buzzers began to sound. "Approaching target."

Violet peered out the car window worriedly. Up ahead,

she could see a light and quickly realised it was a gate situated between two small turret-topped guard towers. Beyond the gates, Violet could see a brick road that was lined on either side by decorative fountains. Water jumped from one infinity pool to the next, all entirely lit from underneath. At the end of the road, if Violet squinted, she could make out a ridiculously large structure. Calling it a mansion would be wrong. The place was a castle, with multiple blue turrets and peaked rooftops, and more windows than a high-rise. Mastermind lived here?

"Call me as soon as you're finished," Mirage said. "I'm setting my timer now... You should be in and out in an hour. Violet, you do the same."

Violet set a timer on Syndrome's watch to let him know they'd arrived. The watch began counting down – 59 minutes and 59 seconds. Syndrome said to get in and out in under an hour and he clearly meant it.

"Good luck," Mirage said, sounding grim as the wailing in the background from Jack grew louder. "If you're not out in an hour, then..."

"Then?" Dash prodded.

But Mirage didn't answer. Neither did Violet. If they weren't out in an hour, Violet knew what that meant: they'd failed... or worse.

"We'll call you as soon as we're done," Violet promised

and the car went silent. The guard booth was directly ahead of them now, only a few yards away. "All right, Dash, you wanted to be Super. This is your chance."

Dash fist-pumped the air. "YES!"

She looked at him sharply. "I'm in charge of this mission. Understand me? You do one thing I tell you not to and you're... you're..." What was an appropriate punishment for a Super? "You're... grounded from future missions."

Dash's eyes widened. "No more missions?"

"No more missions," Violet promised. Guilt took hold as she thought about how this truly would be his first and only mission. She was stealing an invention that would take being Super away from him. She swallowed hard. "So do everything I say in there. This isn't a game. These bad guys will hurt us if they catch us. They're like the ones at the house, but worse."

Dash nodded. "What are we going to say to the guards when we pull up?"

"Ten seconds till approach," the car told them. "Ten, nine, eight..."

"Nothing!" Violet pushed him further into the back seat. "Syndrome said the car would check in at the guard gate itself." She frowned, looking at the driver seat she was sitting next to. When was the hologram going to finally appear? Weren't they cutting this close? Violet skirted as close to the passenger window as she could to get out of the way of the hologram. "Get under those jackets again, and whatever happens, don't make a sound!"

Time to disappear, she thought. Violet held her breath and thought again of something that would help her focus on the task of becoming invisible. Now that she knew what to do, the move was almost effortless. *Mum*, she thought, *I really miss you*. In seconds, she was gone. The suit, miraculously, was gone too, not a moment too soon.

There was a flicker, and suddenly a hologram appeared at Violet's side. It looked like a teen boy with long, brown hair, wearing a Pizza Planet hat and a T-shirt with jeans. "Hi, delivery for Mastermind," said the hologram, sounding a lot like the boys at her school.

"Name?" said a guard, wearing a black security ensemble and black sunglasses.

Violet's heart beat out of her chest in panic. Was this going to work?

"Dude, it's Pizza Planet?" the hologram said, sounding annoyed. "This is 1024 Overlook Drive, no? I got a call for a delivery."

The man checked his clipboard. In the back seat, Violet thought she heard rustling. The guard whispered the delivery information into his watch and a garbled voice responded. "Sorry, we don't have a delivery scheduled from

Pizza Planet. You must have the wrong address."

Violet's heart sank. It wasn't working.

"Says here they ordered two dozen brownie pizzas," said the hologram, and Violet was amazed the computer programming could turn on a dime and respond.

"Sorry, I can't let you in." These guards weren't budging. Violet held her breath.

The hologram sighed. "I can turn around, but it's your funeral dude. If my boss ordered brownies and I was the one who sent the delivery dude away, I'd be toast."

The first guard looked at the second guard. "All right, we will let you through – but just to drop off the delivery at the service entrance. You are not allowed inside. Understood?" The hologram nodded. "Take the road to the end and make a left to the service entrance. It's about a ten-minute drive. You can't miss the turnoff. It's the only one. The next set of guards will take the delivery from there." The guard used a torch to peer through the windows of the car and Violet tried to shrink into herself. *Dash, don't move*, she thought. "In and out. Got it?"

"Got it, dude!" the hologram said. The car roared to life again as the gates opened.

They were in.

CHAPTER SIXTEEN
VIOLET

"Are they gone?" Dash hissed.

"For now." Violet appeared in the front seat again and stared at the hologram seemingly driving the car. She waved her hand and it went right through the projection. "Stay down."

"I can't," Dash groaned. "It's so hot under those jackets! It's making my suit sweaty." "You said you'd listen," Violet reminded him. Her nerves were getting the best of her. "All right. Come out for five minutes, then you have to hide again."

"Great!" Dash said, his head popping up. "So tell me about our mission. What are we doing? Why are we going to Mastermind's? I thought Mastermind disappeared!"

Violet chose her words carefully. "I guess I have to give you a mission report if you're helping me," she admitted, and Dash grinned eagerly. "We're here to find and borrow something of Mastermind's that we need to protect us from the bad guys."

"Borrow? You mean steal! What are we stealing?" Dash pulled out the megaphone. "I'll freeze anyone who comes our way!"

Violet grabbed the megaphone, avoiding the question about what they were actually stealing. "No freezing anyone! As soon as the car stops, I'm going to slip out undetected and cause a distraction so you can zip out of the car unseen."

"No one can see me when I run anyway," Dash said. "Ask Mr Kropp. He never saw me put that tack on his chair. That video didn't prove anything."

"Well, go just as fast as that, then, and meet me at the lift. We're going up to the kitchen, then down the hall, and trying to get down to the lower level. We are looking for a safe down there that has the object we need."

Dash frowned. "A safe? Is it going to just be sitting out there in the open? Because whenever Dad talks about missions he's been on with safes, he's always saying how they're hidden behind a picture, or in a wall, or..."

"We'll figure it out when we get there," Violet said as the car inched towards a tunnel in the side of the mountain.

"WHOA. Look at that!"

Violet looked up. Mastermind's castle looked like something Violet had seen in history books, all grandiose with massive columns, balconies and terraces – there had to be at least twenty rooms per floor. As they neared, the greenery changed too – carved topiaries, many shaped like the letter *M*, sprang up on the sides of the road alongside elaborate flower beds with lime-green blooms and other flowers the colour of the sea. And then, suddenly, the road was dipping down again into the tunnel.

"Is this Mastermind's place? Is it? Mastermind is rich!" Dash said. "So what are we stealing from this safe?" Dash pressed. "Secret plans to a cool new robot that could destroy all Metroville? Something that would put Mum and Dad back in business? Dad really misses being Super, you know."

The words *miss* and *Dad* made Violet's face fall. Dash clearly noticed. "Violet? Do Mum and Dad know we're helping Syndrome or are they going to be mad at us?"

Violet bit the inside of her cheek, trying not to show her emotions. Would Mum and Dad be mad she was trying to steal something that would strip their powers? Change their family legacy?

Yes.

But they were gone and she was the only one here

to pick up the pieces. She didn't have a choice. She grabbed his hand over the seatback. "Don't worry about Mum and Dad. Just focus on the mission. This thing we're stealing from Mastermind will keep us safe. No one will ever be able to hurt us again. That's a promise."

Dash seemed to mull this over. "What does this thing do? What's it called?"

"Entering tunnel," the car said. "Activate cloaking device." The hologram flickered to life again.

"Get down," Violet hissed. "The minute this car stops and I cause a distraction, you move. Okay?"

"You're so bossy!" Dash said.

For a second, Violet couldn't help but smile. Bossy meant she was doing a good job. Maybe her mum would be mad about the nullifier, but she wouldn't be about how take-charge Violet was being. With one hand on her right hip where the comms link was nestled in a pocket, Violet thought of her mum again and disappeared.

The Pizza Planet car glided through the tunnel, slowing down as it reached a service docking area, where several guards were standing around drinking coffee. At the sight of the Pizza Planet truck, they set down their drinks, picked up what looked like electrified sticks, and approached the vehicle. The sound of Dash's breathing made Violet fear they'd be given away. She held her breath.

A guard approached the car. "Can I help you?"

"Brownie pizza delivery for a 1024 Overlook Drive? I've got two dozen boxes," said the hologram.

"Oh, right. Jimmy, they said they were sending this delivery through," said another guard. "Stay in your vehicle, sir. We'll unload from the back."

"Wow, you smell that?" said the third, opening the back of the station wagon. "The boss is going to flip."

"Think anyone will miss one box?" said the first guard as he began unloading.

"Nah!"

They all laughed as Violet felt her heart drum in her chest. How was she going to get out the back without bumping into anyone and get a door open for Dash? She had no choice – she had to open her passenger door. She opened the door fast, jumping out and running as far from the car as she could. *Whish!* She felt a gust of wind go by her. *Dash.* He'd made it. Step one complete.

"Sir? I said stay in your vehicle!" A guard approached the door as she ran fast to the lift up ahead.

"Sorry, dude," said the hologram. "No problem-o."

Violet rushed across the delivery area, past large crates that were all stamped with the word MASTERMIND. Underneath the name were other labels, like COMBUSTIBLE, POISONOUS and HATES PEOPLE. That last box seemed to be growling. She found Dash hidden behind a large yellow crate that said, DON'T GET WET.

He grinned wide. "I did good, right?"

"Yes. Now stay here," Violet hissed, eyeing the guards who had unpacked the pizza boxes and were opening the first one to take a brownie. "I'll press the lift button and then you get in fast and we close the doors."

"Johnnie? Send for the lift so we can bring these up to the boss," called one of the guards, and Violet did a double take.

Sleeping on a chair next to the lift was a guard she hadn't noticed. Thankfully he was snoring, his dark glasses covering his eyes.

"Johnnie!"

With a snort he started to move.

"I'm coming, I'm coming," he grumbled, hitting the lift button before he walked over to the other guards.

"Lift is coming. Let's go," Dash whispered, zipping away before Violet could stop him.

Johnnie stopped. "Hey, did you guys hear something?"

Violet had no choice but to race after him, dashing into the lift and hitting the button to shut the doors while Dash pressed himself against a side wall. As the two doors slid shut, Violet saw the gold outline etched into the metal. Together, the shapes formed an *M*.

"Johnnie!" she heard the guards whine as the doors closed and the lift shot up at alarming speed. A saxophone began to play as lift music filled the space, reminding her of a dentist office waiting room.

"Whew, that was close!" Dash said, jumping up and down. "But we're here! We're inside!" He looked around. "So this is what a villain's place looks like. You know, Dad always said Mastermind was classy, but this just looks like a regular lift."

"Quiet!" Violet pushed him to the ground and disappeared fast as she looked up at a monitor. They couldn't risk being seen. "Here on out, things are tricky."

"They're not already?" Dash whispered.

"The lift should take us to the kitchen, and from there, we have to get down the hall unseen and make it to the lower level," Violet said, and Dash started to grumble. "Yes, I know, go up to go down."

Her heart started to pound again as she thought about what they were up against, but it didn't matter. She wasn't leaving here without that nullifier.

The lift door chimed. "Floor one," it said. "Kitchen."

"Ready?" she asked Dash. "You're going to need to be quick."

"I was born quick," Dash boasted, getting into a running stance to take off the second the doors opened.

"Wow, what's that smell? Is that lasagna?"

The lift opened onto a large kitchen area that looked nothing like their kitchen at home. For one thing, it was about twenty times bigger. And instead of one oven, it had five. There were also at least four supersize refrigerators. In the middle of the room Violet could see three massive islands where dozens of workers in white chef jackets emblazoned with *M*s were running around chopping fruit and preparing every kind of food imaginable. Violet spotted several seven-tiered cakes with lime-green-and-gold frosting, mounds of biscuits and cupcakes stacked on trays, and steaks and salmon being seared on stovetops. Was Mastermind hosting a party? The smell of butter and garlic mixed with chocolate was both nauseating and made her mouth water, but she stayed focused.

Violet became invisible and Dash shot out, moving so fast he must have hit a chef washing a pan, because the man turned around in annoyance to scold another chef, who then started shouting in a French accent about someone swiping the frosting off the cake in front of him, smearing the *M*.

"Hey! Who took my cupcakes?" a chef with a moustache started yelling. "We aren't supposed to eat anything!"

Violet scanned the room. There appeared to be no security cameras in here. That was good. The bad news was the only way to get to the door at the other end of the long kitchen was to walk right through the central aisle, which was clogged with workers. Someone would bump into her along the way, wouldn't they? Dash had already caused a commotion.

"Are you calling me a liar, Eva?" The moustached chef wielded a cupcake menacingly. "Two minutes ago there were twelve cupcakes on this tray and now there are nine. Who ate them?"

At the other end of the room, the door opened. For all she knew, Dash was already through it. She had to move. If her mum were here, she could stretch herself from one length of this room to the other, knocking out people as she went, giving Violet a clear path across. *Mum*, she thought, her stomach tightening. She felt her whole body tingle and her skin warm as she held her invisibility and made her way across the room, dodging chefs and trays of fruit and cupcakes. Soon the door on the other side of the room was in sight. No one even seemed to notice when she pushed it open and dived through to the other side, reappearing in the hallway where Dash was waiting.

"Took you long enough," he said, popping out from behind a giant ficus, eating a biscuit and a cupcake.

"Stay down," Violet said, scanning the long, wide hallway with blue-and-green-patterned rugs and abstract art prints. More than a dozen dark wood doors stared back at them from either side of the hall. Faint music played from unseen speakers overhead and the sound of a film playing filtered into the hall. This had to be the spot Syndrome mentioned on the map. But which door led back downstairs? "We need to find the other lift. Now, it's supposed to be right there at the other end of the hall, but that looks like a regular door and—"

"On it," Dash said, zipping away before Violet could stop him.

The kid was so fast, he was there in seconds, tugging on the doorknob at the opposite end of the hall. "It's locked!" he said loudly.

Violet rolled her eyes. She had to remind herself never to take him on a covert mission again. "Quiet!" she hissed, her voice echoing in the hall. Her eyes roamed left and right as she ran past several closed doors, wondering where everyone was in this place. How could there be so many guards and workers, but no residents in the house? Was Mastermind even here?

Dash was still tugging on the heavy wooden door when Violet reached him. "Hang on," she said, reaching into her other pocket and pulling out the suction cup that Syndrome gave her that could unlock any door. She stuck it over the keyhole, pressed the button and heard a faint deflating sound. Then a click. Dash tried the door again. It opened to reveal a hidden lift with shiny metal doors that also stood open.

"Cool! Come on!" Dash hopped into the lift and Violet followed, pressing the button to close the lift doors as quickly as she could. She watched the long empty hallway until the metal doors slid shut.

She swallowed hard. *Where is everyone?* Music was playing softly in this lift, too, which was much fancier than the first one had been. The walls were wood-panelled and glossy, with large *M*s etched into every surface. The control panel had three buttons in addition to OPEN and CLOSE – UP, POOL, EMERGENCY. Pool? That had to also be the down button. There was a pool on the lower level?

"This should take us downstairs. Let's find that safe," Violet said, pressing the button again and looking around for a security camera. This lift didn't have one.

She felt the whoosh of the lift descending again, and then the doors opened to reveal a darkened hallway where the air was much cooler. A weak light filtered in from a single lamp at the other end of the hall, which was quiet and empty. Violet saw only one door. It was bright green.

"I don't see a safe anywhere," Dash pointed out. "No paintings it could be hidden behind, no rugs over a trapdoor leading to a safe room. I don't think this is the right place."

"It has to be," Violet said, biting her lip. "Syndrome said the safe was downstairs and this is the lower level." She scanned the walls for cameras. What if Mastermind was somehow watching them? Her heartbeat quickened. "Before we go any further, let's try a SpyGuy."

"Yes!" Dash said, pulling one out of his suit. He placed the device on the floor and turned it on.

A laser pulsed and a light wandered over every corner of the room. "Room secure. Violet Parr. Dash Parr located," said the SpyGuy in a robotic voice.

Violet exhaled. They weren't being trailed yet. That was good, but time was ticking. "Okay, great. Let's keep going. Maybe the safe is behind that door. It's the only one down here."

Dash slid into the green door and stared at it. "No doorknob. Just a lock. Can you use that thing again?"

Violet pulled the suction cup out, fitted it around the lock, and heard a click. The door swung open on its own. That was easy. Violet held her breath, half expecting the room to be the actual safe and the nullifier to be sitting on a lit table in the centre like a jewel on display in a film. Instead, she found herself staring at a lap pool that lit up as they entered. The pool looked like glass, reflecting the city skyline that twinkled in the distance beyond the large, wall-size window that had been cut into the side of the mountain under the mansion.

The safe couldn't be in here, could it? It was the only room down here. Was Syndrome's intel wrong? Why would Mastermind keep a nullifier in a pool room? Violet looked around. It was the most beautiful pool location she had ever seen, and eerily silent and pristine. The only sign that people had used the pool before was the monogrammed *M* towels sitting on several of the teak lounge chairs lining the window and a few *M*-shaped pool tubes.

"A pool!" Dash cried. "Inside the house? Mastermind's place is amazing! And look, it has floats." Dash ran over to the other side of the room and grabbed a float shaped like an *M*.

"This can't be right," Violet said, hearing her voice echo. "Why would Mastermind keep a safe in the indoor pool room?" She scanned the walls for paintings (there were none) and hidden compartments (the walls were smooth, no gaps or cracks or anything out of the ordinary), and there were zero rugs. What was she missing? She lifted a pool tube to see the ground underneath, then moved a chair. Nothing there either.

"If I had a safe, I'd put it in here too," Dash said, walking around the pool.

"Why is that?"

"Because no one would ever think something top-secret would be hidden in a pool!" Dash guessed.

In a pool. Violet rushed to the edge and looked down at the water. Could the safe be underwater? Was that even possible?

When it comes to villains, she remembered her dad once saying, *anything is possible.*

If Syndrome was right about the safe being on the lower level, then it had to be in this pool. Violet glanced at the timer on her watch: 42 minutes, 15 seconds. Her heart beat faster. If she couldn't see the safe from here, then there was only one way to see it. She had to dive in. But if they were both underwater, they wouldn't be able to tell if anyone entered the room or they were in trouble. "Dash, how would you feel about taking a swim?"

Dash grinned. "Yes! Can I cannonball?"

"Why not?" Violet said. The SpyGuy said the room was clear. "Jump in and look for a hidden panel, or a door. Anything that could resemble a safe."

"Got it!" Dash took a running jump holding an *M*-shaped float and cannonballed into the pool, the giant splash sending the float careering across the surface of the water.

Violet leant over the side of the pool impatiently, looking for a clue herself while she waited for Dash to reemerge.

His blond head popped up in the middle of the pool. He reached for the *M*-shaped raft to hold on to.

"Found it! There's a door! In the pool! A door!" Dash declared.

Violet grinned. So the nullifier was in the pool! She was still in business. She glanced at the pool room's entrance. It was still closed. The room was quiet except for the sound of moving water, but that nagging feeling returned. Why did she feel like she was being watched even when the SpyGuy said no one was down here? She was probably just being paranoid. There is no way Mastermind would let two kids waltz into the place and steal the villain's most precious weapon. "Can you open the door?"

"I'll try." Dash submerged again, bubbles gurgling up behind him, and then reemerged a few seconds later. "It's locked."

"A regular lock? Or a panel? Describe what you see."

"It's buttons beneath the handle, but maybe it will work with your suction cup," he suggested.

She wasn't sure that device worked on a panel, but he might as well try. Violet threw it to Dash and he caught it, disappearing again below the surface. Her heart was hammering now. She glanced at the watch again: 37 minutes and 22 seconds. Time was clicking away. Dash came back a few seconds later. "It's not working! I tried pressing some buttons but nothing happened."

Violet gave a quick glance to the door again. "Okay, let me give it a try. You keep watch outside the pool. Try the SpyGuy in here too. And, Dash, if anyone comes through that door, use the freeze ray on them. Got it?"

"Got it," Dash said, pulling himself out of the pool. "Take a big breath before you jump in," Dash told her. "The water's deep."

Violet jumped in, letting the momentum of the leap take her straight to the bottom. The water was cool, seeping into her suit, weighing her down as she tried to move forwards while holding her breath. She opened her eyes and looked around. The surface of the floor was smooth and even, until she spotted it: a small door with a handle and a keypad. The door was metal, letters and symbols etched into the keypad that didn't make sense. There were too many of them to even read. She swam towards it and yanked on the handle. It wouldn't budge. She yanked again, putting her feet against the door and pulling, but still it was no use. She had no choice but to float up and get air.

"You get it?" Dash asked the minute she hit the surface.

Violet wiped the water from her eyes. "Not yet. Did the SpyGuy pick up anyone?" Dash shook his head. Violet tried to push the prickling sensation aside and focus. "I'm trying again, but remember: if someone gets in that door, use your speed and get out of here."

Dash's eyes widened. "Without you? No!"

"Dash, listen to me," Violet said, her heart pounding harder. "I can be invisible, remember? Use your strengths." She thought of Mum's advice before she left the other night. "You'll know what to do." Then, before Dash could argue, she took another deep breath and descended below the surface again.

This time, she went straight to the handle and tried to bang out a combination on the keypad. She tried using the letters to spell out the word *Mastermind*. That didn't work. With her breath running out, she looked at the keypad again and noticed something – the buttons could be rotated and when she rotated one, she noticed various lines on the button. Violet thought back to the lift doors closing to form the letter *M*. Could the buttons be turned on the panel till they resembled one giant letter *M*? She started twisting buttons as quickly as she could, her breath running out. She twisted the last button into place, forming the *M*, and heard a click.

There was a hissing sound and suddenly the pool's water was being suctioned out with alarming speed. Within seconds, the pool was half empty. Violet held tight to the latch to keep from being pulled away from the wall. Moments later, her head was above the surface.

Dash called down to her. "You drained the pool!"

"I opened the lock! You needed to turn the buttons till they made the letter *M*," Violet told him. The water dropped to her waistline. She yanked on the door again and it opened, revealing a small compartment. In the centre was a clear glass cube filled with water. Floating inside that cube was a single test tube vial with a bright blue liquid inside that appeared to be bubbling.

The nullifier.

Violet wasn't sure if she should laugh or cry as she stretched out her hands to take the cube. She'd done it. She'd found the nullifier. Within the hour, she'd be back at Syndrome's and they could use it and finally be safe from Mastermind. They'd no longer be Super and in danger, their lives forever changed. She felt a pang of guilt when she thought of Dash's reaction when he'd learn what this little device could do. Would he ever forgive her?

He's going to be mad, but someday he'll understand. She grabbed the cube.

Lights in the pool began to flash red. A door came down over the vault opening and Violet heard a roaring sound. Clutching the cube, she turned around and saw a wall of water from an underground grate rushing into the partially full pool at an alarming rate. Violet floated up to the surface, clutching the cube, assuming the water would stop there. Instead, the water kept rising, sloshing over the side of the pool and onto the floor.

They're going to flood the room, she realised.

"Why is the water still rising? And why are there alarms going off?" Dash pointed to the metal gates coming down over the large glass wall that looked out at the city. "Someone knows we're here!" Water sloshed over Dash's feet as Violet pulled herself out of the pool, placing the cube on the already wet ground to get out. "Ooh! Is that what we're stealing? What is it?"

"Don't touch it!" Violet said, panicking. What if Dash broke it before they could even use it? "We have to get out of here fast."

Dash's eyes widened at something behind her. "Violet? I think the room is flooding."

"I know!" Her heart was in her throat as she looked down at her watch: 22 minutes and 14 seconds. She'd lost a lot of time getting the nullifier, but if they could just get out of the house and make it to the car... She pressed the button on the watch, letting Syndrome know she had the nullifier, then she started to run. "We have to get to that door before we're underwater!"

Holding the cube tightly in one arm, they ran to the door and yanked on it, the water now up to their knees.

"It's locked!" Dash freaked out, pulling on it harder.

"We're doomed! We're doomed!"

"Calm down!" Violet said, trying to think fast. She reached a hand in her pocket for the suction cup. It wasn't there. It must have fallen out when they'd tried to use it on the safe. She whirled around scanning the room for a small red suction cup and spotted it halfway across the room. The water was now at her hips. She thrust the cube at Dash. "Hold this, but don't jostle it around or try to open it. Just hold it!"

"Where are you going?" Dash freaked as Violet began to swim away from him.

The water was ascending so fast now, she felt the current pushing her backwards, but she fought the momentum and reached for the suction cup bobbing away from her. Her hand missed it once, then twice. The third time, she leapt up and grabbed it, then swam as fast as she could back to Dash. The water was already up to his chest. He was holding on to the door handle for dear life with one hand and the cube with the other.

"We're not going to make it!" he screamed.

"We're going to make it!" With slippery fingers, Violet fumbled with the suction cup and put it over the door lock. *Please work*, she thought. *Please work!*

It didn't work.

"Violet!" Dash said as the water sloshed higher, reaching his neck.

Violet felt the water push her up, her feet off the floor now as she tried in desperation again and again. No. They weren't going out like this.

"Help!" Dash pounded on the door. "Can anyone hear us? Help!"

Suddenly Violet realised: she didn't need the suction thingy.

"Dash! Swim away from the door!"

Her brother's eyes widened. "What?"

"Swim away!" Violet yelled. Thinking of Syndrome's tutoring, she focused on all the pain she could muster – everything Mastermind had caused her – and she shot her hands out, firing the largest force field she'd ever made.

The door blew right off, water gushing into the opening, taking Violet and Dash along with it, Dash laughing and screaming, "You did it!" The water dropped them off at the lift, exactly where they needed to be.

Violet found herself laughing too, the stress of the last hour giving way for a moment, as she crawled over to Dash, feeling like a semi-drowned rat. "We did do it!"

"*You* did it!" Dash corrected and looked down at the

cube still in his hand (thank goodness). He reached up and pressed the lift button as red lights continued to flash all around them. "I can't believe how good you're getting with your powers!"

Violet's stomach dropped, her stress returning as they waited for the lift. She had to tell Dash the truth. And she would. When they were in the car. The doors opened almost immediately, and they scrambled towards the lift. It wasn't until she took a step into the compartment that she thought back to the SpyGuy – wondering if they still had it and should use it on the next level before they tried to make a break for it. A blinking metal ball flew past her and exploded in midair.

BOOM!

Violet took to the air, flying backwards. She hit the ground with a thud, the cube rolling past her, but she didn't care. Dash! She had to find Dash. She whipped her head around and saw him lying motionless on the floor. She had to get to him! Violet tried to stand, her head fuzzy, when a guard came running up to her and sprayed something into the air before she could even shout out.

She immediately smelt lavender and then her eyes started to close. *No!* she thought. *I need to reach Dash! The cube! To escape!* She managed to press the emergency dial on the watch to let Syndrome know she was in trouble, but her eyes were fluttering closed as her hands flew out in front of her, breaking her fall as she hit the ground again. The cube was just a few feet away, but she couldn't seem to make her arms work to retrieve it.

Just before her eyes closed, she saw green high heels walk across the floor. Manicured fingers reached down and picked up the cube.

"No," Violet whispered.

The person turned to look at her, but the face was fuzzy. Still, she could hear their voice before she passed out.

"Hello, pet."

CHAPTER SEVENTEEN
VIOLET

Violet was having a dream. She was at the cinema with Kari and Lucy. This time, instead of going to the party and becoming invisible in front of everyone from school, she stayed at the cinema and watched the slasher film alone. Well, not alone, because the minute she sat down, she noticed Tony sitting in the same row. They talked. They shared popcorn. They laughed. Violet didn't freak out or become invisible. When the film was over, he waited ouside with her until her mum came to pick her up. The air was chilly and he stood behind her, to help block the wind. It was a nice dream. Till her mum's car pulled up and instead of her mother, two of Mastermind's guards came rushing out and threw a metal ball at her that exploded, spraying her with a mist that knocked her out cold. She could almost taste the strong scent of lavender as she hit the ground.

Then she opened her eyes for real.

She wasn't at the cinema. She was lying on a green velvet sofa in a wood-panelled study where a fire was roaring in a fireplace, making the room warm and toasty. *Where am I?* Violet wondered, sitting up fast. Her head was pounding, a ringing in her ears caused by either the swim she took or the explosion that went off. Was it an explosion? She thought she remembered an explosion, but the details were fuzzy. She tried to stand, but her head spun and she sat down again. That's when she heard snoring.

"Dash!" she cried, seeing her brother on another velvet chaise opposite hers. He was curled up tight, a smile on his lips as he slept with one hand draped over his eyes like he'd done since he was a baby. Violet tried to be rational: if he was snoring, then he wasn't hurt. He was just asleep. Violet couldn't remember how she got to this room, and that made her start to panic.

Focus. Take a deep breath. Isn't that what Mirage had told her to do when she became overwhelmed? She tried the exercise, taking three counts to inhale and four to exhale. She did it two times. By the third, she felt herself start to relax, and that's when it all came flooding back to her.

The mission. Syndrome. The nullifier. The pool. The guards. The cube.

Mastermind.

They were caught in Mastermind's house.

Warning bells went off in her head. Violet stood up again, looking around for an exit. All four walls seemed to have wall-length bookcases. There were no windows. Where was the door? This was clearly Mastermind's office, with its green-and-blue furry rug and green and blue accent furniture. Framed photos and awards sat on every shelf along with handbooks Violet had never heard of. *A Villain's Guide to Villainy? Ten Steps to World Domination?* Who gave out trophies for things like Greatest Villain Weapon Ever Created or a first-place prize for The Invention That Will Change the Future of Villainy? Violet tasted bile in her mouth when she read the headlines on several framed newspaper clippings. 'Mastermind Escapes Again!' 'Mastermind and Frozone Go Toe-to-Toe!' 'Is Mastermind Responsible for the Metroville-Wide Blackout?' There was even a Mastermind bobblehead and a Mastermind action figure in a plastic box that said THE VILLAIN COLLECTION. Comes with Real-Super-Stopping Laser! (Created by Mastermind!)

This felt like her dad's office, except instead of show-casing accolades for doing good, Mastermind's office contained rewards for being evil. Violet couldn't help but marvel at the memorabilia. There were photographs of Mastermind and the Underminer! Mastermind and Bomb Voyage! Mastermind and… Syndrome? Violet paused. That didn't make any sense. Syndrome wasn't a villain.

He did say he had a history with Mastermind, but she'd just assumed he was afraid of Mastermind like the rest of the world. Violet picked up the framed photo for clues and a faded newspaper article fluttered out from underneath. On it was a large picture with people that looked very familiar.

Mum, Violet thought, heart racing. *Dad*.

The photo was of her parents fighting Mastermind with the headline 'Mastermind Foiled Again by Mr Incredible and Elastigirl! Is Metroville's Hottest Villain Losing Their Touch?' It was an opinion piece in something called *Villain Monthly*. Her anger bubbled to the surface again reading the headline. Is this why Mastermind had targeted her parents? Because her parents kept beating Mastermind?

"I loved that story."

Violet whirled around. Her blood went cold. "You're Mastermind."

The villain smiled. "Hello, pet."

Mastermind was statuesque and was wearing a glittery green nightgown that accentuated her voluptuous curves. The jewel tone of the green perfectly matched her eyes, which were a striking contrast to her olive-brown skin and dark brown hair. Over her nightgown, she wore a loose, sheer robe. Its fur trim covered her shoulders. In the villain's hands was a fluffy white poodle.

This was the person who had destroyed her family. Violet couldn't control her anger. Her hands shot out in front of her, firing a force field without thinking. The field seemingly bounced off something in front of Mastermind and fired back at Violet, causing her to duck. The bookcase behind Violet exploded, sending trophies and picture frames flying. Mastermind didn't move, which only made Violet angrier. She wanted the villain to hurt the way she hurt. *Think of what Mastermind took from you!* she heard Syndrome coaching her, and she fired again, aiming higher, then lower, trying to reach the villain, who barely flinched as Violet shot force field after force field her way. The dog started barking, baring his teeth, drool dripping from his mouth, but still Mastermind didn't move. Dash snored louder, turning away from the destruction, never waking.

"You done now?" Mastermind purred.

Violet looked down at her hands in surprise. She'd never used her force fields to try to hurt someone before. Her thoughts swirled. She imagined her mum or dad reacting to the sight of their daughter trying to destroy another human being. That's not what Supers did... did they?

"Your powers don't work on me, pet. At least not now."
Mastermind gestured to the space around her person and
her pooch. "Personal energy field. It acts as a barrier against
any and all Superpowers I know of. My invention, of course."
She smiled, flashing ultra-white teeth.

The casual grin only sparked Violet's anger again. She
let out a scream so loud, it seemed to come from the depths
of her soul. Mum and Dad weren't here because of her.
She deserved to die. Violet fired at the villain again. She
wanted the villain destroyed. To feel pain like she felt. Violet
fired several more force fields, books flying, glass in frames
shattering, the dog barking, and still Mastermind just stood
there. Violet fired until she had nothing left to give. Then
she sank to the floor in despair. It was no use.

She couldn't destroy Mastermind, and even if she could,
Violet suspected her own pain would never disappear. Her
parents were gone. Killing Mastermind wouldn't bring them
back and yet she wanted her to feel the anguish she felt.

"Impressive. Now are you done, pet?"

"I'll never stop coming for you," she said, her anger
pulsing like a beating heart. Mastermind raised her right
eyebrow, seemingly impressed. "I mean it! You'll never sleep
again because I will not stop till I do to you what you did to
me." She looked at Mastermind with cold, angry eyes. *Think
of what Mastermind took from you!* she heard Syndrome say.

Your family is gone because of them! "I won't rest until you're dead."

Mastermind smirked and put the poodle safely in a plush dog canopy bed. "Oooh! Such rage for such a young girl!" She placed a hand on her right hip. "I love the suit. Your father has one just like it." She winked. "I keep tabs on him, of course. Got a surveillance video of him wearing a suit just like yours from an island off the coast last week. It's part of the reason I came back to Metroville. If your father is working again, maybe there is hope for all of us!" She tapped something on her chair and a screen popped up on one of the bookcases. A video started playing: a man in a brightly coloured suit was running through a tropical forest.

Violet froze. *Dad.* It was clearly her father. He was wearing a bright red suit identical to the ones she and Dash had on. But how could that be? Did Mum bring her dad one of these suits too? Why? Her heart was pounding as she tried to make sense of what she was seeing. In the video Syndrome had shown her, her father was wearing his old suit. He wouldn't have changed suits during the same job, would he? "When was this video taken?" Violet demanded.

"I told you," Mastermind said with a yawn. "A week ago? I think. Maybe two. It's very recent. Everyone in the villain community has seen it. It gives us such hope!"

Violet kept watching. *If this was from last week, then*

why does Dad's hair look different than it does on Syndrome's video from the day he died? Violet bit the inside of her cheek. Something didn't make sense here. Why would it? She was dealing with a villain. Villains lied and cheated. "This is fake," Violet decided.

Mastermind scoffed. "Why would I make a fake video of your father? To watch before bed at night?" She laughed. "No, it's real. Just like you, Mr Incredible and Elastigirl's daughter, are really here in my house and you've managed to steal my greatest achievement." She looked Violet up and down. "I must say, I'm impressed by you, pet."

"Stop calling me pet!" Violet fired off another force field. This one was poorly aimed. She felt like she was losing focus. Why was that video of her dad so different from the one she'd seen?

"I'd be careful," Mastermind said in a singsong voice. "Don't want to hit Dash, do we?"

Dash continued to snore. Violet did a double take. "You know our names?"

"Oh, pet, I've known you since the day you were born! Since each of you – Violet, Dash and Jack Parr – were born." Her green eyes flashed. "I even sent your parents baby gifts. Don't you know? I'm like your villain godmother."

Violet felt another surge of anger mixed with untapped power. Mastermind was mocking her – she'd killed her parents, and now she was toying with Violet's emotions. Her anger and rage mixed with tears. "You hated my parents! You were their biggest enemy!"

"Yes!" Mastermind said, engaged. "And it was glorious. Oh, pet, I wish you could have seen us in our heyday!" Mastermind turned and sat down on a green fur-covered wingback chair. "We were so evenly matched. I knew it from the day I met your mother. She and I tangoed first, of course." Mastermind pressed a button on the right arm of her chair and a panel shot out. She picked up a photograph lying inside and sighed lovingly. "Look at us. Such babies! See for yourself." She held the frame out for Violet.

Violet didn't understand what was happening. She could feel her chest rising and falling fast. She had an overwhelming urge to do two things: strangle Mastermind and grab the picture.

"Oh, pet, don't be so frightened. A photograph doesn't bite." Mastermind thought for a moment. "Hmm, but that would make an excellent weapon." She tapped a strand of pearls around her neck. "Remind me to test killer photograph technology." Mastermind waved the photo again, her expression darkening. "My hand is growing tired, pet. If you don't want to see a picture of your parents, then—"

Violet ripped it from her hands and stared at it. The

photo showed Mastermind and her parents on the ledge of a building rooftop in Metroville, squared off, all three of their faces serious and young. Her dad's hair was longer. Had Dad still worn his hair like this? She tried to remember how his hair looked in Syndrome's video and she couldn't. Was she already forgetting what he looked like?

Mastermind destroyed your family, she thought, thinking of Syndrome again. Violet banged the frame against a nearby table, shattering it as Mastermind watched. The office was in shambles, with one bookcase reduced to rubble and several others half standing, books everywhere. The poodle glared at her from his bed, which was the only thing untouched. Maybe that had a force field around it too. "Stop acting like you care about them!"

Mastermind stood up. "Don't care?" she thundered. "Pet, if I didn't care, you'd be dead right now – and Dash too. You're alive because I *do* care. Too much, I'm afraid. I miss the thrill of going up against your parents! Sometimes they'd win! Sometimes I'd win, but always, they were my fiercest challenge, my smartest adversaries. You can't imagine what it's like, pet, being retired before you're ready," she railed. "Forced to wither away in this tomb of a house for years."

Violet tensed. "You've lived here a long time?"

"Sadly," Mastermind said with a sigh. "The day the

government made Supers illegal, they basically forced villains to be as well." She waved her hand around. "I've been here or occasionally in my other home in France for a change of scenery, but mostly here because my weapons lab is here too. I won't bother you with the details."

Violet didn't understand. Syndrome had told her Mastermind had just got back to Metroville. If she'd been here the whole time, what was the urgency in nabbing her nullifier? Why had Mastermind waited until now to come after her family? Something wasn't adding up.

Violet wanted to throw another force field, but she knew it was a waste of her time. "No one forced villains to retire."

Mastermind cocked her head. "Maybe not officially, but what good is a villain if there are no Supers to spar with? Sure, I tried to pull off a few jobs at first, but there was no one to properly stand up to me." Her eyes brightened. "I am someone who thrives on the chase, pet, and without your parents, there was none. And then I saw that video of your father on the volcanic island! I alerted the rest of the community – the day is coming! Supers must be returning! We all decided to celebrate. Hence, the party I'm having here tomorrow night. We will rejoice as a community. The world realises it needs Supers and villains again. I can hardly wait to be back in business!" She grinned. "And it turns out I don't have to wait long. Before I could even finish planning the menu for the party, you and Dash showed up. I knew who you were, of course, the second you both emerged from the car – facial-recognition technology is one of my specialties. And your Pizza Planet truck was a nice touch, but I knew something was up the minute I saw that delivery van drive up my mountain. My guards wanted to fire on it, of course, but I said, 'Let's see who is inside the car and what they're here to do'. It was so exciting to have a break-in! And then, what to my eyes did appear but Mini Mr Incredible and Elastigirl Junior! I have been watching you two sneak through the house like it's an Oscar-winning film. Your skills are impressive. Invisibility! Superspeed! Force fields!" She shook her head. "You two are a marvel indeed. Your parents must be so proud."

Violet saw red, her rage almost overcoming her. The periphery of her vision seemed to fade, narrowing until the only thing in the world was Mastermind's smug expression. "My parents are dead because of you."

Mastermind stared back at her. "Dead? That's impossible."

Another force field was on the verge of slipping from her fingers. Could it penetrate Mastermind's shield? Would she kill Mastermind if she had the chance? She wasn't a killing machine, was she? She heard Syndrome again in her head. *If you don't stop Mastermind, Mastermind will kill you.* "You killed them!"

Mastermind looked at her strangely. "Killed? Your parents? Mr Incredible and Elastigirl?"

"Yes!" Violet shouted. "You took their powers!"

"Took their powers?" Mastermind repeated. "Oh! With my invention – the Super stripper? The nullifier you tried to steal but failed? Oh, pet, why would I use that on your parents? The threat of that weapon is way more fun than actually using it."

Violet was shaking. "You took their powers," she repeated, "and then when they threatened to keep coming after you so you couldn't do the same to other Supers – like me and Dash – you killed them so they couldn't get in the way! You took my family from me." She broke down, feeling ashamed at herself for crying but unable to stop herself. "And so I tried to steal your nullifier so I could strip my brother's and my powers so you would just leave us alone." She abruptly stopped and shot Mastermind the coldest look she could muster. "I won't let you hurt what's left of my family."

The villain pushed a strand of hair behind her right ear, a dangling diamond earring on full display. "You look so much like your mother when you stare at me like that. It's uncanny."

"Aren't you going to say something about what you did to my parents? Why did you have to kill them?"

Mastermind was quiet. Violet's breathing was shallow. She exhaled slowly and disappeared, racing to the other side of the room till she was standing right in front of Mastermind when she reappeared.

The villain looked delighted. "Oh, pet, that is a wonderful power! Do it again."

"This isn't a game!" Violet yelled as her fingers started to spark. Angry tears spilled down her cheeks. "You killed my parents, and now I want to know why I shouldn't kill you."

Mastermind's expression faltered. "Oh, pet... I don't know where you got this information from, but I did not kill your parents." Mastermind didn't seem that concerned even. She waved her arms around, getting agitated as she looked around at her office – books blown up or scattered, bookshelves broken, splintered wood all over the floor. "And they're not dead either. Believe me, if they were, I'd know. The whole villain community would know. Some would mourn, some wouldn't. I would not be happy losing my greatest adversaries. I was confused about why you needed the nullifier, but this explains a lot."

Violet's breathing became more controlled. She was so confused. "I don't understand. If you didn't kill them... but I saw the video. He said they were dead."

"Who is he? I haven't got into any good villainy in a

while. Unfortunately, I've been here, preparing for the party to celebrate the return of Supers. Fifty villains, all coming here, trampling my begonias."

Violet heard a whooshing sound in her ears. She reached down and retrieved the photograph lying in the broken glass at her feet and stared at her dad's young face again. "My parents are alive? You're lying."

Mastermind thought for a moment. "Or perhaps someone is lying to you. The question is why? Interesting! Let's dissect this." She started to pace, tapping her chin as she walked. "Maybe they want you to think your parents are in trouble so you get the nullifier. But why would you ever think I stripped your parents' powers? Or that I would strip yours and kill you and your brothers?" Her eyes widened with recognition. "Unless... yes, that must be it." She tsked and glanced pitifully at Violet. "Oh, pet. You're more gullible than your mother."

Violet shot a force field at the bookcase right above Mastermind's head for the fun of it. But inside, a small voice was growing louder. *What if Mastermind is telling the truth?* No, Syndrome and Mirage had rescued her at her parents' request. But when did they make that request? Hadn't Syndrome said he'd been hiding when her parents were killed? She tried to gather her thoughts but there were so many of them and they didn't all line up. She had to focus.

Her parents were dead at this villain's hands. She couldn't trust a word out of her mouth. She was a super villain!

So why did Mastermind seem so earnest when she talked about missing her parents?

Behind her, she heard Dash yawn. "Violet, where are—" His eyes widened at the sight of the destruction surrounding them and his sister squaring off against the infamous villain. "Mastermind! Wow!"

"Hello there, Dash," Mastermind said. "You've missed all the fun I've been having with Violet. I was really impressed with your speed tonight! Neither of your parents can manage that. Your father is slow as molasses. Your mother would agree, I'm sure."

"Uh…" Dash looked from the villain to his sister. "Hi? I think."

Violet attempted to put a force field around Dash to protect him, but misfired, hitting the wall behind Dash. It started to give way, and Violet could see an opening to another room. "Where is the nullifier? Do you have it with you?" Violet looked around. "We'll use it on ourselves right now if it will keep you from going after us." Her fingers sparked again. "I will end you before I let you hurt them," she roared.

Mastermind looked at her for a moment, then started to laugh uncontrollably. She held her stomach she was laughing so hard, and her dog started to bark at the lunacy of it all.

Dash and Violet looked at each other.

"I think you broke her," Dash whispered.

"Stop me?" Mastermind. "What a hoot you are, Violet Parr!" Her eyes locked on Violet's. "But seriously, pet, why on Earth would you give up your powers? What fun would that be?"

"Give up our powers?" Dash asked. "Vi, what's she talking about?"

Violet cursed herself. Why had she said that in front of Dash? "I'll explain later."

"I'm not giving up my powers!" Dash yelled at both of them.

"Better tell your sister that," Mastermind said. She pressed a button on her chair again and a panel rose from her desk. "I think she has plans I don't quite understand."

The cube was sitting in the centre.

"Go on, take it," Mastermind said, leaning forwards, almost salivating at the thought. "I'd love to see you try to get out of here in one piece. There hasn't been action in this estate like this in over a decade. So go on, pet. Take the cube!" She leaned on the edge of the desk and tapped her finger next to the cube. "We'll see how far you get in my house with it."

Dash and Violet looked at each other. Mastermind was baiting them. That much was clear. But the bait – the nullifier – was one Violet couldn't take her eyes off of. It was the thing she came for. It was what she told Syndrome she'd return with. It's what she needed to protect herself and her brothers.

Unless she was wrong about everything.

Was she?

There was only one way to find out.

Violet fired a force field at the wall that had started to crumble, making a clear exit, and then lunged for the cube.

Mastermind watched her do it with unbridled glee before pressing a button on her chair. Sirens began to sound. "Let the game begin!"

"Dash! Run!" Violet shouted as she headed for the clearing. Dash sped ahead of her just as guards tried breaking into the room from an unseen entrance. Violet prepared to jump through the opening after him when she heard Mastermind again.

"Good luck, Incredigirl!" Mastermind said, and Violet felt every muscle in her body tense.

She spun around. "Incredigirl? My name is Violet Parr. Remember that."

Mastermind looked pleased. "Noted, Violet Parr."

Violet heard a loud boom – the guards had broken into the room.

"Better run now," Mastermind said, somewhat amused as Violet jumped through the opening in the wall. "I hope you know what you're doing."

CHAPTER EIGHTEEN
VIOLET

Violet and Dash had no choice but to run. As they sprinted down a new hallway, guards came out of doorways in all directions. Violet held her breath, praying she'd find an exit out of Mastermind's maze before that lavender mist guards behind her kept spraying knocked them out.

"Grab them!" shouted a guard, dropping from the ceiling and attempting to grab Dash. Her brother easily sped around them, coming back when he realised Violet wasn't as quick. She moved as fast as she could, shooting force fields at vases and standing lamps in the hallway, hoping the falling items in the guards' paths would buy them some time. But it did slow her down.

"I've got this," said Dash, pulling their dad's freeze ray

from a hidden pocket in his suit. "One for you! And one for you!" he said with glee as he fired rounds slowing guards down so they moved like jelly.

"We have to get back to the car!" Violet shouted, spinning around and firing two force fields at chandeliers above her. They crashed down, narrowly missing the remaining guards on their tail. For a moment, Violet faltered – they could have been killed – and yet, there was something exhilarating about being able to fire at will without blinking an eye. She was getting used to this powers thing.

"Which way?" Dash yelled. "All the doors look the same!"

Another guard came down from the ceiling above, landing in front of Dash. Dash fired the freeze ray again. It worked, but the effects would only hold for so long. Violet spun around looking for an alternate way out, but she was afraid to pick a door. If she chose the wrong room to barricade themselves in, they could be trapped. Her eyes moved instead to an open window, where a curtain flapped in the evening breeze. Could they find another way to the tunnel where the delivery van was parked?

"Dash, fire the shrink button!" Violet instructed as the guards moved in.

"Thought you'd never ask!" Dash clicked the button and the ray connected with the three nearest guards, shrinking them down to the size of mice. The guards behind them froze, panicked. "YES!"

With the extra few seconds, Violet shot a force field at the window, blew it out and looked down. They were on the first floor. "Dash! Through the window!" Dash ran to the window and started to climb over. Violet handed him the cube.

"Stop!" shouted a guard.

Violet shot several force fields at the ceiling and crumbled plaster rained down, blocking the guards' path. "I'm right behind you!" she told Dash just as she felt a hand on her arm.

"Got her!" a guard who came out of nowhere declared.

"Let go of my sister!" Dash yelled through the window, firing the device he had in his free hand. The ray froze the guard on the spot.

"Nice one!" Violet said, climbing out the window and grabbing the cube from him again. They started to run. Where, Violet wasn't sure. She didn't see a tunnel anywhere.

They were on a huge, manicured lawn. Nearby, a large, tastefully lit patio was clearly set for the villain party. A few yards away was a road.

"Where is the tunnel?" Dash cried.

"I don't know! Just keep going!"

Dash sped ahead. Behind her, Violet heard the

sounds of sirens and barking dogs. In minutes, they'd be surrounded. In the distance, ahead of her, she heard a car rev its engine.

Dash was back in seconds. "I found the tunnel, but it's too far away. We're not going to make it! We're going to have to hide."

"There's no time to hide." Violet gulped as she saw the pack of black dogs racing across the lawn towards them. "Run! You can make it on your own."

"Not without you!" Dash shouted, pulling the megaphone out again.

Violet and Dash reached for each other, panicked.

Suddenly they heard tyres. Screeching out of the darkness came a saloon. It raced across the lawn, sending dirt and grass flying. Violet watched in awe as several shots blasted out of the front lights into the lawn, sending smoke bombs that cloaked the grounds in darkness. The car came to a halt in front of them and the passenger door flew open.

"Need a lift?" Mirage asked.

They didn't have to be asked twice. Dash jumped in first and Violet dived in after him, cube in hand, pulling the door shut behind her.

"Hang on!" Mirage peeled away from the side of the house, the gravel under the tyres shooting into the air.

Violet looked out the window. Mastermind's cars were right on their heels.

BOOM! A blast rocked the back of the car, making them skid out.

"Don't worry, I've got this," Mirage said confidently, pressing several buttons on the dash. Two rockets fired out of the exhaust pipe, headed straight at the cars that were giving chase.

Violet and Dash watched as the villain's cars got wrapped in a large spiderlike web. Their tyres were spinning, lights flashing, but the web had trapped them.

"I've always wanted to try that one!" Mirage said giddily as she raced away. "That should take care of them. Let's get out of here."

"I thought we were doomed," Dash said, throwing himself back on the seat dramatically. "We were locked in Mastermind's office and she gave Violet the cube back and Violet blew out the walls – Bam! Bam! Bam! And then we were running and running and diving out a window and… WOW." He threw a hand over his eyes. "What a night."

Mirage kept her eyes on the road, glancing at Violet for a split second. "You were stuck in Mastermind's office? Are you okay?"

"Yes. Thanks for coming for us," Violet said, looking down at the watch. "I wasn't sure whether this would work."

Mirage patted Violet's hand with her free one. "I got here as fast as I could. I'm so glad you're okay. And you have the nullifier!"

"Yep, the nullifier." Violet sank back against the seat, clutching the cube firmly in her arms. Now that she was safe, her mind was whirling.

Why would I kill your parents? Mastermind had said.

Mastermind killed your parents and you're next! Syndrome had claimed.

The question was: who was telling her the truth?

"Violet?"

Dash's concerned voice was the first one Violet registered.

"Can you hear me?" Dash waved a hand in front of her face, but her stare was locked on the road ahead, or lack of road, she should say. Mirage was clearly making her own road in her quest to get away.

No, I'm not okay, Violet wanted to say. *I'm confused.* Who was telling her the truth? Had she just got into the car with someone she could trust or who was trying to kill her? Her hand moved to her pocket again, where somehow, her mum's comms link was still tucked away.

"Dash, sit down!" Mirage shouted as she turned the car wildly to the left and the car practically took air. "We're almost off the grounds and in the clear. Then we just need to get down the mountain." In the distance, Violet could see the city.

A staticky sound filled the car, followed by a familiar voice.

"Mirage? Are you there? Where are you?" It was Syndrome.

Mirage hit a button and put him on the speaker. "I've got them! I had to blast my way out using the car's weapons, which I've never had to fire before, but I did it."

"Does Violet have the nullifier or no?" Syndrome asked.

"Yes, she has it," Mirage told him.

"Yes!" Syndrome cheered. "Ha-ha! *That's* what I'm talking about! I knew I was right about you, Violet! I knew it! Did I train you well or what?"

Violet closed her eyes, trying to block Mastermind's voice from her mind. *Someone is lying to you. The question is why? Maybe they want you to think your parents are in trouble so you get the nullifier.*

What if Mastermind was telling the truth? Could that mean – no – was it possible? Could her parents actually be alive?

Her heart drummed at the thought, as ludicrous as it might be. She desperately wanted it to be true, but she didn't want to give herself false hope. Mastermind was a villain and her parents were dead at her hands. She couldn't trust a word out of her mouth. So why did something feel terribly wrong?

"Why don't I hear celebrating?" Syndrome's voice filled the air.

Dash spoke up. "Because ever since Violet talked to Mastermind, she's been acting weird." He nudged her. "You still didn't say what the cube does. What's a nullifier?"

"Weird?" Syndrome's voice was tight. "Violet? You okay, kid?"

Violet couldn't summon the words to answer him – had she just stolen something that would protect her and her brothers, or destroy them? Suddenly she wasn't sure.

Mirage glanced at Violet again. "I think she's coming down from the adrenaline rush. Almost being killed after stealing from a villain will do that to a person."

"Mirage, can I speak to you off-speaker?"

"Kind of driving a getaway car at the moment," she said, her eyes on Violet again.

"Then pull over." Syndrome said flatly. "We need to talk. Now."

Mirage sighed. "Hang on. There's a scenic overlook on the mountain up ahead."

"How soon till you're back here, anyway? We need to get that nullifier ready right away. Right, Violet? Your request is priority number one… if you still want it."

Violet didn't respond. She was itching to look at that

picture from Mastermind's office again. She'd stolen it on her way out the door and folded it in her suit.

Mirage peeled off onto a dirt path that served as a scenic overlook to the city. They were the only car there, but in the distance, Violet could see the lights of Metroville calling to them. "Don't move," she told the kids. "I'll be right back after I deal with… *this*." Mirage pulled a small silver gadget out of her bag that looked like a portable phone and walked a few feet away, where Violet could see her motioning angrily.

"You are acting kind of weird," Dash said quietly. "Like really weird. For you, at least."

She didn't laugh. "I'm just tired. I've never used my powers like that before."

"You. Were. Awesome!" Dash declared, hopping up and down on the back seat. "You were sending guards flying! Went invisible! You broke walls! Knocked down doors!" He folded his arms across his chest. "I wish I could make force fields."

"No, you don't," Violet said, but there was that needling sensation again that told her the opposite. That making force fields and controlling her invisibility *was* cool.

"Hey, Violet?" Dash looked at her pensively. "Why were you yelling at Mastermind about… about" – he hesitated, his eyes darting at the car floor – "killing Mum and Dad?"

Violet looked up in surprise. "I thought you were asleep."

"I was pretending," Dash's eyes were full of worry. "Is it true? Are Mum and Dad...?" He couldn't say the word.

Violet grabbed his hand. There was never a good time to tell him the truth. This clearly wasn't it either, not when she had more questions now than answers. But there was something she needed to know as the clock ticked down. Soon they'd be at Syndrome's, and she'd have the chance to use the nullifier – the question was, should she do it? Was giving up her powers worth it to keep them safe? "Dash, if you knew a way to keep us safe so that no villain would ever come after our family again, would you do it?"

His face scrunched up. "I guess. What would we have to do?"

Violet inhaled sharply before speaking. "Give up our powers."

"No!" Dash said, instantly mad. "I like being Super! I'm faster than everyone we know!"

"But it's not like you can use your speed," Violet reminded him, trying to help him see reason. "It's why you can't run track or play football. You're too fast. If you weren't Super, you could join the team."

"Who cares about the team? Syndrome says speed is my best friend!" Dash countered. "He likes how fast I can run."

"He's just saying that," Violet replied gruffly. Why would he tell her brother that when he knew Dash was giving up his powers? "We all know Supers are illegal. Being Super is why we have to move so much! And why Mastermind's after us. If we gave up our powers, we'd be safe. Don't you want to be safe?"

"Not if it means we have to be boring!" Dash yelled.

"You'd be normal!" Violet shot back, getting upset despite trying hard not to. She needed him to understand what was at stake without scaring him. "All powers do is cause problems!"

"Maybe for you," Dash said. "I think they make me special. Mum said they're a gift. They're who we are. Why would we give back a present?"

Violet bit her lip. Mum did say that. As opposite as Mastermind seemed from her mum, hadn't she kind of said the same thing? *Why would you ever think I stripped your parents' powers?* Something wasn't adding up.

Outside the car, Violet could see Mirage still gesturing wildly with her hands. A gust of wind lifted Mirage's hair and Violet froze. Was Mirage wearing a wig?

"Viiiii-let?" Dash waved a hand in front of her face again. "You froze again and I didn't even use Dad's device on you. Are you listening to me? I'm not giving up my powers."

"Shh!" Violet hissed as Mirage walked back towards the

car. "We will talk more about this later. Don't say anything in front of Mirage."

"But—" Dash tried.

Violet shook her head vehemently. "Not. Now. I'll talk to you about it later."

Dash folded his arms across his chest and flopped back against the seat again. "You say that about a lot of things."

The driver's door opened, and Mirage placed the phone back in its holder on the console and turned the key in the ignition. "Everything all right?"

Violet and Dash nodded, but Violet couldn't look her in the eye. Why would she need a wig? Was Mirage who she said she was? Violet felt herself starting to panic.

"Okay, let's get to the house." Mirage sounded way too cheery. "Syndrome is flying back and should be arriving at the same time we do. He's anxious to get that nullifier ready."

"Wait. If you're with us, where is Jack-Jack?" Heat flushed Violet's cheeks as she berated herself. How could she forget about her baby brother?

Mirage froze. "Oh. He… I…"

"Did you leave him alone?" Violet shrieked.

Mirage looked sheepish. "I hired that babysitter friend of yours – Kari?"

"Oh." Violet exhaled. Jack was safe, then. Kari was the best.

Mirage looked at the clock on the camera and frowned. It was after 10:30 PM. "Although, I was actually supposed to pick him up an hour ago, but then Syndrome said you were in trouble and…" She looked at her phone again. "I think she left me a message." She blinked hard. "Actually, I think she left several messages." She pressed a button on the car dash and the messages began to play.

Mirage? This is Kari. I just have a question about Jack-Jack. Call me.

A click, and then a second message started.

Mirage, it's me. Jack-Jack is fine, but weird things are happening!

Violet and Mirage looked at each other warily. *Weird things?*

Another click, then another message.

Jack-Jack is still fine, but I'm getting really weirded out! AHH! When are you coming back?

"She doesn't sound good," Dash commented.

Mirage looked ill. "Probably just ran out of nappies."

I'm not fine, Aunt Mirage! Stop! Put that down! The sound of Jack-Jack crying could be heard in the background. *Stop it! You need to call me!*

"That doesn't sound like Kari at all," Violet told Mirage. "She never gets flustered babysitting. She once fashioned a nappy out of napkins in a pinch." Another message played.

I need help, Mirage! Jack-Jack was wailing now. *I'm going to call the police! Aaah!* The line went dead.

"We have to go get him," Violet told her. "What if Jack-Jack is hurt?"

"But Syndrome wanted us to get back to the house," Mirage reminded her. "I can't disobey orders."

Violet pulled the cube to her chest. "I'm not handing over the nullifier till I get my brother."

Mirage sighed and pressed a phone button Violet hadn't noticed before. "Syn?" she said when he picked up. "We have to go pick up Jack. The sitter I left him with is having an issue."

"The baby is fine, Mirage." A tinge of annoyance creeped into Syndrome's voice. "The important thing is you get the nullifier here. We'll pick him up later."

"It's after ten," Mirage said. "I was supposed to get him an hour ago, but then I had to drive a getaway car and—"

"Sweetheart, get me the nullifier." Syndrome cut her off. "I'm in charge. Remember? Then you can make some overtime if you need it so badly and go get the kid. Understood?"

Mirage hit a button and Syndrome's voice cut out.

"Bad connection," Mirage said as the phone in the car immediately began to ring again. Mirage grabbed the SpyGuy on the seat next to her and smashed it against the dash. It let out a puff of smoke and the ringing stopped. "Oh, look at that. The phone in the car isn't working," she said in an eerily pleasant tone. "Let's go get your brother."

CHAPTER NINETEEN
MIRAGE

One thing Mirage had learnt from Monique's acting classes was that yelling was a cop-out. True, if one was cast in an action movie playing the part of a captain whose ship was about to be lost at sea, that would require some shouting. But for most other roles, including Supportive Employee Asked to do Insanely Strange Things and Pretend to Be a Babysitter, Mirage understood that it was more effective to keep the volume of your voice within a medium range. With the kids staying at Syn's house, she'd tried to keep her decibel level down and speak in soft, even tones. She wasn't sure how much longer she could keep this acting job up.

Violet offering up that babysitter's number tonight was

a godsend. True, it was too late to get to Monique's class, but at least handing Jack-Jack off to Kari gave her an hour of peace. That baby was always disappearing and reappearing in strange places like the lift. And Syn couldn't care less how stressed she was about what they were doing. "You can handle it," he'd say, brushing her off.

She didn't want to handle it. She wanted to be at acting class and dating a guy who put her needs first. Instead of thanking her, the man was now yelling at her on the phone.

"What is going on with Violet?" Syndrome demanded the minute she'd taken him off speakerphone and was walking away from the car. "What does Dash mean by 'weird'? Do you think Mastermind told her something? How would Mastermind know I'm behind this? I mean, yeah, I've tried to bully her into selling me this device for nearly a decade, and she knows I've tried to steal it before, but she'd never guess I had Mr Incredible's kids in my back pocket. Would she?"

In the last three days, she'd decided something about her full-time boss and occasional date: the man sounded manic and a tad paranoid.

"I don't think so," she said through gritted teeth.

"You don't think so? I need you to be sure! What am I paying you for if you can't figure out a kid's mood swings?"

What am I paying you for? She was an underpaid

employee playing the role of Babysitter. Now he wanted her to play the role of Therapist after just completing the role of Action Hero on a Rescue Mission? ("I can't be seen on Mastermind's property," he'd said earlier, "and if those kids perish with my nullifier, this whole plan – the bonus money you're counting on – is gone. You understand me?") She needed that bonus. She'd just left a deposit on an elite-level acting camp.

And so she'd played Action Hero on a Rescue Mission. And now she was playing Babysitter Therapist Who Must Pick Up Annoying Baby. And he was still giving her a hard time! Now that Mr Incredible and his poor wife, Elastigirl, were dead, she suspected he'd want her to play Babysitter forever. What could have been so important that he'd leave Violet on her mission alone so he could race back to his island?

For a moment, she'd considered walking out and leaving Syn to clean up his own mess. But then she thought of Violet and Dash. Syn had pitted them against Mastermind, one of the greatest super villains Metroville had ever seen. She'd remembered reading stories about Mastermind as a kid – she'd once made a building disappear. If the kids actually survived breaking in and had got the nullifier, how could she just leave them there?

This job was making her soft.

"Look, Syn, you need to relax," Mirage tried again. "Violet is a teenager. They get moody! I'm sure she's just tired. You would be too if you were the one who went after the nullifier yourself. You sent children to do a job we've been working towards for a year now." Quiet rage seeped into her voice despite her better instincts. "We had a plan, and then you got ahold of the Parr kids and you lost your mind!"

There. She'd finally said what she'd been thinking all weekend.

"I was improvising!" Syndrome had drummed in her ear. "I don't need to explain my reasoning. Or why Mastermind hates me. There was no way I could go get the nullifier myself. It's a long story."

One she didn't care to hear.

"Just talk to Violet. Make sure she hasn't turned. I need you to find out," Syndrome said sharply.

"Even if she has turned on you, what does it matter? You already convinced her to give up her powers, didn't you?" Mirage was getting agitated. "Didn't you?" She was getting a strange vibe here. "Isn't that why you wanted me to take these kids in the first place?"

He didn't answer her.

"You are still getting them to strip their powers, aren't you?" She clutched the receiver, a cold feeling coming over her. *What are you up to?* she wondered.

"Just do your job," Syndrome replied. "Let me worry about the rest – it's my company. Stop focusing on your scenic route home and talk to the girl."

"Scenic route?" she fumed. "Oh, I'm sorry I was a little busy *trying not to die*."

He huffed loudly. "Just get back here."

"We're less than thirty minutes away," she told him. *You are a smart, capable babysitter-turned-action-hero dealing with a difficult boss. You are unflappable. You can do anything you set your mind to*, she told herself, adopting Monique's interior monologue techniques.

"Make it twenty," he said and hung up.

CHAPTER TWENTY
VIOLET

Mirage was quiet the rest of the drive to Kari's house. Dash passed out from exhaustion. It was getting late – it would be almost eleven by the time they got to Kari's.

Once they were off the mountain, the car cruised along. The only lights came from the yellowish headlights and streetlights. It was all rather soothing and easy for Violet to get lost in her own thoughts. She couldn't stop thinking about that picture of her dad and the video footage Mastermind had shown her. Why would her dad have worn two different suits during the same job? Why did his hairstyle look different? Was there a chance her parents could be alive, and if they were, what had happened to them? Why hadn't they tried to reach their children? The comms link burned a hole in her pocket. As ridiculous as it was to want to try it again, she had an overwhelming urge to give it another shot.

Finally, Mirage pulled down Kari's street. Several houses were dark, but Kari's house had every light on. Violet frowned. What was going on in there? Mirage pulled in the empty driveway and cut the engine. The silence woke Dash, who sat up and yawned.

"Here," Mirage said, tossing him and Violet each a jacket to put on over their Supersuits. "Just be quick. If we take too long, Syndrome might send out the cavalry."

Violet wouldn't put it past him. She looked at the cube on the seat beside her. Did she trust Mirage not to take the nullifier and leave them in the dust? The nullifier was the only collateral she had at the moment. But if she took it inside, how was she going to explain to Kari what this liquid-filled cube was?

"Violet?" Mirage's voice was gentle. "Are you sure you're all right? Do you want me to go in and get Jack-Jack for you?"

For the moment, Violet decided that she trusted her. She managed a weak smile. "No, she's my friend. I'll get Jack. Come on, Dash."

"Why do I have to go?" he whined.

Violet wasn't stupid. Her brother was more valuable than a nullifier. She would leave the cube, but she was taking him with her. "Because I need you to help me carry all his stuff. Jack is probably sleeping."

Mirage nodded. "See you in a few."

Violet hurried up the path with Dash and prepared to knock. As she got closer, she heard Jack-Jack crying and Kari shouting. Violet frantically knocked. "Kari? Are you okay? It's Violet."

Kari flung open the door. Her hair, normally so neat in her classic ponytail, was unkempt, pieces falling around her face. Her eyes darted around nervously. The smell of something burning wafted out the front door.

"VIOLET!" Kari hugged her so hard, Violet thought she cracked a rib. "You came! I've been calling Aunt Mirage over and over and OVER and she hasn't called me back."

"Aunt Mirage?" Dash tried not to laugh.

Violet turned (Kari was still holding on to her pretty tight) and gave him a sharp look. "Yes, our aunt. Mum's second cousin." She tried to look positive. "She was watching Jack since… since my mum and dad are…" She didn't know what to say. Violet felt like she couldn't lie to yet another person. It was exhausting.

"Looking for a new house?" Kari asked. "I heard about the fire! My mum was driving by your house on her way home from food shopping. I asked for pizza for dinner and we didn't have any frozen pizzas, so my mum said, 'Can you

just eat something else?' And I was like, 'No, I want pizza!'
So she was like—"

"Kari?" Violet interrupted. Once her friend was off on
a tangent, it was tough to rein her back in. Kari kept going.

"'Then I have to go to the store', and I said, 'We're
out of eggs anyway'. My dad likes eggs on the weekends,
and so—"

"KARI," Violet said sharply. "Mirage – Aunt Mirage
– played your messages for me and… is everything okay
with Jack-Jack?" She peered beyond Kari into the house.
The living room was foggy. She could hear Jack-Jack
babbling. Why did he sound like he was overhead? Was he
upstairs?

"No, it's not." Kari's right eye started to twitch. "Sorry
for freaking out, but your baby has problems."

Violet paled, and she and Dash looked at each other.
"Problems?" What did that mean? She opened her mouth
to speak and started to choke on the smoke. "Is something
burning?"

"Yep!" Kari had a crazed look in her eye. "The house is
destroyed! Not sure what I'm going to tell my parents when
they get back from dinner. The living room couch is singed.
I've had to use the fire extinguisher in every room because
your brother keeps bursting into flames!"

"Flames?" Violet repeated. Kari wasn't making sense.

Somewhere in the house, Jack-Jack squealed. Violet motioned to Dash and he seemed to understand she wanted him to find the baby. He zipped past them.

"I thought it was a regular babysitting gig. It started out that way, with reassuring the parents – or in your case – the aunt – and everything. After she left, we were ready for some cognitive development. I played Mozart." Kari's eyes widened. "But when I turned around, he was gone."

"Gone?" Violet repeated, trying to understand.

"Violet?" Dash's voice sounded worried. She could hear Jack-Jack giggling. "I think you should see this."

"I found him on the table and I thought, 'That's weird. I didn't know he could climb', so I put him back on the floor and…" Kari started to blink rapidly again, "I tried flash cards, but then… he… he… burst into flames! And started running around laughing, making me chase him." She started shaking.

Now it was Violet's turn to laugh. "You're joking. Right?" Kari didn't laugh. "Jack-Jack spontaneously went on fire?" Kari had lost it!

Kari's eyes narrowed and she let go of Violet. "The baby was exploding! I mean it! Have you ever seen him explode?"

"Explode? No." Violet tried to keep a straight face.

"Or shoot lasers through his eyes?" Her eyes were really wide now. "Sit on the ceiling? Or… or… float through a wall?" she whispered.

Violet had that weird prickling at the base of her neck again. Float through a wall? "Kari?" Violet put a hand on her arm to steady her. "Are you all right? Have you been babysitting too much? Babies can't float through walls."

Kari wasn't amused. "I'm telling the truth!" she shouted. "The baby was UPSIDE DOWN on the ceiling! I had to use a fire extinguisher to put him out because he kept bursting into flames! I called my parents when your aunt didn't answer, but they didn't believe me!" She was hysterical now. "Then I called Lucy and she said she'd get here as fast as she could, but that was a half hour ago."

"Lucy? Is coming here?" Violet felt her heart start to beat fast again.

"Yes. She asked where you were and I said I didn't know. You haven't been in school the last two days so I thought maybe you were sick, but then your aunt wanted me to watch Jack-Jack, so I thought maybe you were somewhere with your parents? Your family is confusing!" She waved her hands wildly. "She said she'd been trying to reach you. Her uncle couldn't reach your dad and was worried. But she wasn't worried about a baby who could SHOOT LASERS OUT OF HIS EYES."

If Lucius was looking for her dad, maybe he knew what

really happened to her parents. Violet's watch started to flash. That was probably Mirage wondering what was taking so long.

"Violet!" Dash sounded more urgent now. "You need to get in here!"

"Are you listening to me?" Kari said more urgently. "Jack shot lasers out of his eyes!" She started to laugh and cry at the same time. "This isn't worth the triple pay your aunt offered me." She motioned to the charred living room rug. "What am I going to tell my parents?"

"VIOLET!" Dash shouted, and Kari and Violet heard Jack squeal again. They looked at each other and ran into the other room.

Violet almost fell over at the sight.

Jack-Jack was sitting upside down on the ceiling eating a biscuit.

"Jack-Jack has powers!" Dash said excitedly, then realised Kari was there and stopped.

"Powers? What do you mean, *powers*? What is going on with him? He needs a doctor!" Kari freaked.

Violet wasn't sure what to react to first – Dash outing them, or the fact that Jack-Jack was just like the rest of the family – he wasn't normal. He was a Super! Even more surprising, if Kari was telling the truth about the things she'd seen Jack-Jack do tonight, then Jack-Jack didn't just have one power or two, like her and Dash. He had several. What exactly were they dealing with? How was she going to keep Jack-Jack safe if she didn't know what he was capable of?

Jack-Jack saw Violet and clapped his hands, the biscuit falling to the floor. "Num-num?" he said worriedly, then burst into tears and disappeared.

"Jack-Jack?" Dash called. "Jack-Jack? Where are you?"

Violet spun around. "Jack-Jack?" There was no baby anywhere! "Jack-Jack?"

The baby walked right through a wall and came toddling towards her. Violet resisted the urge to scream, swooping down to pick him up and praying Kari didn't pass out.

"Num-num?" Jack-Jack said again.

"See! He can walk through walls!" Kari cried. "And all he wants is biscuits. I only have a few left and there's been no time to bake more! The house has been on fire!"

The baby started to turn red, then pounded his fists. "Num-num!"

He disappeared from Violet's arms and reappeared several feet away. Still yelling, his eyes suddenly shot beams clear across the house, shattering several vases in Kari's mum's china cupboard in the dining room. Kari screamed. Violet and Dash looked at each other. This was bad. *Really* bad. How was Violet going to explain all this? What was she going to do about Jack-Jack? The baby looked at her and sneezed. A stream of fire came out of his nostrils. Before Violet could react, Kari had a fire extinguisher in her hands and had covered the floor in foam.

"I told you I was right about your brother! There is nothing wrong with my skills as a babysitter!" Kari was beyond hysterical now.

Violet handed Jack-Jack off to Dash. "Get him to the car. Fast," she whispered, then she turned to Kari and thought fast. Dash grabbed the remaining biscuits from the table on his way out the door. "Kari, I'm really worried about you." She put her arm around her. "When was the last time you slept?"

"Last night," Kari said suspiciously. "Why?"

"I think you're overtired. You've been working too hard! Babysitting all the time." She led her friend to the stairs. "I think once you've had a good night's sleep, you'll see everything here is just fine at the house."

"I can't go to sleep. Lucy is coming over," Kari said.

"Call her back and say you spoke to me and I'm going to call her," Violet told her. "You need to get to bed and forget all about this bad dream."

"Bad dream?" Kari said, her voice calming a bit. "Yeah, that makes a lot more sense."

Violet went with it. "Yes, a bad dream, and I'm in it

because… because you're mad at me. For ditching you at the party."

"Yeah! I am still mad about that," Kari said, taking her first step upstairs. "You're right."

"Very mad and I should apologise. You will tell me to apologise," Violet continued, stepping backwards towards the door. She felt terrible about leaving Kari with this mess. She'd find a way to make it up to her at some point, but she had to keep their identities safe and she couldn't think of another way to do it. She needed to get back to the nullifier and figure out how to reach Lucy and see what her uncle knew about her parents. Violet would talk to Lucius about what happened with Mastermind. "I will call you and apologise big-time."

Kari yawned. "Good. And you'll have your aunt pay me? She owes me a lot of money for this."

Oh, more than you know, Violet thought, taking one step out the door. "Sleep tight!" She pulled the door shut behind her and found Dash was waiting with Jack on the steps. The baby had crumbs all over his mouth.

"We're out of biscuits," Dash said. "Mirage better drive fast."

"What took so long?" Mirage yelled through the open window. "Syndrome is going to be manic wondering where we are."

Violet and Dash looked at each other. Should they tell her? Before Violet could decide, Dash did it for her.

"Jack-Jack has powers!" he crowed, jumping in the back seat with the baby and seat belting him in.

"Powers?" Mirage repeated. "The baby?" She looked at Jack-Jack with a renewed interest that made Violet uncomfortable.

Jack-Jack just babbled to himself. Thankfully not about biscuits.

"Well, we don't know for sure," Violet hedged. "But we should get back to the house fast just in case." She put her hands around the cube again. It was right where she left it, thankfully. In a short time, her brothers' and her Super problem would be solved. She should be relieved. So why was Mastermind's monologue still eating at her? She held the cube tighter.

"He can burst into flames! Walk through walls!" Dash continued, not getting that Violet was trying to keep things quiet. Jack-Jack just laughed. Then he sneezed and burst into flames that quickly sizzled out.

Mirage's jaw dropped. "Wait till Syn sees this."

CHAPTER TWENTY-ONE
VIOLET

Violet made a decision: Mastermind was lying to her. It was the only logical answer. That's what she told herself as Mirage pulled into the secret entrance to Syndrome's place. Mastermind had played with them the way a cat plays with a mouse before killing it. This was all a big game, and telling Violet her parents might still be alive was part of the trap. Violet had her most prized possession. What choice did Mastermind have but to make her question what she was doing?

Violet was Team Syndrome for a reason. He'd helped her get this far. She had to trust she was doing the right thing. When Mirage pulled into the cave, Syndrome was waiting for them downstairs in the carport, flanked by several workers in headgear. He cheered the second he saw the car.

"You did it!" He ran to the car door to open it. "I can't believe it, but you did it!" He high-fived Dash. "And you! Going rogue! You sly dog!"

Dash looked worried. "So you're not mad at me?"

"Mad?" Syndrome leant down to his level. "You killed it and helped Violet save an invention from a villain. You should be proud of yourself." He looked over at Violet, who still hadn't exited the car. "So where is the nullifier?"

Violet stepped out of the car, hesitant to let go of the cube she'd worked so hard to get. "Right here."

Syndrome stopped bouncing and looked at the cube reverently. "Mastermind's greatest achievement," he whispered, taking it gently from her. "I'd started to wonder if this thing even existed, but here it is." He eyed Violet. "You're sure this is the nullifier?"

"Oh, she's sure. Mastermind told her to take it," Dash boasted.

"Mastermind told you to take it?" Syndrome repeated, surprised.

"Yes!" Dash spoke up again, to Violet's annoyance. "She was kind of like, 'Let's see you try to get away'."

Syndrome frowned. "Why would Mastermind just hand

over her greatest invention?" He brought the cube up to eye level. "Do you think this is a fake?"

Violet hadn't thought of that. "I don't think so. I think she was bored and wanted a thrill."

Syndrome rolled his eyes. "Sounds like something she would do. She misses villain action. She thinks her place is so hard to infiltrate. I wish I could have seen the look on her face when she realised Mr Incredible and Elastigirl's kids broke in!"

"She was excited. She said she sent us baby gifts when we were born," Dash offered, and Violet shot him daggers.

"Wait, she knows you two exist?" Syndrome did a double take. "You didn't tell me that."

"Because we didn't know that either," Violet reminded him. "I've never seen her before tonight, and I hope I never see her again."

"She trapped us in her office," Dash continued. "And then when Violet blew out a wall with a massive force field so we could get away with the cube, she sent her guards after us! They chased us through the halls and I got to use my dad's old weapons! Shoot, I think I left some at Kari's," he said with a frown.

"Kari's?" Syndrome was sounding more and more tense.

"The babysitter who watched Jack," Mirage said. "Speaking of which—"

Dash was still talking and clearly had Syndrome's ear. "And then when we tried to get away, we had to go out a window! We thought we were trapped! But Mirage came skidding in across the grass, shooting weapons from the car and we sped away. It was the BEST. DAY. EVER!"

Violet pulled Jack from the back of the car. He'd started rubbing his eyes on the ride home. She had to get him to bed, but she wanted to talk to Syndrome more. She didn't want to say too much in front of Dash, but she wanted to make sure they used the nullifier right away, before Mastermind had a chance to steal it back. She felt Syndrome clap a hand on her shoulder.

"What about you? You haven't said much about this epic getaway." Syndrome's tone was more serious than it had been moments ago. "All okay?" He glanced at Jack-Jack in her arms.

"Num-num?" the baby said, looking at her. "Num-num?"

"I'm just ready for this all to be over," Violet admitted, sounding as exhausted as she suddenly felt. She felt like she'd lived a thousand years in just the last few days. "How long before you'll be ready to help us use that thing?"

He peered at the cube closer. "Let's get it upstairs and

we can talk." He headed to the lift and the guards and everyone else followed.

"Num-NUM?" Jack said louder, overtired and beyond cranky now.

"No more num-nums," Violet told him. "You're going to bed." She'd have to explain what happened at Kari's to Syndrome, but she didn't want him getting distracted. The nullifier was more important than telling him about Jack, who'd had powers for a hot second.

"NUM-NUMMMMM," Jack started to screech as the lift doors opened, and then he screamed, his face turning red.

"Jack! Stop. No more num-nums!"

"He's going to explode!" Dash said. "Or turn into a devil. Did you see him do that, Vi? I saw it when I gave him the last biscuit."

Syndrome paused. "A devil? What are you talking about?"

"I'll explain on the way up. Why don't we go up first?" Mirage suggested, eyeing Jack worriedly. "And Violet, why don't you and the baby take the next one. Seems like he needs a minute."

"But—" If anyone was going to tell Syndrome about Jack, Violet wanted to do it.

"Mirage is right. That baby is giving me a headache.

Come on, Dash," Syndrome agreed, stepping into the lift with the cube. Dash followed, along with Mirage and the guards.

Jack-Jack was screaming in Violet's ear now, making it hard for her to argue. This was her mum's area of expertise. What did she do in this situation? She held tight to Jack with one hand and dug into her pocket with the other, searching for her mother's note again. Maybe there was something she missed on here about the biscuit issue. There was no way her mum gave in to Jack having unlimited sweets.

The lift dinged when it reached the main floor, and Violet pressed the button, sending it down again while Jack yanked at her hair. She found the note and pulled it out as the lift doors opened in front of her. Jack gave her hair a sharper tug.

"Jack-Jack, please!" she begged as they stepped inside and then *BOOM!* The baby floated out of her arms and disappeared through the lift ceiling. "JACK-JACK!" Violet shouted as the doors closed. She couldn't have the lift ascend without the baby. What if he was in the lift shaft? "JACK-JACK?" She heard him babbling somewhere outside the walls. She hit the emergency stop button and the lift went dark. Great. Just great. "Jack-Jack, I'll give you a num-num!" She was clearly no Kari when it came to babysitting. "Two num-nums!"

Jack-Jack popped out of the floor, bathed in a ray of light for a moment, and Violet grabbed him.

"Num-num?" Jack-Jack said, sounding calmer now.

"Two num-nums," Violet promised, relieved. She really hoped Syndrome still had biscuits. She could barely see her brother in the darkness, but something was glowing other than the baby. It was the note from Mum.

Violet peered closer. There was a name and number on the page written in black light. This was why her mum had been so adamant about Violet holding on to her note! It had a message only for her. Violet read it quickly. *In case of emergency, call Rick Dicker at the Agency.* It was followed by a phone number.

So Mum did have an emergency backup plan, Violet realised, and it wasn't Mirage or Syndrome. It was the Agency, which Mirage claimed was no longer even in business. Violet faltered.

Was Mastermind telling the truth that she hadn't kidnapped Violet's parents?

If she hadn't, who did?

"Num-num?" Jack questioned again as the lights flickered on and Violet hurried to put the note back in her pocket. The lift flew upwards.

"Soon," Violet promised. She tried to understand – if her mum had wanted them to call the Agency, why was Mirage's card the one on her Dad's desk? Were her parents working for the Agency? Or were they working with Mirage and Syndrome? Her thoughts were all jumbled and she couldn't make sense of them. Was Mastermind – a true villain – being honest with her that she would never use the nullifier on Mr Incredible and Elastigirl because she liked sparring with them? So that it could be Super versus villain like it had always been for her parents?

Then again, who cared what Mastermind wanted? She was still a villain, and they were Supers. If they were normal, villains wouldn't be ringing their doorbell anymore. She could keep her brothers safe, just like Mum wanted.

"Num-num?" Jack asked again.

Violet held him tight, as if that would help keep him from disappearing again. His powers were a problem. All their powers were. It was clear: giving them up was the right thing to do. But first, Syndrome had some explaining to do.

CHAPTER TWENTY-TWO
VIOLET

"The baby has powers?" Syndrome said as the lift doors opened to let Violet and Jack out. He'd adopted a Super stance, hands on hips, feet planted slightly wide, cape billowing behind him in the breeze coming from the open patio doors.

"Uh..." Violet was caught off guard. She was the one who had the questions here, and she intended to ask them and get this nullifier going ASAP. "Yes, but..."

"What kind?" He took Jack from her arms before she could react. He held the baby awkwardly, under his armpits as Mirage had, keeping him at arm's length as if he could bite. "What can he do?"

Violet didn't want to get distracted. "Just a few things so

far. Now, the nullifier..."

"He can walk through walls!" Dash supplied. "And he can shoot lasers from his eyes! Turn into a devil. And travel through dimensions! I think!"

"Fascinating," Syndrome said, staring at Jack-Jack with renewed interest. "He's like the Super of all Supers."

Violet didn't like how that sounded. "Can we talk about Jack later?" Violet tried again. "I really need to talk to you."

Jack sneezed and fire shot out.

Syndrome screamed and dropped the baby, but instead of Jack-Jack falling, he floated up and into the ceiling and disappeared. "Are you kidding me?" he said excitedly. "Where did he go?" Syndrome asked, looking up at the sound of Jack-Jack's voice from somewhere above.

"Not sure, but if you offer him a biscuit, he'll come back," Dash suggested.

"Baby? Want a biscuit?" Syndrome asked.

BOOM! Jack-Jack appeared in his arms.

"Incredible! Did you see that?" he asked Mirage. "I called him and he just came to me! Someone get me a biscuit!"

"No biscuits!" Violet snapped and everyone looked at her. "Sorry. I'm just tired. We all are." She reached for Jack-Jack and took him back. "He needs to go to bed. Dash too. I have something I really want to ask you."

"Sure. What do you want to know?" Syndrome sat down on the sofa. "Dash, buddy? Why don't you get some shut-eye? Big day tomorrow."

"Syndrome says we're going on a trip!" Dash told Violet.

"A trip?" Violet said at the same time Mirage did.

"To an island! A volcanic island!" Dash said, clearly excited.

Violet's stomach clenched. Syndrome's island? That's where her parents were killed. She had to believe that to be true, because if it wasn't, why hadn't they tried to reach her? Was the island where Syndrome planned on letting them use the nullifier? She didn't want to ask these questions in front of Dash. "Dash, can you put Jack-Jack to bed for me so I can talk to Syndrome?"

Dash groaned. "It better not be about giving up our powers!"

Violet froze. Out of the corner of her eye, she could see Syndrome watching her.

"I just fought a super villain and won," Dash reminded her as he picked up Jack-Jack and the baby rested his head on his shoulder. "I don't want to give up being Super."

Syndrome laughed awkwardly and ran a hand through his red hair. "All right, kiddo. We hear you. Let me talk to your sister."

"Fine," Dash said, shooting Violet a look before walking out.

Syndrome turned to Violet with full attention. "You told your brother about the nullifier?"

Finally! "Not exactly, but that is kind of what I wanted to talk to you about. I—"

"You're taking the kids to the island?" Mirage interrupted.

"*We're* taking them to the island," Syndrome said, not looking at her.

"I'm off tomorrow, remember?" Mirage said, but he ignored her.

Syndrome leant forwards, his eyes on Violet's. "What did you tell your brother?"

Violet sighed. He wasn't going to let this go. "I told him giving up our powers would keep us safe, just like we talked about."

Syndrome scratched his chin. "How did Dash react?"

Violet glanced at her boots. They were covered in mud from running around Mastermind's grounds. "He wasn't happy. He doesn't understand what we're trying to do."

"Keep you all safe," Syndrome supplemented.

"Yes," Violet said, glad to be on the same page about this. "There's always going to be another Mastermind. If we're normal, no one will care who our parents are – *were*."

She paused. "But I did have some questions about that."

Syndrome stood up in front of her, cutting her off. "How did it feel tonight? Using your powers the way they're meant to be used? Knowing how to control them? Busting into and out of a super villain's home with just a few days of training?"

Violet felt like he could hear her conflicted thoughts.

"You can admit it," Syndrome said. "It felt incredible, didn't it?" He was practically nose to nose with her now.

Violet couldn't lie. "Kind of, but—"

"I knew it would!" Syn patted the nullifier. "If you fought Mastermind once and won, imagine what you could do if other villains came knocking? Think of what you and Dash could do! And now that Jack has powers? You three could be an unstoppable trio! With the right training? And me as your mentor? You'd be the strongest Supers in Metroville. No, forget that. The WORLD!"

Violet felt uneasy. "I thought you said we were in danger because of our powers. That our parents being upset about losing their powers cost them their lives. And that's why getting the nullifier and using it on ourselves so that Mastermind would leave us alone would keep us safe. Now you're saying the opposite."

"Because look what you can do!" Syndrome boomed. "If the four of us were a team – with my inventions and your skills – no one could mess with us. Not even Mastermind. And now that we have the nullifier, if any other Supers tried to get in your way, we can easily get rid of them."

Violet's blood ran cold. "Now you sound like Mastermind."

Syndrome cocked his head to one side. "What does that mean?"

"Mastermind said she'd never take my parents' powers and she didn't understand why Dash and I would think she'd want ours. She said..." Violet looked down, Syndrome's stare unnerving her, "that someone might be lying to me." The room was so quiet, she could hear Dash and Jack in the other room.

"Violet," Mirage started to say.

"Stay out of this, Mirage." Syndrome's voice had bite. "What are you saying, Violet? That I'm lying to you? Because it kind of feels like you're suggesting Mastermind is more trustworthy than me. More than the guy who saved your life and is now trying to do it again by showing you how to use your powers to their full potential. Your Super mummy and daddy never did that. Trust me: you have so much to offer, and we can do it together."

"But that's not what you said when you rescued us," Violet reminded him, her heart starting to pound. "Why would we steal the nullifier if we're not going to use it to protect ourselves?"

Syndrome ignored the question. "Don't you see how well we work together? Dash loves me! Jack will too. Where are you going to go if you leave here? Your parents are dead. Dash set fire to your house trying to protect you from my guys instead of going quietly the other morning."

Wait. Did he just say *"my* guys"? Violet's heart started to beat faster.

"We've got a good thing going here. Look at what we pulled off in one weekend!" he continued. "If you come with me to the island, I can promise you, we can do so much more. And maybe I'll even have a few surprises in store."

Violet felt her skin warming, her throat constricting. Mastermind hadn't tried to kidnap them. It was Syndrome's goons posing as Mastermind's. Why? *To make us think we were in danger,* she realised. It all was starting to come together – why her mum's note suggested calling the Agency if they were in trouble, why that video of her dad and mum felt a bit off, why her dad looked different and was wearing his old suit in that video Syndrome showed her. That's when she knew: Mastermind wasn't the villain of this story – Syndrome was.

"Violet?" Syndrome watched her. "What are you thinking?"

Violet's voice was a whisper. "You said, 'my guys'."

"What?" It was Syndrome's turn to look confused.

"You said 'my guys' came to our house," Violet repeated, feeling shaky. "Mastermind didn't come for me and my brothers. You did, which must mean… you kidnapped my parents, too."

Syndrome laughed. "Do you hear yourself? That's insane!"

"You kidnapped my parents so you could use the nullifier on them after I stole it for you," Violet realised. "Which means… my parents are alive." She felt like she was going to pass out. Was that what happened? Her suspicions were confirmed when Syndrome didn't answer her.

"Syn?" Mirage stood behind the sofa listening. Was it just Violet's imagination, or did Mirage look as surprised as Violet felt? "Is this true?"

"Are my parents alive?" Violet tried to keep her voice steady.

"Syn?" Mirage tried.

"*Mirage*," he said through gritted teeth. "Let me deal with this."

Deal didn't mean answer. Violet's head was spinning. "You were in a picture with Mastermind in her private office," Violet put together. "You knew how to get to Mastermind.

You said, 'Every villain has their weakness. Mastermind's is brownies'. Yours is my parents," she realised.

If her parents were alive, then why did Syndrome want the nullifier? *To steal her Mum and Dad's powers*, she guessed.

Her eyes shifted to the nullifier. Syndrome's did the same. Violet forced her body to disappear. She moved fast trying to grab it. Syndrome lunged in front of the cube and took it first.

"Don't even think about it, Violet," he said quietly. "We may not be able to see you, but we do know you're here and so are your brothers. Guards? Go get the boys for me. I want to keep them safe while their sister rethinks her position." A bunch of guards came running and headed to the boys' door.

Dash! Jack-Jack! Violet's head appeared first in a panic. "No!"

"So what's it going to be, Violet?" Syndrome said calmly. "Are you going to quit with the questions and join me? Or are we going to have a problem?"

"Sir?" A new guard came racing into the room, interrupting them.

"I'm in the middle of something important!" Syndrome thundered.

"There's been another breech," the guard said. "It's another Super, sir. One who can make ice. He's trying to break them out!"

One who can make ice.

Frozone? Violet's heart skipped a beat.

Break them out.

Violet looked at Syndrome again. *Them.* As in more than one. And that's when her gut told her she was right. "Frozone is there to break out my parents – they're really alive," she realised.

Syndrome threw his head back. "Oh, Violet... I wish you hadn't just said that." He pressed a button on his wrist and a laser beam lifted her off the floor, immobilising her.

"Syn! What are you doing?" Mirage shouted.

"Lock the other two in their room," Syndrome told the guards as he held tight to the beam that was holding Violet, who couldn't speak or move.

She was completely helpless as she hovered above the sofa, caught in the buzzing beam.

"Neat trick, huh?" Syndrome said, walking around the room while the laser held firm. "Immobi-ray. I created it. I've created a lot of things. The only thing I haven't been able to create is a nullifier that strips Supers of their powers."

"Syn, she's a child!" Mirage begged. "Just tell her she's wrong. Her parents are dead."

"But that's the thing. She's right." Syndrome started to laugh. "You are one smart cookie, Violet. You figured me out!"

"That can't be," Mirage sputtered. "You said—"

"I know what I said!" he snapped, and Mirage grew quiet. "But when you went to get the kids from the Parr house, I started thinking – why should I kill Mr So-Called Incredible and Elastigirl when I can completely destroy them by turning their children against them? I mean, using their children to steal Mastermind's nullifier and then make them watch as the kids use it on them? It's a brilliant idea, no?"

"I can't believe you lied to me, too," Mirage hissed. "You're a monster. I quit!"

Syndrome shot a laser at her with his other glove, the stream of energy catching Mirage and immobilising her. "Oh, sweetheart, I'm sorry to hear you feel that way. Especially when you're not innocent in any of this." Mirage rose into the air, a look of shock on her face. "Violet, that's not even Mirage's real hair! She's a blonde actress! I hired her to trick you. Does it *get* any better than that?"

Violet struggled against the invisible hold, feeling a scream build inside her that she couldn't release. From the other room, Violet heard Dash shouting and Jack-Jack crying.

"Sorry, Mirage. You can't quit. You're fired." He turned the laser holding Mirage towards the open sliding-glass doors and with a press of the button, ejected Mirage off the porch.

Violet watched in horror as Mirage disappeared over the side.

"Bummer. I'm going to miss her. But not paying her overtime." He turned back to Violet. "Oh, don't be sad. I'm going to give you exactly what you always wanted, and I'm finally getting what *I've* always wanted. Your parents took away my future. I'm simply returning the favour and taking away their kids. Oh, don't worry. I'll be the perfect mentor to your brothers. Supportive. Encouraging. Everything your dad wasn't with me when I was simply Buddy Pine."

Violet froze. Buddy Pine. Now she realised why she'd heard the name before. That was her dad's Super fan stalker. Buddy Pine was Syndrome!

"Who knows? In time, your brothers might make the perfect sidekicks." He pressed a button and the beam lowered and slammed Violet to the floor. "You could have been one too, you know. You were doing so well with your rage. Oh well."

With a buzz, the beam flickered out, releasing its hold. Violet's whole body felt cold and numb. She tried to lift her head, but she was too tired to move. Syndrome opened the cube in front of him, a hissing sound releasing from the cube as he lifted out the nullifier. A guard handed him an oxygen mask, which he placed over her face before she could protest. Violet started to squirm, but she couldn't even manage to scream. The guards held her down and she watched in horror as Syndrome poured a drop of the green nullifier into a vial, then attached it to the oxygen mask hooked up to a tube and a small machine. A compartment with water underneath started to bubble and its mist started to enter her lungs. It tasted like lavender, which was Mastermind's signature scent, it seemed. Her whole body started to tingle then burn as if she were on fire. She began to convulse on the floor.

"Sir! Sir!" Another guard came running in. "We got him! That Super – Frozone? We got him! The captives are secure."

"Excellent! Get them off the island and move them to my beach house. I want them to see their boys one more time before we use the nullifier on them, then finish them for real this time." He patted Violet's back. "Thanks for letting me test this on you first, though."

Violet's insides felt like they were burning. She couldn't breathe. Was she dying?

"Now, now, don't panic. I didn't kill you. Yet," Syndrome said soothingly, which made her want to punch him. "In thirty seconds, it will all be over, and you'll have what you always wanted – no powers!" He looked at a guard. "When I'm done, lock her up and have her transported to the island. She'll be no problem dealing with then." Syndrome just stood there watching, smiling eerily, his blue eyes piercing beneath his black mask. "She can stay in her parents' old cell until I figure out what I want to do with her."

Violet felt like a fish out of water. Her head pounded, her limbs screamed, till she finally lost consciousness.

CHAPTER TWENTY-THREE
VIOLET

Violet awoke gasping for air.

She sat up fast, letting a breath fill her lungs as fast as she could, gulping oxygen down like iced tea. It took her a moment or two to realise where she was.

She was in bed, in the bedroom she'd been staying in at Syndrome's place the past few days. On the floor, two guards were knocked out cold. She didn't know how that happened, but she wasn't going to look a gift horse in the mouth. Daylight was streaming in the window, which meant she'd been asleep for hours. Not good.

Syndrome. The nullifier. Her parents. Her brothers! She had to get to them.

Violet jumped out of bed.

Oww.

Her whole body ached, as if she were getting over the worst case of the flu she'd ever had. She felt hot, then cold, then hot again, and she was sweating. She dabbed at her forehead with a tissue and looked in the mirror. She looked the same, but inside, she knew she was different.

Violet tried to become invisible using every technique she knew (which, annoyingly, were Syndrome's tips) and nothing happened. Next, she shot her hands out in front of her, attempting to fire a force field. All she felt was achy.

Her powers were gone.

A sob escaped her lips. She had got what she'd always wanted and yet... she didn't want it anymore. Her arms felt like weights hanging from her shoulders. She just wanted to lie down and sleep, but she couldn't. Mum and Dad were alive! Alive! Violet started to cry, relieved and then worried all over again. They were alive, for now, but if she didn't get to them, she knew what would happen. She had to hurry. Syndrome was moving them to the beach – isn't that what he had said? He was going to strip their powers and run off with Dash and Jack-Jack, and Violet was the only one who knew his plan. Mirage was dead. There's no way she had survived that fall. Frozone was captured. It was all on her.

And she had no powers to help her.

Syndrome had destroyed her family and she'd basically

let him walk in and do it. He was despicable. A pure villain, plain and simple, and she had fallen for his lies. Maybe Mastermind was a super villain, but at least she had been up front about it.

Was there any way to reach Mastermind now? Not alone. Not without powers. And even if the car was still downstairs and the coordinates were in it, what would she tell Mastermind if she found her: hey, I know I stole your nullifier and lost it, but can you help me? No. She needed to come up with a different plan and fast. She was almost certain Syndrome's other guards were getting ready to haul her away to the island any moment.

What was she going to do?

You're going to get out of here and help them, a voice in her head said. She had no choice. If Frozone had been captured, who was left to help her square off against Syndrome? Who was smart, capable, headstrong and unafraid to stand up for themself?

Violet heard a phone begin to ring.

She looked around wildly, hoping to silence it before it alerted the guards.

On her nightstand were two items: the SpyGuy that Syndrome had given her the day she arrived (which she never bothered using) and a small slim silver gadget that was ringing. It was Mirage's portable phone. Violet picked it up and stared at the buttons. On top was a green one and a red one. Green meant 'go', so… "Hello?" Violet answered.

"Aunt Mirage? Is that you?" Kari's voice was so loud Violet had to hold the phone away. "This is Kari McKeen? The babysitter? The one who watched Jack Parr for hours – overtime, I might add – and didn't get PAID! You owe triple!" She heard a voice in the background mumbling something. "I mean, six times my pay! On account of all the damage in my house because… you know." She whispered that last part.

"Kari!" Violet hissed, not wanting to alert the guards that she'd woken up. Any second they could bust through that door. She had to speak fast. "It's Violet! I need your help."

"Help? I need YOUR help! Getting my house back! My head is kind of foggy, after what happened – my parents said maybe there was a gas leak in the house? They don't even remember letting me babysit. But I remember your aunt and she owes me money! How could you leave Jack here when he's… he's… strange?"

"Give me the phone!" someone barked. "Violet? Violet is that you?"

"Lucy!" Violet watched the door again for signs of guards. "It's me!"

"I'm so glad we found you," Lucy said as Kari continued

yelling in the background. "I thought something happened to you. When Uncle Lu heard about your house and he couldn't reach your dad... he went after him. Now Aunt Honey is all upset because no one has heard from Uncle Lu in a day and we're really worried about him, too."

"I know where he is," Violet blurted out.

"You do?"

"Kind of," Violet said and felt her lower lip start to quiver. "It's the same person who took Dash and Jack-Jack. They have my parents too, and that's probably where Frozone is trapped as well. I'm afraid if we don't get to them in time..." *They'll lose their powers or worse.* "I have to get to them as quickly as possible and I don't... I can't... I am not sure how to..." She felt so overwhelmed, yet for the first time, none of her powers manifested along with her emotions. It was a disorientating feeling.

"Calm down. Where are you?" Lucy said.

"I don't even know the address. I just know I need to get out of here." How was she going to get around the guards without powers? Surely the two on the floor in front of her weren't the only ones around.

"Can you use your Super smarts and get to us, then?" Lucy pressed as Kari kept yelling. "We can meet somewhere public. It's safer. How about the Happy Platter?"

The Happy Platter! It was in downtown Metroville. She

didn't have her powers, but she could figure out how to get there. She needed her friends' help. "Okay. I don't know how, but I'll be there in a half hour. We have to hurry."

"Okay," Lucy said. "We'll be there too."

"Bring my babysitting money!" Kari shouted in the background.

Violet grabbed Mirage's phone and her SpyGuy. Then she sneaked out of the room, expecting to be stormed. Instead, leaving the house was too easy. Almost as if someone had planned to help her non-Super self leave the premises. When Violet stepped out of the bedroom, she found more guards passed out on the floor, all snoring loudly as if they'd been hit by a sleeping spray. She didn't question her luck. The lift took her down to the parking garage. She expected to have to ride Dash's skateboard all the way to the diner, but instead, she found a car much like the one Mirage drove waiting for her with a large note taped to the window in messy handwriting. Her name was in large print.

Need a ride, VIOLET? Tell the car where you need to go! Homing device on this car has been disconnected so your location cannot be tracked. Hope that helps! - A friend

A friend, huh? It felt like a trap, or someone who wasn't loyal to Syndrome was helping her. She hesitated for the briefest of moments before sliding into the front seat and pressing the navigation button, which had also been marked. "The Happy Platter, Metroville, please!"

She was saying please to a car. Whatever. It worked. In seconds the engine was purring and the car was cruising out of the garage, heading to the city. All the while, Violet kept worrying. How was she going to find Syndrome's beach house? She reached for her powers, willing herself to go invisible, to hide from the impossible challenge she had to face, but her body did not disappear. Her powers were truly gone. Solving this problem was going to be entirely on her normal self.

The Happy Platter, its tall, neon sign a landmark in the city, was just a few corners away. She peered out the passenger side window cautiously. She didn't see any of Syndrome's goons, but they could be in disguise, couldn't they? Clearly they'd been the ones dressed in tuxedos at her house, posing as Masterminds' goons. How could she have fallen for such a ruse?

"The Happy Platter, home of the famous forty-ounce burger and cookie dough milkshake, on your left," the car announced, rolling to a stop right in front of the diner. Violet heard the doors unlock. "Shall I wait for you,

Violet Parr?"

"Yes!" Violet told the car, feeling funny treating it like a dog. "Wait right here. I'll be back soon. Don't leave with anyone else!"

Inside, the reception was jammed. She could see the dining room was packed. She stood on her tiptoes to try to find Kari's familiar dark-blonde ponytailed head among all the people sitting in red leather booths and heard someone calling her name.

"VIOLET!" Lucy shouted from across the room, standing up and waving. "Over here!" Next to her, Kari had her head in her hands and was staring at her red placemat.

Violet hurried over and Lucy pulled her into an embrace. Violet held tight, not wanting to let go.

"I've been so worried," Lucy whispered. "Are you okay?"

"No," Violet said, feeling her eyes well with tears. "Everyone I love is in trouble and it's all my fault."

Lucy's brown eyes crinkled worriedly. "We're going to figure this out. Together." She held up a faded brown messenger bag. "I've come prepared for anything."

Before Violet could ask what was inside the bag, Kari interrupted them.

"Hi, Violet," Kari said in the dullest tone possible.

Violet did a double-take. Her friend looked like she hadn't slept in weeks. Dark circles rimmed her large eyes, her ponytail was askew, her hair frizzed and her clothes wrinkled. She looked way worse than she had last night.

"Uh… hi?" Violet looked at Lucy and whispered, "What happened to her?"

"She's… struggling," Lucy whispered back. "She told me about Jack-Jack. When did *that* happen?"

"It's been a long weekend," Violet said wearily, "but there's no time to explain. I have to find my brothers and my parents and I don't know how and I've lost… I've lost…" She couldn't say the words *my powers*. She started to hyperventilate.

"Just sit down," Lucy instructed. "You look as bad as Kari. Eat something. I ordered pancakes for all of us."

"I don't have time to eat," Violet said, sitting across from Kari as Lucy slid in next to her. She was hungry, though.

"You have to," Lucy said, sounding motherly. "It will help." She pushed a glass of orange juice over to her and Violet took a sip greedily. "You need your strength."

Strength. The word caused Violet to laugh, semi-hysterically. Kari glared at her.

"How can you laugh at a time like this? I'm so mad at you. Your aunt owes me a lot of money. And a new house!" Kari said, sitting up suddenly and looking stormy. "My parents think I had a fire in the kitchen or was playing with matches or knocked over a candle – all things I never touch because, hello? Babysitter Guide 101?" Her right eye was twitching. "That fire was caused by—" Her voice lowered to a whisper, "your brother bursting into flames! Going through walls! Shooting lasers with his EYES." She pointed a finger at Violet's face and accidentally poked her in the nose. "I know what I saw. Don't try to deny it! And I didn't even get paid!"

If Violet wanted Kari's help – and she needed Kari's help – she had to tell her. She'd deal with the consequences later. Didn't her dad say the Agency had a way to wipe people's minds? Could she make Kari forget once they got through this? She hoped so. She had no choice. Desperate times called for desperate measures.

"You're right," Violet said. "I'm sorry for laughing." She glanced around the diner to make sure a waiter wasn't nearby. "Jack-Jack *is* special. He's a Super."

Kari blinked rapidly. "A Super? As in *the* Supers? Like the ones with powers? The ones that are illegal?"

Violet and Lucy both nodded.

"Yes." Violet said. It felt good to tell someone the truth. "He's a Super baby, and the night you babysat him? That was the first time he demonstrated any powers. If I had known he had any, I wouldn't have suggested Mirage – who is not actually my aunt, by the way – let you babysit."

Kari's jaw dropped, and it took her a few moments to close her mouth. "So that means if Jack-Jack is Super, then you and your family are…?"

"Super too? Yes," Violet admitted. "We're all Supers, and so is Lucy's uncle." Might as well throw it all out there!

"Umm… we're not really supposed to tell anyone, but since I found out by accident, I haven't had my mind wiped or anything," Lucy said, playing with her fork.

Kari sat up straight. "Mind wiped?"

"Let's not scare her." Violet patted Kari's arm.

Kari looked from Violet to Lucy and back again, unable to form words.

"To be clear," Lucy spoke up, "I'm not Super like Violet."

"You're a Super?" Kari repeated, staring at Violet. "A *real* Super? What can you do? Like fly? Or shoot lasers like Jack-Jack?"

Violet bit her lip. "I used to be able to shoot force fields and I could become invisible. That's actually what happened Friday night at the party. It's why I disappeared."

Kari threw her hands up. "I thought I saw you running outside without your head, but I told myself I was seeing things." She threw herself back against the pleather-cushioned seat. "My parents think I'm losing it."

"You're not. I am a Super." She looked down at her hands. "At least I used to be."

"What do you mean, used to be?" Lucy asked.

Violet quickly filled her friends in on all that had

happened the last few days. Lucy was aghast, but Kari seemed fascinated, despite the peril everyone was in.

"I can't believe I'm friends with a Super!" Kari raised her voice. "I was right! I was right!" She seemed to be telling the whole diner as Lucy shushed her.

"Correction: I'm a former Super," Violet reminded her miserably. Why did it hurt so much to say that?

"You'll always be super to me," Kari said giddily. "Do you realise how lucky you are?"

"Nope," Violet said grimly. "Maybe that's why I lost my powers in the first place."

"I'm sorry, Violet," Lucy said. "That's awful. I know Uncle Lu would have called you back if he hadn't been away with Aunt Honey for his anniversary. He got back Saturday, and when he couldn't reach you guys and he saw your house, he took off. Aunt Honey hasn't seen him since. She's really worried."

"She should be," Violet said quietly and took another sip of orange juice. "Syndrome has some sort of vendetta against my parents, and I gave him a weapon that could strip powers! And basically begged to have my powers taken away!" She looked at her friends again. "Who knew the one thing I always wanted to get rid of – my powers – was something I would need to save my family?"

"What are you going to do?" Kari asked.

"I don't know," Violet admitted. "That's why I'm here – I was hoping you could help."

"What can we do?" Kari asked. "We're not Supers."

"Didn't you hear her?" Lucy reminded her. "She's not either anymore. We will help. Somehow. Isn't there anyone we can call for backup?"

Violet thought for a moment. "I have the number for the Agency, but where am I telling them to go? I don't even have an address for Syndrome's beach house." She pulled the phone and SpyGuy out of her bag. "All I have is this."

"A SpyGuy!" Kari said. "I always wanted one of these. It takes videos." She pressed a button and the screen came to life. Suddenly Dash appeared, his face so close to the screen he appeared to be touching it.

"Violet? It's me!"

"Dash!" Violet cried, grabbing the SpyGuy. "What is he saying? Can you turn it up?" Kari adjusted the volume.

"If you get this, he's taking us to some old shack at Metroville Beach that he turned into a secret hideout. It used to be a restaurant called Nigel's." He looked back worriedly. "Hurry!"

"Nigel's. I remember that place. Horrible chips," Lucy said with a shudder, pouring syrup on her pancake stack.

Kari hit some buttons on the device. "Here it is. There's even a locator." The screen flickered and suddenly Violet saw a blinking dot like the one she had seen on the homing device.

"There he is," Violet said, touching the screen. She started to get up. "I'm going."

"Alone?" Lucy asked. "That's crazy. Just call the Agency. Have them storm the place."

"I'm going to call, but this can't wait. What if they don't get there in time?" Violet insisted. "I helped my family get in this mess, I have to get them out of it."

"Well, if you're going to do that, you might need whatever is in this bag," Kari said and placed it on the table. "Dash left this at the house the other night."

"Dad's weapons!" Violet cried, spying the megaphone inside and the peace button.

"I also have these," Lucy added, putting the messenger bag on the table as well. "I took it from Uncle Lu's. I don't know what this stuff does, but it must do something."

Violet peered in the bag. There were all kinds of gadgets in there. "Thanks." She felt stronger already. She looked at her friends. "But I don't want to do this alone. I could really use some help. I know what I'm asking is dangerous."

"I'm in," Lucy said immediately.

"Me too!" Kari added. "I've always wanted to see an actual Super in action. Even though you're not Super. And we're not sure your brothers will be either by the time we get there. Or whether your parents are okay. Or whether this Syndrome guy will try to kill us. Or—"

"Kari! We get it." Lucy looked at Violet. "We will help you with whatever you need. Starting with this. Here." She began playing with Violet's hair, pulling a black headband out of her bag and placing it on Violet's head, pushing her hair out of her eyes. "Now you can at least see who you're fighting."

Violet touched her head, turning to the window to stare at her reflection. The headband didn't look half bad. The girl in the reflection was someone she hardly ever spent time looking at. Violet had been hiding her whole life. From her powers. From her secrets. From what she couldn't control. But she couldn't hide anymore.

Don't think. And don't worry. If the time comes, you'll know what to do. It's in your blood. That was what her mum had said on the machine.

"All right, this is what we're going to do—"

"Pancakes?"

All three girls looked up.

Violet almost swallowed her tongue. "Tony!"

"Hi." Tony placed a platter of pancakes in front of her.

His hair flopped in front of his eyes and he smelt like bacon grease and pancake syrup. He was wearing a white dress shirt with a red bow tie, and his shirt was monogrammed with the word TONY across his right breast pocket. For a moment, Violet forgot all her troubles.

"Did you order more buttermilk pancakes?" he asked.

"Um," Violet stammered.

Lucy nudged her in the back. "Yes. Thanks, Tony. Have you met my friend Violet?"

Kari started to giggle.

"I know Violet," Tony said. "Hi."

He knew who she was? Her heart fluttered. How could she be drooling over a boy at a time like this? She snapped to attention and smiled. "Hi, Tony."

"Hi," he said again, and they stared at each other a moment. His eyes got bigger. "Oh, I forgot more syrup! Be right back."

Kari grinned. "I think he likes you!"

Did he? Like her? Violet wasn't sure, and at the moment, Violet couldn't wait around to find out. Sure, she wanted to talk to Tony Rydinger, but today was not that day. Violet could feel her confidence growing, a plan forming to change her family's fate. "Quick. I have a ride out front. A driverless car. Let's go!"

"A driverless car?" Kari crowed.

Violet threw some money down on the table and grinned at Tony's retreating figure on the other side of the diner. "I'll explain everything on our way to Nigel's."

CHAPTER TWENTY-FOUR
VIOLET

"Syndrome is a genius," Kari declared.

"Kari," Lucy warned. "You're not helping."

"Sorry, but he is!" Kari said as the Pizza Planet delivery car flew through Metroville and she attempted to get the car to work with the SpyGuy so they could make it to the right place. (It was so complicated, Violet wished there were a gadget that could help you navigate directions.) "He's made an invention that can tell you whether anyone is in the room, and it also acts as a homing device. Too bad we can't get the car to find the location."

"Car, please head to Nigel's at the beach," Lucy tried for the umpteenth time.

"Location not found," said the car again.

The girls groaned.

"What are we going to do?" Lucy asked. "Get out and walk?"

"That would take hours," Kari said.

Violet took the SpyGuy from Kari's hands. "Is there a way to zoom in on this thing? Maybe if we can see Nigel's up close, we can find some other landmarks to give the car." She pressed the screen and the image magnified.

"Keep doing that!" Lucy said.

Violet kept pressing till they could see Nigel's on the edge of a cliff at the beach. Violet glanced at the surrounding area. There were no other landmarks. Just rocks. "Uh, car? Can you take us to the beach by the giant boulder?"

"Location not found," the car said again.

Violet kept trying, moving her finger over the screen to see what else was nearby. She noticed something tall. "Oooh! Look!"

Kari leaned over the device. "I know where that is! Car! Can you take us to the Metroville clock tower?" She looked at the others. "It's a beach monument that my mum and dad used to meet at all the time. They used to walk all the way to the water taking turns carrying the beach chairs and—"

"Directions to the Crow Beach Chair," the car said.

"Let me try," Violet suggested. "Car? Can we get

directions to the Metroville clock tower?"

"Directions to the Metroville clock tower," the car said and made a hard left.

Kari threw up her hands. "That's what I said."

"Maybe it likes my voice," Lucy said gently and checked the SpyGuy again. "It looks like from the clock tower it's a straight path down to the water and Nigel's." She frowned. "Doesn't look like it's an actual road, though, but we will make it one."

"Now that we're going to the right place, let's talk gadgets," Violet said and pulled out Lucy's bag. "Luckily, I know what all these things Lucy brought are for. These are comms links." She held up the one that was identical to her mum's. "Even if we're separated, we can be in touch, and these things are smaller than a tube of lipstick, so they're easy to hide."

"Cool!" Kari said, swiping one immediately.

"Even though the homing device on this car has been turned off, the second we approach the restaurant, Syndrome will know," Violet guessed. "I'm sure he has tight security. Even if he doesn't know it's me, he will come after this car, and I'm not sure comms links, freeze rays and shrink buttons are enough against him."

Lucy frowned. "I'm not loving this negative attitude.

Can we be positive here?"

"You're right. Sorry." Violet looked at Dash's tricks and wondered. How did she outtrick a trickster like Syndrome? She thought for a moment.

Beat him at his own game.

"Wait a minute: maybe our gadgets will work if we can at least get the car onto property sight unseen. Mastermind allowed a delivery truck on her property, even if she was suspicious. So what if we call Syndrome at Nigel's and use me as bait?" She was spitballing, but the ideas were coming fast.

"Give you up?" Lucy questioned from the back seat. "You have no powers."

"True, but I do know what he's planning. I could threaten to tell the Agency all his secrets and where he's at. What's he going to do – flee? Abandon his beach house, regular house and volcanic island? Where would he go?" It was kind of how he'd forced her hand too – *where are you going to live?* he'd said.

"He owns a volcanic island?" Kari asked incredulously.

Lucy thought a moment. "It's risky. He might have somewhere else to go and then we'd have no clue where he was taking your family."

"But could he get everything he needs out of the beach house in the next twenty minutes?" Violet questioned.

"Because we'll be there in ten. So maybe we call as Mastermind and say she has me and she wants to make a trade – nullifier for me; and if he won't trade, she'll let me tell the Agency all my hideouts. If I were him, I'd let a car with me onto the property."

"That's a lot of ifs," Lucy said with a sigh. "But it could work."

"But how do we get Syndrome to believe Mastermind is calling?" Kari asked.

Violet grinned. "That's where the world's best impressionist comes in. Lucy, you can call Syndrome as Mastermind and say you want to make the switch."

Kari piped up again. "But didn't Violet say her mum knew it was really Lucy calling from the movies the other night?"

"Hey. Who is the negative one now?" Violet questioned and looked at Lucy. "My mum knew you did impressions. Syndrome doesn't know you. I think it will work."

Lucy bit her lip. "Well, I am a good impressionist. But I haven't heard Mastermind's voice in forever. Uncle Lu used to show me video interviews he did with clips of her, but it's been ages. All I remember is that she went everywhere with a white dog."

"A poodle?" Violet asked. "She still does."

"Wait a minute," Kari said. "Is this Mastermind?" She

pulled up a video clip on Dash's SpyGuy and handed it to the others. "I found this on Dash's device when I was replaying his message. You're in the video too. I thought this was that Mirage woman you were talking about. But now that you mentioned the poodle. Look."

There was Mastermind in her office, gesturing wildly with one hand while holding the poodle with the other. Mastermind's back was to the camera, which meant that Violet could see herself across from Mastermind. She didn't look as scared as she remembered. Dash must have secretly filmed this. "This is her. Turn it up!" Kari hit a button and Mastermind's velvety voice filled the car. "Try this."

As she listened, Lucy began mimicking Mastermind under her breath.

"Problem solved," Violet said, exhaling. "Next: we call Nigel's and pretend to be Mastermind."

"Car!" Kari thundered. "Call Nigel's. I think I ate there once before it closed. My grandma got food poisoning. I think it was the salmon. My mum always says, never trust frozen salmon. If it's not fresh, it's no good."

"Calling Salmon Nigel," said the car.

"No! Violet corrected. "Car, call Nigel's at the beach."

"Hang on!" Kari said. "Didn't you say we need to call that Agency thing too?"

"Yes," Violet slapped her head. Even if they couldn't

get there as fast as she could, maybe they'd be her backup. It was worth a shot. "Car, call this number." She recited the one on Mum's note.

The phone rang twice, and then there was a voicemail. "Hello. You've reached Rick Dicker. Please leave a message."

"Hi." Violet cleared her throat. "This is Violet Parr. Helen and Bob's daughter. My parents and brothers are in trouble. A villain named Syndrome has them at Nigel's at the beach in Metroville, and if we don't get there quick, he's going to use a weapon Mastermind created that will strip their powers. I've already lost mine, but I'm going after them. Hurry!" She hung up. *Please send backup*, she thought.

"Okay, my turn," said Lucy. "Car, call Nigel's!"

"Calling Nigel's," said the car. The line picked up immediately.

"Hello, pet," Lucy purred. "Mastermind. I've got the girl and I'm putting her in that heap of junk you call an invention and sending her to you at your beachside lair. In exchange, I expect my nullifier. If not, well, we both know I know where you are – and news flash: I've already had Violet call the Agency and give them your location. If the nullifier isn't in that car and on its way back to me within the hour, I'd start packing up or your party is over. The girl will be there shortly, pet. Make sure you let the car onto the grounds." She hung up. The three high-fived.

"I make a great super villain," Lucy crowed. "I can't believe I just pretended to be Mastermind!"

"Now all we have to do is go save my family," Violet said. She felt a familiar sense of rage flicker to life. It wasn't her powers, but it was an energy beating inside her. A determination to finish this, no matter the cost. She couldn't imagine a world where Dash and Jack-Jack would grow up as villains. Where her parents, who were still alive (alive!) could lose their lives because of her mistake.

They passed the clock tower and the car made a quick left, then a right onto a bumpy, sand-covered path lined with tall beach grass. It was clearly not an actual road.

Violet had an idea. "Car! Stop, please." The car did what it was told. Violet looked at the others. "I think you two should get out here. If you're in the vehicle when I arrive at the restaurant, you'll immediately be captured, but if you get out now, you might find another way in. We all have comms links so we can communicate once we're inside." She grabbed the tiny happy face pin that was a shrink ray. "I'll hold on to this. It might come in handy."

"But you're going to be alone," Lucy reminded her.

"I've been on my own for days, but I'm not alone anymore." Violet smiled. "I have backup now and gadgets to help me till you show up."

At the end of the day, Syndrome wasn't a Super either.

He was just a guy with a vendetta. She was a girl who loved her family. If she thought about it in the most basic of terms, she had a shot. She tried to sound confident. "I'm going to be okay."

"Okay. Kari and I will be right behind you." Lucy peered out the window of the car and looked at the beach grass before opening the door and stepping out. "Come on, Kari! Let's go infiltrate a super villain lair!"

Lucy was fearless. If anyone should have been born with powers, it was her.

Kari slid out from the front seat beside Violet, clutching a SpyGuy. She looked at Violet. "Don't die till we get there, okay?"

Violet grinned. "I'll do my best."

Kari squared her shoulders and looked at Violet. "I'm going to find your brothers. A good babysitter never loses her charges."

"The world's *best* babysitter," Violet corrected, hugging her before letting her out of the car. "Car? Continue to Nigel's." The car started moving again, her friends watching as the car rolled away.

Violet was alone and barrelling towards what she knew was a super villain lair. She'd faced Mastermind and escaped. She could do the same when it came to Syndrome. She had to.

Up ahead, she could see a blue wooden restaurant at the edge of a rocky cliff overlooking the ocean. It had a large wraparound deck with splintered wood, faded paint and dirty windows. Clearly the place hadn't been open in a while. A massive pelican-shaped sign was hung at one corner, danglingly precariously over the ocean. Not the type of place Violet expected Syndrome to have another lair, but she supposed the rent was free. Outside, she saw four guards patrolling the perimeter. She shoved the happy face shrink ray and comms link in her pockets, which was probably the best feature of this Supersuit. She could have changed out of it for this mission, but Super or not, this suit was a part of her now.

The car rolled to a stop in front of the car park and the guards approached the vehicle. Violet's heart was pounding as they peered inside.

"Tell the boss it's really the girl. We've got her," one reported.

She heard mumbling on the other end of the guard's headset.

"Get her out of the car. He wants her inside the hangar," said the first guard to the others.

A hangar? Where would a hangar be inside a beach shack? she wondered, scanning the area. She imagined something almost like Mastermind's place – built into the side of a cliff.

The guards each approached one of the four doors with electrified sticks. Violet felt her palms grow clammy. *Right about now would be a great time to have powers*, she thought, her heart lurching at what she'd so freely given away. If she could have become invisible or used a force field, she could have busted right past them. Instead, she'd have to fight any way she could.

One of the guards yanked her out of the vehicle. Violet smelt the sea air as someone grabbed her left arm and another grabbed the right.

"Don't make any moves," a guard warned.

"She doesn't have her powers, remember?" said another. "What's she going to do?" They laughed.

Violet was determined to prove them wrong. Her mind was spinning as they approached the rickety deck and a set of double doors that had pelicans painted on them. Did she try to do something now? Or did she wait until she was inside?

"Take her down to the hangar," said the first. "Two of us have to stay up here to keep watch. Boss is pretty sure Mastermind will show up."

She was down to two guards. Those were better odds. Violet felt her heart thumping as she approached the stairwell. She walked quietly down the first winding set, then started down the second where the air was cooler. She could hear talking in one of the guard's headsets but couldn't make out what they were saying. They were halfway down the second set of stairs, when Violet twisted out of the hold one guard had on her using the element of surprise.

"What the…?" The first guard let go just as she landed a roundhouse kick into his waist. The goon went down, his electrified stick rolling away. Violet turned and kicked the second guard's stick out of his hand, grabbing it herself.

"We need backup!" the second guard shouted. "We need – who? Wait. We've got the girl! Who is upstairs? More kids?"

Lucy and Kari had made it! Violet heard more shouting through the earpiece. She pulled the happy face button out of her pocket and shrunk the second guard down to the size of a rat. All she could hear now was squeaking.

"Backup!" the first guard said getting up. "She's armed! She's—"

"Got you," Violet replied cheerily, turning the button on the guard and shrinking him as well. She started running down the stairs as fast as she could. If she reached the hangar before Syndrome was alerted, maybe she had a shot. At the bottom was an entrance to a large cave. She hugged the exterior and peered inside. Computers lined one wall of the hangar, and several Omnidroids lined the other. There was even a helicopter parked in there. At the other end of the hangar was a partially open large metal door out to the beach and the water. At least a dozen goons were working on computers, but there was no sign of Syndrome, her brothers or her parents.

Violet slipped through the doors and saw exactly what she was looking for. In the centre of the room stood a glass chamber attached to several tubes. Inside the central chamber, suspended in bubbling liquid, was the nullifier. Violet started to run towards it but stopped when she saw something out of the corner of her eye.

Her family.

They were trapped behind electrified bars on the opposite side of the room. Jack-Jack was wailing from her mum's arms, Dash was talking a mile a minute and her dad was screaming at someone Violet couldn't see. But they were all alive! They were here! She'd found them! She let out a sob and they turned towards the noise.

"Mum, Dad," Violet whispered, her eyes filling with tears.

"Violet!" Dash cried out before he could help himself.

Violet froze, making eye contact with a guard at a computer.

"Run!" her mum instructed, and then her dad started to yell too, but it was too late. Syndrome crossed the room in mid-flight while several guards ran on foot.

"Look who showed up!" Syndrome crowed. "The whole family is together now for the big event! You can have the seat of honour, Violet. Guards! Get her!"

Violet spun around, prepared to kick her way out of there. Instead, someone elbowed her in the back. She went down hard and looked up in surprise.

It was a woman with short white-blonde hair. Violet recognised her immediately, despite the hair change. She smiled as she leant over Violet and zip-tied her hands. "Hello, Violet. Miss me?"

CHAPTER TWENTY-FIVE
MIRAGE

Four hours earlier...

How could she have let herself be bested by a boy?

That was her first thought as Syndrome turned her immobi-ray on her, picking her up like she was a pest and shooting her through the glass doors with the intention of killing her.

This is what she got for taking a stupid temp job that had nothing to do with acting and everything to do with an egomaniac who forgot to pay overtime and expected her to deal in villain work. She'd missed appointments with Monique. Stopped talking to friends. Worked eighty hours over the last few days all because a guy she'd gone on a few half-decent dates with sweet-talked her into kidnapping a trio of Super kids with the promise of triple pay.

What had she been thinking?

This twerp needs to go, she thought, but instead, it was her going out the window, hurtling towards the edge of a patio where a twenty-foot drop awaited her. She was sure she was about to die, or at least wind up in traction for years, losing all good roles that could possibly come to her. All because she'd let this jerk gamble with her life instead of his own.

Money makes people do stupid things, she thought as she flew through the air and waited for the world to go dark.

Instead, she hit a beach umbrella she'd forgotten to take down the night before and fell into the infinity pool. Surprised, she rose to the surface, sure the guards were going to haul her away or zap her again. Instead, no one came. As she caught her breath and tried to ignore the pain in her leg, she listened to what was still going on inside the house.

Syndrome was busy monologuing to poor Violet about how she deserved to lose her powers and how he'd finish what he started with her parents and take everything they cared about. Then he used the nullifier (the thing actually worked) on Violet, reducing the kid to a puddle of her former self. All Mirage could do was listen. Dash was yelling from his room, the baby was crying (all he did was cry, really), and she was alive to hear it all. Syn had no clue.

God, the man had such a Napoleon complex.

That's when Mirage came up with a plan.

She didn't consider herself a vengeful person, but Syn deserved to pay for what he'd done. She'd wasted a year of good acting experience at this bonkers job, swayed by a few pricey dinners. On top of that, he'd lied to her – lied! He'd told her the kids' parents had died. And she'd believed him! Monique had taught her better than that. How could she not have seen through his ruse? Or questioned the parts of his story that didn't add up? She felt like a fool. Even Violet had put two and two together after visiting Mastermind.

Mirage wasn't sure how long she floated in that pool, clinging to the edge, feeling her body turn blue, but she waited till the house grew quiet. She figured most of the workforce was in the process of packing up equipment and transporting it to Nigel's for phase two of Syn's world domination.

Or should she call it what it really was – Mr Incredible domination.

At that thought, she sprang into action, full of rage, grabbing one of the electrified sticks from a charging port on the porch and stomping into the living room. She knocked out one guard, then three more before anyone could report in. Then she used this sleep spray Syndrome created to make sure they stayed asleep for hours. She carried Violet to a bedroom, made sure her vitals were strong and left her with the means to get out of the house when she awoke. She might not awake till morning, but hopefully she knew how to use a telephone. Poor girl. She'd been duped and Mirage had played a huge role in that. She didn't feel guilty about much, but messing with a child was a line she hadn't wanted to cross. The girl had lost her powers and it was partially her fault.

It made her wonder...

Maybe she had one more part to play before she ditched this gig.

I'm Mirage, she thought, *and I'm the vengeful ex-girlfriend hell-bent on making her dweeb boyfriend feel as small as his actual stature.* (The guy definitely wore lifts in those ridiculous boots of his.) This was a role she would relish. Her last as part of Syndrome Industries.

Her confidence soared at the thought. "I quit!" she told herself, shouting it to the quiet house. "I quit!" she said again, making her way downstairs and knocking out several other guards on her way to one of the cars and spraying sleep spray on them. She scrawled a note for Violet, and punched in a password that would allow Violet to take the car wherever she wanted to go. She turned off the homing device on the vehicle so if Syndrome learnt Violet was missing, he couldn't track the car. "I quit!" she said as she jumped into her work car. She found the coordinates she'd used only the night before. A plan was forming and it was wickedly good. What she had in mind was risky, but as long as Mastermind didn't kill her on sight, Mirage had a feeling she would see reason. "I quit!" Mirage said once more for good measure.

She was done taking orders from that tyrant, and she was going to see to it that Syndrome's dreams went up in flames.

Vengeful ex-girlfriend was going to be her greatest role yet.

CHAPTER TWENTY-SIX
VIOLET

Violet heard her mum, her dad and Dash shouting, but she was too stunned to do anything but stare at Mirage, who was leaning over her.

"Don't say anything," Mirage said quietly. "I'm doing the talking."

Violet's heart was pounding and her back hurt from where she'd been hit by someone she had been certain was dead. Instead, the woman looked ready for a night out. She was wearing a chic grey fitted romper and heels. The dowdy babysitter look had obviously been a ruse. "You're alive," Violet whispered. "And your hair... it looks great."

Mirage touched her short blonde coif. "Give me a moment, Violet, will you? I have some business to attend to." Mirage motioned to Violet as she looked at Syndrome, who was racing towards her. "I have a delivery for you."

Violet didn't understand what was happening. Was Mirage with her or against her?

"Sweetheart!" Syndrome said. "Now, just hold on. I knew you'd be okay – you are okay, right? I aimed for the pool. I didn't want to hurt you, just shut you up since you seemed to be taking the kid's side."

Mirage continued to stare at him.

While they argued, Violet had to find a way out of this. There was a large clock on one wall. In the centre of the room several guards kept working away at computers, preparing the nullifier on the table for use. It didn't seem like her family had lost their powers yet, but she couldn't be sure.

"I was sending a team back to check on you," Syndrome said. "I've just been busy getting everything ready for the big show! Ta-da! Look at that! The nullifier chamber ready for its first test run. We're using that Frozone guy to test it out. Can't have any mistakes like we did with Violet here." He nudged her with his foot. "You're supposed to be dead!" He laughed.

"Buddy, I'm warning you!" her dad shouted across the room. "You touch my kid and you will not live to see tomorrow!"

"Don't call me Buddy!" Syndrome yelled. "And what are you going to do from behind bars? After you nearly broke out twice on my island, you think I'd use the same holding chamber on you the third time? That jail cell you're in is pure zero-point energy. I can lift it up and move it or hurl it into the sea with one press of a button, and your powers can't help you there." He tapped his gloved hands. "Ask your daughter how well it worked out to test me on this technology."

"Or you could ask his girlfriend," Mirage murmured. "Ex-girlfriend."

"Sweetheart," he tried.

"Don't call me *sweetheart* and I won't call you *Buddy*." She motioned to Dash and Jack-Jack in the cage. "I thought you were keeping the children as your own personal pets."

He ran a hand through his hair and glared at the cage again. "Turns out a baby is too much work. Especially when it can turn into a devil, and Dash, he wouldn't see reason."

"I like my powers, but I'll never be a super villain!" he shouted. "Get him, Violet!"

Violet tried to stand up, but Mirage gave her a look that seemed to say *stay put*.

Syndrome reached for Mirage's hand. "Don't you see? With these guys out of the way, we can have everything we ever wanted."

Mirage raised her right eyebrow. "We?"

"Yes! I won't be focusing on Supers anymore because they'll be gone. I've got the one I wanted!" He motioned to Helen and Bob again. "I have the whole family! Now we can put this behind us and you can focus on acting. I can pay for your classes. Or you don't have to work at all if you don't want."

Mirage seemed to be mulling the offer over. "Keep talking."

"Sir! We got two more." Two guards came in, each one holding on to a struggling Lucy and Kari.

"Violet!" Lucy said when she saw her on the ground.

"Wow!" Kari said, taking in the space: the electrified cage, the hangar and all the Omnidroids. "It's like a movie!" She saw Violet on the floor then glanced at Syndrome and Mirage. "Who are you guys? Are you the villains?"

"Kari!" Helen shouted. "What are you doing here?"

"Hi, Mrs Parr, Mr Parr! I'm here to help Violet! I had no idea you were Supers, but I said to myself, if they are in trouble, even if their baby is a handful, I should help them because Violet is the best friend I have. I'm highly capable and responsible. I'm not going to be scared of a villain I've never even heard of. I jumped out of a moving car! And I hit someone with a freeze ray. It only lasted a few seconds and I got caught but—"

Mirage stuck a Taser to her neck and knocked Kari out cold. "She talks too much."

"Don't touch her!" Lucy cried as Kari fell to the floor. "Rick Dicker is on his way. Violet called him. The Agency is coming!"

"That's my girl!" Helen said from her chamber, and Violet smiled. Mum. Mum was here!

"So Mastermind wasn't kidding. You really called the Agency, huh?" Syndrome asked, blowing the moment. "Smooth. Well, I guess they'll arrive in time to see the world's greatest Supers reduced to NOTHING! First up, your uncle. Bring in Frozone!"

Two guards wheeled out a second electrified crate that had Lucius trapped inside.

"Uncle Lu!" Lucy shouted, trying to pull away from the guards.

"What the heck is going on here?" Lucius was yelling as he attempted to freeze the bars (it didn't work). "Lucy? How did you get mixed up in this?"

"Uncle Lu!" Lucy shouted. "I'm here to save—" Mirage Tasered her, too.

"Lucy!" Lucius screamed as his niece dropped next to Kari.

"Two problems solved. Anyone else want to be shut up fast?" Mirage brandished the Taser and the guards backed up. So did Syndrome. "I accept your offer," she said. "Finish off this family and we walk out of here as partners."

He cocked his head. "Partners?"

"Partners," Mirage repeated. "No relationship – we both know it would never work out between us. You're too much of a workaholic. But as a boss? You command stage presence. You get things done."

"I do," he agreed, calming.

"Make me your partner, fifty-fifty, your company and mine," she continued. "Forget acting. We can build weapons together. Use this nullifier to reduce these Supers to nothing – and we can take over the world. Your name will go down in history for destroying Supers." Mirage locked eyes on Syndrome. "What do you say?"

"You won't get away with this!" Helen cried, but Mirage ignored her.

"Do we have a deal?" Mirage pressed Syndrome.

Violet didn't understand. Whose side was Mirage on?

Syndrome smiled. He held out his hand. "My name going down in history? I like the way you think. We have a deal, but I will miss our dinner dates."

Mirage pressed a hand to her heart. "I'm touched. How about one more kiss for old time's sake?"

Syndrome leant in.

Mirage Tasered him in the neck. Syndrome's eyes

widened in surprise as he started to fall backwards. Guards started running from all directions.

"What did I ever see in you?" Mirage whispered to Syndrome as he fell. Then she spun around and headed towards Violet, a needle in her hand. Violet cringed, trying to get away, but Mirage was quicker.

"This is going to hurt," she said, stabbing Violet in the neck before she could even react. "You can thank Mastermind for that."

Suddenly Violet was twitching. It felt like she was burning from the inside out again, the serum flooding every inch of her body. She felt tingling, saw flashes of light, her body flickering in front of her eyes.

Wait. Was she turning invisible?

Was she getting her powers back?

Mirage stood back and smiled as Violet lifted her bound hands, watching in wonder as they came in and out of focus, fingers appearing and disappearing over and over. She felt her hands spark. The electricity broke through the binds on her hands, making them loose. She stood up fast just as the first guard approached her, levitating from the sheer force of the force field that shot out of her hands. The beam hit the ground beneath the guard's feet, sending him flying.

Her powers were back!

Violet looked at Mirage in wonder. "You fixed me."

Mirage smiled. "Not exactly. You'll have to fix these Super issues you have yourself – I have no clue if these powers are good or bad, but you know what? As long as they don't affect me, I don't care. Just promise me one thing, Violet: whatever you do, do it for yourself. Never change for a guy, Violet. Or overtime."

She wasn't sure what Mirage meant by that, but whatever. "Deal," Violet said.

"In the meantime, I'm taking the nullifier back to its rightful owner and getting out of here before that Agency arrives." She winked. "Good luck, kid," she said, striding away as more guards flooded the room. She headed right for the cube, stepping over Syndrome's downed body and picking up the cube from the table in the centre of the room.

Violet spun around, firing more force fields at the guards approaching Mirage. For a woman now in heels, Mirage moved in a surprising flash and disappeared. It was easy to get away when so much was happening. Violet's family was shouting, weapons were firing, lasers shooting through the air. From the corner of her eye, she saw an Omnidroid come to life, then another one. Violet fired again, taking out one of the legs on the first droid, then she sprinted across the room to the chamber her family was in.

"Violet! I don't care what you did or didn't do, but you have to get out of here," her mother cried as Jack-Jack screamed in delight at the sight of her.

"How do I break this cage or turn it off?" Violet asked her dad, ignoring her mum's directive.

"We're not sure," her dad said. "I think it's one of those computers across the room, but I'm not sure which one."

"Then we'll take them all out." Violet ran for the computer bank, sliding under an Omnidroid and blasting every computer on the wall. Rocks rained from the ceiling of the cave, hitting guards and sending people running. Violet turned around. Her parents and Lucius's cage deactivated. The bars disappeared.

They wasted no time reacting.

Lucius ran for Lucy and Kari, shooting a wave of ice across the floor, which he skidded across before grabbing the girls and getting out of there.

Violet's parents handed Jack-Jack off to a protesting Dash and headed right for Syndrome, who had stood up and started pressing buttons wildly on his gloves, his boots rising into the air. All the Omnidroids came alive at once and began to fire as the helicopter started up, its blades whirring. Her parents tore after the robots, trying to take them out as the walls of the cave began to crumble around them.

He's going to try to escape, Violet realised. *And we're going to be trapped in here.*

Syndrome flew off his feet, firing lasers in every direction, not caring who he hit. He aimed at Jack-Jack and Violet screamed. The laser missed.

Violet's eyes narrowed at the nearest Omnidroid.

That coward wasn't getting away.

CHAPTER TWENTY-SEVEN
SYNDROME

Losing the kids was a downer. He could admit that.

Oh, the plans he'd had for those two boys! Dash would have taken some working over, but the baby was the perfect age for moulding. Give him a year somewhere tropical with no television sets and he'd have those kids convinced their parents and sister were the villains and he was their saviour.

But some dreams have to die.

Destroying Mr Incredible was more important.

And now Mirage had aided Violet and ruined that dream too. His secret hideout was crumbling, Mirage had the nullifier and was probably taking it for herself. What a waste. He could scream, he could monologue or he could get out of there and regroup. Find another way to destroy this family. Because, oh, he would destroy them. He wasn't done.

"You won't get away with this!" he shouted as he flew across the room. "I will find you again! I'll take your kids!" he declared to Mr So-Called Incredible. "I will get your powers! I will! I'll destroy you!" he claimed as he grabbed hold of the helicopter door and dived inside.

He was almost at the control panel when he felt the blast.

Violet was shooting force fields at him. He had taught her too well. Syndrome whirled around and settled into the driver's seat, firing a rocket at the kid from the front of the helicopter. Violet dived out of the way and Dash came out of nowhere and moved her clear across the room. Parts of the cave were crumbling now. If he didn't fly out of here fast, he'd be under the rubble. He got the helicopter into the air.

Sirens wailed in the distance. Syndrome looked out at the beach through the opening in the cave. A line of Agency vehicles was headed his way. He was getting out just in time. He slowly started to fly out of the cave.

The helicopter got yanked backwards. Syndrome turned around in surprise as the helicopter spun through the air. Then he saw them.

The whole Super family was high atop his most advanced Omnidroid, riding it like a pony, their faces menacing, their stances determined. Elastigirl had a fistful of wires in her hands and Violet was holding a remote while Mr Incredible pressed the buttons on it. Syndrome knew what was about to happen before it did.

Mr Incredible grinned, shouting over the sounds of the helicopter, which stopped when a second Omnidroid tentacle grabbed hold of it.

"Fly home, Buddy!" he crowed and pressed another button.

The tentacle flung the helicopter into the air, knocking Syndrome from the chair and sending him flying into the back of the cockpit. He knew he should have tried to hit something on his wrist or shouted out to Mr Incredible (*You can't think of a better line all these years later?* he'd have said). But it was too late. All he could do was scream as the helicopter spun and tumbled into the sea.

CHAPTER TWENTY-EIGHT
VIOLET

Violet watched as Syndrome was pitched into the ocean at high speed. The Omnidroid powered off and lowered to the ground where her family jumped off.

Dash grabbed her arm. "Is he... dead?"

"I... don't know," Violet chose to say as Agency cars pulled into the hangar. Syndrome had been squeezed like a bottle of mustard and then hurled hundreds of miles an hour into the ocean. At the end of the day, Syndrome wasn't Super. She couldn't see how he could get out of that one.

"Violet!" Her mum was running towards her.

Violet felt herself start to cry at the sight of her mum again. "Mum!" she said, running towards her too.

Her mum wrapped her arms around Violet twice for

good measure. "My girl," she said softly, smoothing her hair. "It's all right. Shhh." Violet couldn't stop crying. Her mum pulled away and stared into Violet's eyes. Her own were rimmed with tears as she looked around at the hangar, the Agency swarming the place and Syndrome's guards on the run. "Dash told me everything. You have been through a lot more than you bargained for these last few days. You did good. Real good."

"No, I didn't," Violet sobbed. "I almost cost you your powers! I lost my powers! I sided with a villain."

"You made a mistake and you learnt from it." She touched Violet's chin, tilting it up to her own. "I couldn't ask for more. You are going to make a great Super. Well, if we are ever allowed to be Supers again after this one." They laughed.

A small golf cart was zooming towards her as Agency members exited their cars. A man that looked very familiar – salt-and-pepper hair, grave face, pale skin, wearing a suit – was striding towards them.

"Everyone all right?" he asked, looking from Violet to the others. "I've been briefed on what happened."

"We're fine," her mum said. "The kids are too."

"Mastermind has a nullifier that can strip Supers' powers," said her dad.

Dicker looked at Violet. "Your daughter filled me in.

Where is the nullifier now?"

"I think back with Mastermind," Violet explained. "Or on its way there." She left Mirage's name out of it. It was the least she could do after all Mirage had done for her in the end. "I don't think Mastermind actually intends to use it."

Dicker eyed Violet. "Oh? What makes you say that?"

"She kind of told me so herself," Violet said. "She misses the Super-villain game. She had nothing to do with what happened here. It was all Syndrome, and he's…"

"Finished," Dicker said for her. "Well, we'll follow up with Mastermind." He motioned to Lucius who had skidded back into view on a sheet of ice with Lucy and Kari in his arms.

"Uh, about my friend Kari?" Violet said, swallowing hard at the fact she had to come clean about something that had been drilled into her head since she could talk. "She might need her memory wiped."

Her dad raised an eyebrow. "Might?"

Violet bit her lip. "I had no choice! I had no powers! I needed backup! I had to tell Kari who I was." Her cheeks flamed.

"Violet!" her dad started to protest, and for once, her mum actually shushed him as if she was on Violet's side. Violet attempted a smile.

"I'll take care of it," Dicker said as he pulled a strange

contraption with a suction cup out of his bag. "All in all, it seems like you kids did all the Super work this weekend and without the fanfare of the rest of the world knowing. Nice job, kid," he said to Violet. "Only Mastermind is aware of what went on here, and it sounds like she's not going to talk anytime soon. She'd kill to be back in business."

"The important thing is we're all right," Violet's mum said, glancing at her dad as they pulled the kids close. "And we're together."

"Alive to fight another day!" Dash declared, and Violet smiled.

The kid was corny but he was right. After the last few days, Violet finally felt like she could breathe again. Controlling her powers was something she'd soon ask her parents to help her work on, but the important thing was she had her family back. "Another day sounds good," Violet said, and this time, she meant it.

CHAPTER TWENTY-NINE
MIRAGE

One month later...

"Tell me what's happening. Can you see them? I can't see anything."

Mirage lowered her cat's-eye sunglasses. "That's because you're sitting in the back seat hiding under a cashmere blanket."

"I don't want them to see me. If I've managed to avoid them this long, I can go a bit longer." Mastermind giggled with glee, sounding like a child. (Mirage was done with children after last month, so the sound was jarring.) "But tell me what's going on."

Mirage sighed. They'd parked the saloon down the

street from the Safari Motel for tonight's stakeout and had been waiting over an hour for movement, but they finally had some. Helen had opened the curtains in the hotel room giving Mirage a view inside.

Mirage couldn't help but smile when she saw Violet, her hair pushed back behind her ears, the girl standing by the door, dressed up like she was going to a party. And was that an actual smile she saw on her face? *Atta girl, Violet*, she thought. Helen looked happy too. She didn't know her the way she did Bob, and she knew the children way better than she knew him, but she was happy to see the family back together. Even if they had lost their house in all this Syndrome nonsense.

Thinking of that egomaniac still made her blood boil.

"Mirage? I'm waiting, pet…"

"Don't call me pet."

"Sorry." Mastermind leant forwards, looking like an old-school ghost under the sheet. "But I need to know what's going on."

"Fine. Helen and Violet are in their motel room. Violet is dressed up, so I'm assuming they're getting ready to leave."

"When they do, we follow," Mastermind instructed.

After working for Syndrome, Mirage promised herself she'd never work for another egomaniac, or do anything other than acting again.

But it turned out auditions were rough. And bit parts paid next to nothing.

On the other hand, working for egomaniacs paid well. And Mastermind was nothing like Syndrome. Mirage knew it the minute she showed up at the villain's compound and explained what was going on with Mr Incredible, Elastigirl and the children. Mastermind hadn't hesitated to give Mirage an antidote to the nullifier on one condition – when the dust settled, Mirage would bring the nullifier back to Mastermind for safekeeping. "I don't want any more Supers losing their powers," she commanded. "I need them if I'm ever getting back to work."

Mastermind's plan was a good one – not unlike Syndrome's in a way – draw Supers out of retirement, get them back to work by creating situations that governments couldn't ignore. True, Mastermind could blabber on a bit during dinner about the "Villain Glory Days," but if she could make Supers and Villains legal again, they'd be rolling in dough. And unlike Syndrome, Mastermind had been willing to make Mirage her full partner. "You've got gumption," she'd said. "We could work well together."

For the last month, they had. The villain planning was exciting, Mastermind's compound top-notch (the pool alone!), and Mirage wanted for nothing. She could get used to this sort of life. And a villain partner.

Violet opened the hotel room door and she walked out with Helen, who was carrying Jack-Jack. Mirage put her sunglasses back on, started the engine and slowly rolled down the street, following Helen, Violet and the baby from a safe distance. "Put on your seatbelt," she told Mastermind. "We're going for a ride."

CHAPTER THIRTY
VIOLET

"Are you sure you have everything you need?" her mum fretted as she pulled out of the car park of the Safari Motel and drove down the street with Jack-Jack babbling in the back seat. "Money? The phone number for the hotel? The address of where you're going?"

"Yes, Mum," Violet said for the umpteenth time.

"And you know what time I'm coming to pick you and Kari up, right?" Her mum turned left and headed towards their old house since the party Violet was going to was the next street over.

"Yes," Violet promised. "I won't be late. I know Dad is out with Lucius and you'll have Dash and Jack-Jack with you."

Her mum smiled. "I'm just checking. It's what mums do."

Their house had been condemned after the fire Dash had accidentally started for a very good reason (as she and Dash pointed out over and over again). It would have to be rebuilt and according to Dad, that could take a year. The Agency had stepped in – saying a satellite had fallen on the house or something to that effect – so their neighbours didn't know about the villain threat, but it meant they had no place to live. Lucius and Honey had offered to host them, of course, but there was no room in their flat for the five Parrs. So for the last few months, they'd been camped out in a hotel room at the Safari Motel. High points of living at a motel: lots of Chinese food takeout and daily use of a pool. Kari loved coming over to swim. She didn't remember a thing about her Super outing, or even the fact that Violet's family had powers, which Violet felt bad about, but Rick Dicker insisted that it was safest for her this way.

"And Lucy knows to keep an eye on you?" Mum continued the pestering.

"Yes, Mum," Violet said again and laughed. "We went over this. I'm not a baby. I can handle myself at a party. High schoolers are nothing compared to a super villain."

"I'm not so sure about that," her mum joked. "Ask me again when your brothers are in high school." Jack-Jack squealed and banged a toy against the car seat, happily occupied in the back seat. Her mum patted her hand. "But you're right. You can handle a little ol' party. I can't wait to hear all about it later."

And her mum would since they were basically all living in one hotel room right now.

Her mum pulled up to a familiar house on a residential street. Kari was waiting on the path. She gave Violet a wave. Violet could hear music inside and people. Through the windows, she could see the house was packed. Her heart started to beat faster. That was a lot of people. She'd have to talk to some of them. Maybe Tony would be there.

Violet pulled down the mirror in the car visor and checked her headband. She'd started wearing headbands a lot. She decided she liked how she looked with her hair out of her eyes. She also couldn't help but look in the mirror to see if anyone was behind them (call it a useful Super habit). That's when she noticed a car roll to a stop and turn off its lights half a street back. Violet squinted to see. Was that a blonde wearing sunglasses at the wheel? Mirage?

Nah. She had to be seeing things. She hadn't heard from Mirage since the day they'd taken Syndrome down.

"Ready?" Mum asked.

"Ready." Violet kissed her mum on the cheek and got out of the car. "Bye, Jack-Jack!" He squealed again.

"Have fun!" Mum called, watching her go.

Violet took a deep breath and closed the visor. She looked different. She felt different. She wasn't afraid to be different either. And maybe, just maybe, she was ready to talk to Tony too. Who knows? If she was lucky, they'd hit it off, make plans to go to the cinema, maybe share a popcorn. Anything was possible.

Jen Calonita is the author of the award winning *Secrets of My Hollywood Life* and *Fairy Tale Reform School* series. She lives in New York with her husband, two boys and two Chihuahuas named Captain Jack Sparrow and Ben Kenobi. A huge Disney fan, Jen dreams of moving the whole family into Cinderella Castle at Walt Disney World. Visit her online at: www.jencalonitaonline.com and Twitter @jencalonita.

ALSO AVAILABLE IN THE TWISTED TALES SERIES:

WHAT IF ANNA AND ELSA NEVER KNEW EACH OTHER?

Following the unexpected death of her parents, Elsa finds herself
the sole ruler of Arendelle and mysterious powers begin
to reveal themselves.

Elsa starts to remember fragments of her childhood that
seem to have been erased – fragments that include
a familiar-looking girl.

Determined to fill the void she has always felt, Elsa must take a
harrowing journey across her icy kingdom to undo a terrible curse...
and find the missing Princess of Arendelle.

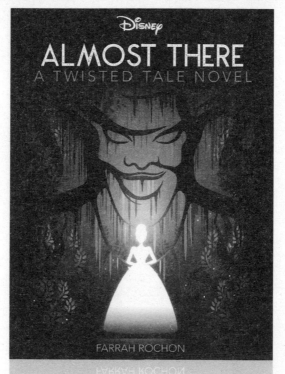

ALSO AVAILABLE IN THE TWISTED TALES SERIES:

WHAT IF ALADDIN HAD NEVER FOUND THE LAMP?

Aladdin is a Street Rat just trying to survive in a harsh city, while Jasmine is a beautiful princess about to enter an arranged marriage. Their worlds collide when the sultan's trusted adviser suddenly rises to power and, with the help of a mysterious lamp, attempts to gain control over love and death.

Together, Aladdin and Jasmine must unite to stop power-hungry Jafar tearing the kingdom apart in this story of love, power and one moment that changes everything.